For Emily, Jack, Ruby and Tilly.
My awesome gang.

Prologue

Walking back through the town, Julia Coleman swung a paper bag of pastries while swigging a takeaway coffee from a polystyrene cup. It was a beautiful morning, with only a few sporadic clouds floating along in the cobalt sky. Early afternoon the temperatures were predicted to hit a whopping twenty-five degrees, and even though it was every girl's dream that the weather was perfect on their wedding day, the bride was already beginning to panic that she would be sweltering inside her wedding dress. Julia had caught sight of the dress just moments before she'd headed out and it was, quite simply, a gown fit for a princess. Layers of ruffles that floated all the way to the ground, a bateau neckline and floral beaded bodice. The only two words to describe it were simply stunning. It all seemed set to be the perfect day. Except for the fact that Julia's good friend, Anais, was marrying a man who Julia didn't like particularly much – Flynn Carter.

Julia paused for a few minutes on the bank of the River Cree. Sitting down on a rickety old bench, she tilted her face up towards the sun. This was a place she'd spent many a Sunday alongside her grandfather fishing for salmon. The town of Newton Stewart, southwest Scotland, held such wonderful memories for her. Julia had grown up in the town but moved away to Fort William to study tourism and hospitality at the college there. It was only when her grandfather had passed away that Flynn Carter, a property developer, had appeared in Julia's life.

Her grandfather had worked hard all his life but had no wealth to speak of, except the house he lived in. At the time of his death the property market had crashed, no one was buying or selling, and his house had been left standing empty for nearly two years. This was when Flynn Carter had made Julia a ridiculous offer for the house, which was built on a decent plot of prime land. Flynn was ruthless, had offered cash, thousands below the asking price. According to Flynn the deal could be done and dusted as soon as possible. He was mechanical with his negotiation, showed no compassion or room for manoeuvre, and to add insult to injury made the offer available for only forty-eight hours.

Julia had been torn. The money from her grandfather's house would be the only way she could follow her own dreams to begin her own hospitality business, but Flynn Carter had made it crystal-clear that her grandfather's house would be demolished if the sale went ahead. Those forty-eight hours had been the worst of Julia's life. She'd

STARCROSS MANOR

CHRISTIE BARLOW

One More Chapter
a division of HarperCollins*Publishers* Ltd
1 London Bridge Street
London SE1 9GF
www.harpercollins.co.uk

This paperback edition 2020
First published in Great Britain in ebook format
by HarperCollins*Publishers* 2020

A catalogue record of this book
is available from the British Library

ISBN: 978-0-00-836273-7

Printed and bound in Great Britain by
CPI Group (UK) Ltd, Croydon CR0 4YY

barely ate or slept weighing up all the scenarios, trying to figure out what was the best thing to do. This was her grandfather's home, a place she'd felt safe and happy as a child, a place full of such happy memories. Julia had prayed another buyer would miraculously appear, but they hadn't, and time was ticking. In the end, Julia felt that accepting Flynn Carter's offer was her only choice, but she hadn't enjoyed being railroaded into making a decision in such a short space of time. Flynn Carter preyed on the vulnerable, snapping up houses at next-to-nothing prices to further his property empire. But for Julia, any money was better than nothing, to give her that chance of starting her own business. As she signed the legal papers at the solicitor's she felt nothing but anger towards Flynn Carter. She knew the property was worth more and so did he, but it would be too much of a gamble for Julia to keep hold of it just in case the housing market miraculously recovered anytime soon.

Julia remembered standing on the other side of the road, watching the bulldozers smash her grandfather's house to smithereens, the tears rolling down her cheeks. A house where she'd spent a happy childhood now a huge pile of rubble. It completely broke her heart; and as much as she longed to get her own business up and running, it still hadn't made the decision any easier.

Once the property was sold Julia had invested the money in a small bed and breakfast business and settled into the small town of Heartcross in the Scottish Highlands. The last time she'd seen Flynn Carter had been the day in the solicitor's office, but today he was marrying her oldest school friend, Anais Brown.

Anais had always been the popular girl at school, the one with the perfect clear skin and russet hair that bounced just above her shoulders. Her figure a perfect size ten, her waist tiny and eyelashes to die for. Not only did Anais have the beauty but also the brains, her grades always top of the class.

Julia was bridesmaid at the wedding alongside their old friend Mia; all three of them had been as thick as thieves through school and sixth form. And last night had been a hoot, too. It was safe to say that when Julia had turned up outside Anais's cottage, the familiarity of their friendship had instantly fallen back into place and the lagher and conversation had flowed all night.

All the stops had been pulled out for this wedding, with no expense spared. Even though Julia wasn't fond of the groom, it was still going to be a magnificent day, starting with the horse-drawn carriage to take them all to the church. Anais was a single child, which made it all the more special that her two oldest school friends were there to share her special day.

Carrying on down the bank of the river Julia took a quick detour over the wooden bridge towards a cobbled courtyard. But as she turned the corner, she felt her heart beat faster. A couple of years ago this was where her grandfather's house had stood, but now the place was completely unrecognisable. At first, happy memories flooded her mind, she pictured herself skipping up the street, playing ball against the front of the house and her grandparents shouting her in for lemonade and fruit gums. But then a wave of sadness hit Julia. Because now, in its place, stood an extravagant hotel with magnificent stone lions on guard at the impressive entrance.

'The Carter Hotel,' she read, a five-star rating engraved proudly under the name followed by the name of the proprietor. Flynn Carter.

The man who had provided her with the chance to make something of her life, but who had done it by taking advantage of her. He'd got her grandfather's house at a steal due to the economic climate, but he'd known he was forcing her hand. Judging by this place he was most definitely a successful businessman and Anais was about to embark on an amazing life with him – clearly, she'd want for nothing.

Anais, who worked at the local estate agents, had met Flynn at work. At the time Julia had been shocked to say the least when Anais had telephoned to tell her she'd met the love of her life, especially when she revealed her new fiancé was Flynn Carter. Anais had been the one who'd held Julia's hand through her grandfather's death and she knew how heartbroken Julia had been when Flynn had bulldozed the house. But Anais had fallen madly in love and had gone from being in a relationship on Facebook, to being engaged in what seemed overnight. But as Anais had pointed out, 'he was the one', despite Julia's reservations and surprise at the quickness of it all, and she could only be happy for her friend.

Feeling her tummy rumble and in need of a couple of paracetamols after drinking way too much alcohol last night, Julia began to walk back towards Anais's cottage when her phone began to ring. Julia rummaged inside her bag and pressed the phone to her ear. Anais could barely get her words out through the tears and gulps of air. The only thing Julia could understand was that Anais was saying that the wedding was off. But how could the wedding be off? Julia's throat was suddenly dry, and her lungs felt squashed as she broke into a sprint. What the hell had happened in the last twenty minutes whilst she'd been out to grab coffee? When she'd left the cottage everything had been absolutely hunky dory, Mia had been just about to take a shower whilst Anais was packing her suitcase ready for the honeymoon ahead. It didn't make any sense at all.

Pushing her legs to go faster, Julia felt hot and sweaty and even though her heart was beating rapidly against her chest there was no way she was slowing down until she got to Anais. She arrived back at Tollgate Cottage at a super-speed and flung open the garden gate to the honey-coloured stone terrace.

Hoping for Anais's sake that this was all just down to last-minute nerves – even though there wasn't any time for wobbles, they were all due at the hairdressers in just under an hour and the church in four hours' time – Julia burst through the front door. 'Where are you?' she bellowed, kicking off her trainers and hurrying up the hallway towards the living room.

Catching her breath, with her hands on her hips, her

eyes widened and her jaw fell open. Julia was rendered momentarily speechless. There lying on the floor was Anais's wedding dress cut to shreds, now barely recognisable. Anais was curled up in a ball on the floor, hugging her knees, the tears sliding like a tsunami down her cheeks. Mia was sitting next to her, clutching a box of tissues.

After saying 'Christ on a bike!' (twice), Julia dropped to her knees. Anais looked so dejected and Julia grabbed her hands and forced her to look at her.

'What the hell has happened here?' asked Julia, not beating around the bush. She wanted answers. 'Mia?'

Mia shrugged. 'I was in the shower and came down to this,' her eyes swept around the room.

Anais's swollen eyes bulged, and she swallowed. 'He's gone. It's over,' Anais blurted, taking gulps of air as she tried to catch her breath.

Julia heard the words but didn't understand. 'What? Why? How? I've only been gone twenty minutes or so.'

'And that's all it took. He swanned in here and right back out again after delivering his news.'

'And the news is…'

'He's seeing someone else.'

Julia exhaled. 'No! Flynn seeing someone else? But he's devoted to you. You told us he was devoted to you. He was the one, you were the one.'

'Well, not any more he isn't.'

'And he thought the only time to tell you would be today, on your wedding day?' Julia was perplexed. What an absolute rat. Julia knew that the man was ruthless and not to be trusted. Look at the way he'd conducted business with her, and now this. Maybe, just maybe, Anais had had a lucky escape, even though it really wasn't the right time to be pointing this out to her.

Through her tears, all Anais could manage was a nod.

'Who... how long?' Julia had lots of questions spinning around her head.

Mia held the box of tissues towards Anais who grabbed a handful, blew her nose and shrugged. 'Some girl and I've no idea.'

'What – you didn't ask him?' continued Julia, probing gently.

'He didn't give me a chance, he told me the facts then left.'

'Did you not try to stop him?' Julia looked towards Mia.

'I never clapped eyes on him, he was in and out before I'd even finished my shower.'

Julia was shaking her head in disbelief. 'Ring him, we need to find out the answers.'

'No,' insisted Anais. 'What's the point? He's cheated on me... He's seeing someone else. I wouldn't have him back now anyway, or give him the satisfaction of thinking I'm bothered.'

Even though Julia hadn't favoured Anais's marriage to Flynn she still felt distraught for her friend. She knew in a few hours' time there was going to be a church full of people waiting to celebrate their marriage. Anais's mum was already at the hairdressers and her dad was currently on the way to the florist to pick up the bouquets and buttonholes... this wedding had cost a fortune and Flynn was walking away, leaving Anais to cancel everything and deal with the aftermath. What type of person was he?

'What about all the guests? What do you want me to do?' Julia's voice was soft.

Once more Anais broke down and began to wail.

'Sorry... sorry,' said Julia apologetically, focussing back on Anais. 'I didn't mean to make it worse.'

'How could he do this to me? How am I ever going to be able to show my face again?' Anais wept.

Julia slid her arm around Anais's shoulders and pulled her in for a hug. 'Shame on him. He's let a good thing go and one day he'll regret it. You will find someone who worships the ground you walk on... someone that deserves you.'

'Believe me, at this moment in time, I'm in no rush,' sniffled Anais, giving a strangled sob before dabbing her eyes and reaching for the bottle of champagne on the table. 'I need a drink,' she said, her voice cracking as she passed the bottle to Mia who popped the cork then poured the liquid into the leftover cups that were still on the table from last night.

All of them took a very large gulp and sat in silence for a moment before Julia spoke. 'Okay,' she said, with authority, taking control, 'we need to inform the guests, have you got a list? We can start ringing around.'

With a pained expression Anais nodded to the seating plan on the coffee table. 'All the names are on there, but I wouldn't have everyone's phone number. Maybe the easiest thing to do would be to post in the Facebook event. The news will spread like wildfire... it gets it over and done with in one click.'

Julia felt just terrible for her friend and could see Anais's heart was breaking. Julia thought this type of stuff only happened in the movies, she never thought it would happen in real life, especially not to someone she knew. Who the hell did Flynn Carter think he was? He might be a ruthless businessman, but this was another level. He'd humiliated Anais, kicked her to the kerb. It was unacceptable to treat anyone this way, especially on their wedding day. Julia didn't know how she would cope if something like this ever happened to her – it was a girl's worst nightmare.

The second Julia posted that the wedding was cancelled in the Facebook Group, Anais's phone began pinging out of control with notifications. Once more, Julia took control and switched off the phone before topping up the tumblers of champagne.

Flynn Carter would get his comeuppance one day. Julia believed in karma.

Chapter One

FIVE YEARS LATER

J ulia breathed in a lungful of the late summer air as she arrived back at the bed and breakfast and sat on the wrought iron chair outside the back door. Closing her eyes, she felt the sun beating down on her face. The last person she'd expected to see in the pub in her little village of Heartcross that very morning was Flynn Carter. She'd frozen momentarily, in complete shock and had to look twice to make sure she wasn't imagining things. She really wished she'd been hallucinating but he was very real, and he had been standing just a few metres away from her. Flynn was a face from the past she'd never expected to see again. He hadn't acknowledged her even though Julia had recognised him the minute she'd set eyes on him. The man that had demolished her grandfather's home and jilted her friend on her wedding day was now renting a cottage on Love Heart Lane for the next twelve months. What the hell was he doing in Heartcross?

Opening her eyes Julia stared out across the beautiful garden and smiled. The scenery was simply stunning, the high mountains rose steadily in the background, towering above the grassy pastureland, and the River Heart tumbled over the rocks. Foxglove Farm nestled in the distance and Drew was out on the quad bike riding over the fields with his son Finn clutching to his waist. This place was her own little piece of paradise, bought and paid for with the money from her grandfather's house. Julia's bed and breakfast was her whole world. The three-storey elegant country-style house dated back to the mid-1800s and was set in just over an acre of land, including the garden and its very own brook.

Julia had fallen in love with this place the second she saw it, and with its characteristic bedrooms and impressive living rooms with oak beams that ran the length of the ceilings alongside rustic log fires, she'd immediately put in an offer. Within months her own bed and breakfast business was up and running, and she never looked back.

Since Heartcross had been catapulted many times into the news over the last eighteen months, business was booming. The 'No Vacancies' sign had hung outside on the gate for months and Julia was continually turning customers away, so much so that she had decided to take the plunge and have plans drawn up for a two-storey extension on the back of the house with a luxury private annexe situated at the bottom of the garden. She couldn't wait to extend her little empire and was waiting patiently with her fingers firmly crossed hoping the all-important letter would land on the mat and the planning permission would be granted.

'Penny for them?'

Julia looked up and grinned. Eleni was standing in front of her wearing a long, lemon floaty dress with a beautiful bodice pulled in by a tight waistband. She was sporting a huge smile and swinging a parasol above her head, shielding herself from the afternoon rays.

'You look like someone from the 1920s,' Julia said and wished she was bolder with her dress sense. 'In fact, you look like you should be on a film set... *Pretty Woman*, whereas I...' Julia looked down at worn-out jogging pants and a T-shirt that was splattered with bleach stains. 'Goodness knows where I should be.'

'Are you calling me a prostitute?' Eleni put her hand on her chest in mock protest then giggled. 'And don't put yourself down, you are rocking the grunge look, it's very popular you know.' Eleni tipped Julia a cheeky wink before propping her parasol up against the wall. 'So come on, what have you got on your mind?' Eleni tilted her head to one side.

'Me, I was just thinking about life in general,' admitted Julia, 'and how far I've come in the last few years. This place makes me happy, the rooms are full, and it brings me joy every day... you know what, life is good.'

'Good for you! Those hikers come back time after time, and that's down to you,' smiled Eleni pulling out a chair and parking herself next to Julia.

'You're too kind. What did you want to be when you grew up? What was your ambition Eleni?'

'Me? That's easy. I wanted to become Mrs Harry Styles or Prince Harry's partner in crime. As you can imagine my parents weren't keen on either, hence the reason they kind of kicked me out and I ended up fending for myself with every Harry running for the hills.'

Julia chuckled. Eleni Gladmore was in her early twenties, was always the comedian, and had begun working at the B&B only a few months ago. She was as reliable as the church clock and currently lived in a small flat in the town of Glensheil on the other side of the bridge.

Initially Eleni was hired on a month's trial, but the second she'd stepped inside the B&B she had fitted in perfectly. With her wicked sense of humour and amazing baking skills – not to mention that she cooked up the best Full Scottish breakfast – Julia had hired her on the spot. It was lovely to have such company on a daily basis, and the pair of them spent most of their time smiling through the daily chores and dancing like loons as they cleaned and polished the house. They shared stories of their lives past and present, not to mention their religious Friday 'working' lunch in the pub.

Eleni reminded Julia of Merida, the Disney character from *Brave* with her long, wild, curly red hair, blue eyes, pale skin and slender body.

'How's your afternoon been?' asked Eleni.

'Interesting to say the least,' affirmed Julia.

'Go on... spill the beans because it can't be any worse than my afternoon.'

Julia looked over towards Eleni. 'OMG, how did it go?... The date?'

Eleni rolled her eyes. 'It was over before it began, but that's another story. Come on then, so what's happened in the little village of Heartcross? A nuclear bomb... the Queen booked a room or... please don't tell me Prince Harry actually turned up in the village... anything is possible after Zach Hudson.' Zach Hudson was a celebrity heartthrob who'd turned up in the village to film a new documentary – but after his dog was run over, Rory the local vet had saved its life and the two had become great friends, and now were off saving lions in Africa.

Julia couldn't help the smile on her face. 'Prince Harry is taken, if there was a nuclear bomb, I wouldn't be here to tell the tale and, no, the Queen hasn't booked into the B&B.'

'So what is it then?'

'Flynn Carter...'

'And who is Flynn Carter?' asked Eleni, none the wiser.

'A property developer, who's just rented out Rory's old house on Love Heart Lane.'

'Do you know him?'

'Yes, unfortunately I know him, and never in a month of Sundays did I ever think he would cross my path again.'

'Oooh, you look kind of angry. What exactly has this Flynn Carter done?'

Julia explained the history behind Flynn's ruthless

business dealings and his dumping of Anais on their wedding day.

'And this all happened five years ago,' asked a wide-eyed Eleni, listening to the story.

Julia nodded. 'I know I have all this,' she swept her hand in front of her, 'because of his money, but in my opinion, he didn't play nicely. I should have walked away. I feel he cheated my grandad, in a way; he'd worked hard all his life.' Julia raised an eyebrow. 'And then there was what he did to Anais too.'

'What sort of man does that? He actually dumped her on her wedding day?' Eleni looked horrified. 'That's every girl's worst nightmare. And the girl he ran off with, did he marry her?' asked Eleni.

'There's no wedding ring,' replied Julia, knowing that she'd clocked his hand when she saw him in the pub. 'According to all sources, he's bought the old Boathouse and is turning it into some sort of water sports centre. And rumours are Starcross Manor is being renovated into retirement flats. Whether that has something to do with him or not, I have no idea, but it seems likely since he's moved into a house on Love Heart Lane.'

Eleni whipped her phone out of her bag and began to tap away, staring at the screen with intensity. 'Mmm, Flynn Carter... property tycoon... businessman of the year twice running in the last two years, according to this... owner of a five-star chain of hotels... spa, golf course in Florida...' Eleni let out a low whistle. 'M-I-L-L-I-O-N-A-I-R-E,' she strung the word out. 'JEEZ!'

Eleni now had Julia's full attention as she passed over her phone and pointed at the screen. 'That man is wealthy, but yes, you're right he's not married, according to Google.'

Julia spent the next couple of minutes scrolling through Google. There was no mistaking Flynn Carter was a successful property developer with a string of five-star hotels under his Gucci belt, and his very first one still remained in Newton Stewart where her grandfather's house had once stood.

'Surely, he must have something to do with Starcross Manor,' said Julia, thinking that the rickety old Boathouse on the edge of the River Heart was never going to generate an income as much as all his other successful businesses listed on the internet. 'There's no other vacant land this side of the bridge.'

'Maybe he's just had enough of the hectic rat race and is looking to enjoy the quiet village life,' suggested Eleni.

Julia gave her a look. 'And that's what I love above you youngsters... innocence. You mark my words: Flynn Carter is not looking to enjoy the quiet life. That man is ruthless, he'll be up to something. There's a reason he's turned up here... we just don't know what that reason is yet.'

Jokingly, Eleni wagged her finger. 'Cynical, that's what you are. What happened to your jilted friend, by the way?' she asked, taking her phone back from Julia then continually scrolling through every image of Flynn Carter on the internet. 'He's definitely got that handsome, sultry, brooding look going on, hasn't he?' She turned the phone back to Julia, who had to admit he was physically attractive.

He was the kind of guy who would turn heads wherever he went.

'Anais moved on, got married, has two boys. Her Facebook is always filled with exotic holidays and fast cars. Looks like she lives a great life and is very happy.'

'That must had been nerve-racking, getting married again. I'd be a nervous wreck putting myself through that again. Were you bridesmaid again?'

Julia shook her head. 'No, not that time. It was an intimate affair, the two of them took themselves off and got married on a sandy beach in Jamaica. I can't say I blame her.'

Eleni was still staring at Flynn's image on her phone. 'There's something about this Flynn Carter, an air of confidence about him. A snappy dresser too,' continued Eleni, finally putting her phone down.

'Time will tell why he's here, but my gut feeling isn't good. Cup of tea or a glass of homemade lemonade?'

'Lemonade for me please,' answered Eleni.

'And how was your date?' remembered Julia, standing up.

Eleni rolled her eyes. 'Not my type – would you believe he had a tattoo on his chest of George Michael.'

'What? Don't be daft… really?'

'I kid you not. Only ten minutes into the date he ripped open his shirt and began singing "I'm Your Man", pure embarrassment. Apparently at the weekend he doubles as a tribute act for Wham! But that is the first and last date, believe me.'

Julia couldn't help but chuckle. 'Oh my God, that's hilarious, the youth of today.'

'You aren't that much older, you know.'

'I have at least twenty years on you. And before you ask: no, I've not thought any more about my birthday.'

This year Julia was hitting the big 4–0. It didn't faze her going into her fourth decade, and she would prefer not to make too much of a fuss, but there was no way her friends Isla, Allie and Felicity were going to allow it to slip by unnoticed. She wasn't opposed to a few drinks down the Grouse and Haggis pub, but already Isla was researching weekend festivals, racing car days, and clay shooting weekends. After a few gin and tonics and in a drunken stupor, Julia had agreed to leave the birthday preparations in their capable hands, much to their delight.

'I wouldn't worry, I'm sure the girls have got it all under control,' grinned Eleni.

'I'm sure they have,' replied Julia, raising an eyebrow. 'And I'm sure you are in the thick of it all. I'll get the lemonade.' As Julia disappeared towards the kitchen, she twisted her long blonde hair and secured it in a bun. Woody, her faithful Cocker Spaniel, was hot on her heels hoping for an afternoon treat, and sat to attention next to the kitchen cupboard looking up longingly at the treat jar on the shelf next to the fridge.

'How can I resist those adorable eyes,' she muttered, ruffling the top of his head before unscrewing the lid and tossing him a biscuit, which he swallowed in one gulp.

'No more, otherwise we will both be on a diet,' chuckled Julia, reaching for the glasses.

The kitchen was Julia's favourite place in the whole of the B&B, with its farmhouse sink and chequerboard floor. There was one Aga and two ovens, two fridges and the aluminium pots and pans hung from the wooden rack fixed to the ceiling. At the far end there was a real fire with an emerald green wingback armchair situated to the left, a battered brown leather sofa and a small coffee table which housed numerous magazines alongside the book she was currently reading.

She poured two glasses of lemonade and placed them down on a green floral tin tray alongside two pieces of cake Rona had dropped off from the teashop. Once back outside Julia handed over a huge wedge of cake on a white china plate.

'You could never be on a diet in this place, could you?' said Eleni, sinking her teeth in immediately, then letting out the biggest 'mmm' of approval.

'Life is too short for all that diet malarkey. Love me… love my wobbly bits. I just need to find someone to love me now,' laughed Julia, who had had numerous dates in the past couple of years, but nobody who had set her world on fire.

Wiping the crumbs from around her mouth, as well as the blob of cream that was resting on her chin, Eleni slipped a pile of envelopes towards Julie. 'Maggie's just dropped these off. She apologises for this morning's late delivery of post, apparently she got caught out by a flat tyre on the van and was late starting her rounds.'

Julia flicked through the post. 'Bills and more bills,' she exclaimed, shuffling through the piles of letters. Then Julia placed a brown letter down on the table in front of her and stared.

'What's that one?' asked Eleni, with intrigue.

'That one is from The Highland Council.' More than likely this letter was the decision that Julia had been nervously waiting for.

'Is that what I think it is?'

'I think it is,' replied Julia nervously, still staring at the letter.

'Well come on then, open it!' urged Eleni, pushing her plate to the side and folding both arms on the table.

'I daren't, what if it's not good news?'

'And what if it is?' Eleni shook her head in despair. 'If you aren't going to open it then I will.' She crept her hand forward slowly, but Julia quickly grabbed the letter and slipped her finger under the edge of the envelope and tore it open. She held her breath as she scanned the words as quickly as possible, and there was the decision, right before her eyes in black and white.

Julia tipped her head back and briefly closed her eyes. 'Planning permission for a two-storey extension has been granted,' Julia waved the letter above her head. 'Whoo-hoo! Oh my God. They said yes!' Excitement surged through Julia's body, it had taken her nearly three years to save and secure a loan from the bank, but now the wait was finally over. She stood up and punched the air and began jigging on the spot.

'Congratulations! This is brilliant,' squealed Eleni. 'I'm so happy for you, but I suppose this means I'm going to have twice as many bedrooms to clean.'

'Absolutely you are!' Julia was over the moon. She'd already organised numerous quotes from a handful of builders and now one of those quotes was going to become reality. She couldn't wait, her little business empire was finally expanding.

'When do you think all the building work is going to start then?' asked Eleni, taking a sip of her drink.

Julia paused and thought about it for a second. 'Hopefully as soon as possible.' Since Heartcross had become a famous village she'd already turned away numerous bookings and she didn't want that to happen again. Even though there may possibly be building work during the Christmas period, it would be worth it, knowing she would double her income by March.

'I think we need to celebrate,' suggested Eleni, looking over the letter. She was genuinely chuffed for her boss.

'We could grab a drink at the pub after I've taken you for a driving lesson... my treat,' suggested Julia.

'Now you're talking! What's the plan? Shall we use the carpark again up at Starcross Manor, you never know, we might even bump into that Flynn guy,' replied Eleni, flicking through the pages of the free newspaper that had been delivered alongside the post.

'In fact, there he is, the man himself.'

'Huh,' answered Julia, rubbing the side of her jaw.

'Have you still got toothache?' asked Eleni, turning the newspaper towards Julia. Staring back at her was the face of Flynn Carter.

'Yes, but never mind that, what's he doing in there?' asked Julia, her eyes quickly scanning the article. Immediately her eyes were drawn to his. He had the look of a movie star, a charismatic smile and she had to admit, he was extremely photogenic. 'There's no getting away from this man,' she said, feeling a little irritation towards him – there he was, invading her little world once more.

'The old Boathouse,' continued Eleni, 'an all-new singing and dancing water sports centre for the tourists. That will be a massive hit with the locals too.'

Judging by all the articles she'd read, it was obvious Flynn knew a good business opportunity when he saw it. Since the bridge had collapsed last year and Heartcross had been catapulted into the news, the amount of tourists climbing the mountain had multiplied, and re-opening the Boathouse would no doubt be very popular with all the activity junkies that frequented the area.

'There's definitely fun to be had, especially in the summer months…' Eleni pointed to a line in the article. 'Look, he's said here… opening up within the next month. He's definitely sticking around.'

Julia looked over the article. 'I still don't trust the man. Flynn Carter doesn't do anything unless there's something big in it for him. There's more to him being back in Heartcross than just the Boathouse, mark my words.'

'Watch this space,' replied Eleni, closing the newspaper. 'Right, shall we get this driving lesson underway? Then we can get to the pub and celebrate your good news.'

'Absolutely,' agreed Julia, still thinking about Flynn.

'But you do know if he's moved into the village, you are going to come across at him at some point?'

It was like Eleni had just read her mind.

'Yes, I know, and between you and me I'm not looking forward to it.' Julia knew in such a small village that she was bound to bump into him, but she wasn't sure if Flynn would even recognise her. Julia wished she knew the real reason why Flynn Carter had descended on their village. Maybe it *was* just because of the Boathouse. Only time would tell.

Chapter Two

Eleni's mirrored aviator shades looked cool as she placed them on the bridge of her nose and pushed the key into the ignition. Julia had to admit the first couple of times she'd taken Eleni out that she'd thought she'd made a huge mistake offering to teach her to drive, but thankfully, as time went on, she'd started to improve. Julia watched as Eleni strapped herself in then checked the mirrors. She put the car in first gear and eased out of the driveway, and kangarooed a short distance before driving smoothly.

'Sorry,' she apologised. 'That clutch thingy has a mind of its own sometimes.'

'You don't say,' answered Julia, keeping her eyes fixed firmly ahead.

Eleni indicated left and headed through the High Street. Outside the Grouse and Haggis there wasn't a spare table in sight, everyone was out in full force taking advantage of the sunshine.

'Turn right at the end of the road and concentrate, you're driving too near to the kerb, you'll end up clipping the wheels,' Julia instructed.

'Yes boss! And don't look so terrified, this is about our tenth lesson you know.' Eleni slowed down then turned right, thankfully pulling off from the junction smoothly this time. Teaching Eleni to drive reminded Julia of her own father teaching her to drive. It had ended in tears and countless arguments, and it finally came to a head when her father had insisted he drove the car out of the garage as it was rather a tight squeeze, but unfortunately ended up running over her mother's bike. Julia hadn't helped the matter by laughing so hard she nearly wet herself. Her father had slammed the door then immediately tripped over a watering can and twisted his ankle. He was heard muttering expletives as he'd shouted for Julia's mother, who'd then spent the rest of the day sat in Accident & Emergency. After that, Julia had saved up for her own lessons with the money from her part-time job at the local bakery, and had passed her driving test first time.

'Fifteenth to be precise, not that I'm counting or anything,' stated Julia, still with her eyes fixed firmly on the road ahead. 'It's a good plan to head towards Starcross Manor, we might be able to practise some emergency stops, there's plenty of space up there to drive around.'

Eleni followed the winding lane through the woodlands and manoeuvred her way past the gatehouse and approached the tree-lined driveway where an impressive elegant manor house stood straight in front of them.

'Starcross Manor. This place still takes my breath away, and just look at that lake,' exclaimed Julia. The Georgian manor house standing in front of them was magnificent, set in a hundred acres of green lush grass which incorporated formal gardens, a deer park, woodlands and a wildflower meadow. The driveway leading to the entrance was grand, sweeping into a wide circle with an ornate fountain in the centre which wouldn't look out of place in the grounds of a royal palace. Huge stone steps led to the large double oak doors within a broad porch of stone pillars. Ivy clung to the walls of the building. 'It's like something out of a romantic novel.'

'I thought you wanted me to keep my eyes on the road.' Eleni took a swift look over towards Julia and grinned.

'I do!' Julia wound down the window and stared out across the lake as they drove past. It teemed with life. A proud, plump mallard sailed across, followed by five baby hatchlings, frogs jumped from one lily pad to the other whilst flashing green and blue dragon flies hovered above. A weeping willow bejewelled the water and with the sporadic clouds sailing above, the scene reminded Julia of a Monet painting.

'Have you seen the sign?' Eleni nodded to the wooden sign hammered into the ground 'Sold.'

'Yes, it sold at auction last month. It'll make a lovely retirement home. I wouldn't mind ending my days in a place like this.'

'What's that over there?' Eleni took her hand off the wheel and pointed to a freshly cut lawn at the side of the property.

'A hot air balloon, well I never. I'm not sure if it's landed or just about to take off. Can you see anyone around?'

Eleni was still staring across the fields when Julia screamed out and pulled at the steering wheel.

Time slowed.

Thud.

Eleni's eyes darted forward as she hit her foot hard on the brake causing the seatbelts to tighten and the car to screech along the gravel until eventually it stopped.

Julia squeezed her eyes shut, her chest tightened, her breath quick and shallow. She grasped the side of her seat to try and regain control. 'Shit.'

'Oh my God, I'm so sorry.' Eleni's voice was shaky, barely catching her breath. 'What have I hit?'

Instantly, Julia felt all the colour drain from her face, her heart was hammering so hard against her ribcage she thought it was going to burst out of her chest at any given second.

'Are you okay?' asked Eleni, her knuckles white as they gripped the steering wheel.

'I think so, are you?'

Eleni could only manage a nod.

For a moment, they both sat still.

'Please take a look,' Eleni's voice was earnest.

Julia, still trying to calm her beating heart as she unclipped her seatbelt, flung open the car door. Tripping up over her own feet she hurried to the front of the car and breathed a sigh of relief. 'It's okay, we've… you've… just hit a cardboard box full of papers.'

Eleni exhaled. 'Thank God for that,' she said, resting her head back on the seat rest. 'I need a moment. I think I'm in shock.'

'What the hell do you think you are doing? It's not Knockhill Racing Circuit. You nearly smashed my car into smithereens,' bellowed a voice from behind them.

Taking a sharp intake of breath, Julia's eyes widened and for a moment she was frozen to the spot, unable to move. Walking towards them was an angry-looking Flynn Carter throwing his hands up into the air. She watched as he loosened the top button of his shirt, and stared at the battered cardboard box, the papers inside now strewn all over the ground. Flynn was shaking his head in disbelief.

A petrified-looking Eleni slowly climbed out from behind the wheel, she fumbled to answer then blurted, 'I'm so sorry, it was my fault. I wasn't looking where I was going…' She bent down and began scooping up the papers in her arms. She was physically shaking as she handed Flynn a pile of crumpled documents. 'I'm learning to drive, but it seems I'm not doing very well.' Eleni attempted to lighten the mood but looked like she was about to burst into tears.

Lifting a single eyebrow, Flynn's face softened, he looked between them both. 'No, I'm sorry; I didn't mean to shout, forgive me. And where are my manners – are you both okay? You must be feeling a little shook up.'

Julia knew he had every right to raise his voice and stepped in. 'Honestly, we're fine, just relieved we've not actually run over a human being, an animal, or hit your car,' she said, reaching down and picking up the rest of the papers that were flapping lightly in the slight breeze. 'I hope these aren't anything too important.'

'Only my accounts,' he replied, taking the papers from Julia and holding her gaze.

Turning slightly pink, she felt herself tingle as his hand brushed against hers. 'Do I know you?' he asked, as his gaze intensified. Julia felt her heart skip a beat as she stood there for a second in an awkward silence. Her thoughts were racing all over the place before she decided to come clean.

'We met a while back now.'

'Did we? I can't place it... when and where?' he asked, his eyes still firmly fixed on Julia.

'Well, actually, I was a bridesmaid at your wedding.'

Flynn frowned in concentration then took a cautious step back as his eyes swept over her entire body. Then he locked eyes with her once more. 'Bridesmaid?'

She was momentarily thrown by the strength of his gaze causing her heart to thump a little faster. 'Well actually that's not quite true because the wedding didn't take place... Anais Brown?'

Flynn raised an eyebrow and seemed to bristle at the sound of Anais's name.

'Julia...' she said.

'Julia...' he repeated.

'Julia Coleman.'

'Julia... of course, please forgive me. How are you? You look great... It's great to see you.' He stepped forward and kissed her on both cheeks taking Julia completely by surprise, the aroma of his aftershave not going unnoticed.

'What are you doing here in Heartcross?' he asked, clicking his car key and placing the squashed box of papers in the boot of his car.

'I live here, I own the B&B in the village.'

'Really? You live here? Such a small world,' he turned back towards them with a warm smile. 'I just don't believe this. How long have you been here?'

'A good few years now,' she replied.

'The local B&B you say?'

Julia watched as he rolled the sleeves of his shirt up over his forearms. He raked his hand through his fringe and pushed it to one side, his eyes still looking down on her.

'You must be busy this time of year, especially with the gorgeous weather we are having.'

'Very,' she replied, knowing she was still staring at Flynn.

'Are you in a rush?' Flynn looked between the two of them. 'And do forgive me,' he stretched out his hand towards Eleni, 'I'm Flynn.'

'Eleni,' she replied, warmly.

'Let me show you around the grounds. Would you like to take a look?'

For a second, Julia hesitated. This was the man she had

numerous reservations about, but she was dying to take a look around Starcross Manor.

Flynn smiled and acknowledged her hesitation. 'Come on, I'll show you the deer park, it's a place of outstanding beauty,' he suggested, still staring at Julia.

They began to walk and followed Flynn through a tiny stone archway which led through to a courtyard with twisted vines of coloured roses entwined in the wooden-built lattice roof above their heads. 'It's beautiful,' exclaimed Julia looking up. In that split second, she tripped up the step and clutched the back of Flynn's shirt to steady herself.

He looked over his shoulder and gave her a lopsided grin. 'You okay?'

'Sorry, I was too busy looking at the roses instead of watching where I was going.'

Julia knew she was clumsy, but this was embarrassing. Flynn led them through a paved garden that was enchanted, littered with potted blooms, the whole place was colourful. Just up ahead was a wooden door which let them onto the winding side of the valley and around a quiet millpond, into a wilderness garden.

'This place, it's like a maze,' remarked Eleni, taking in her surroundings, 'the history of the place is intriguing.'

Julia was in awe, her eyes wide. 'These gardens will have taken many years to nurture and cultivate into such gorgeous places of beauty.'

'They are amazing, I fell in love with this place the second I visited,' admitted Flynn, once again catching

Julia's eye and causing her stomach to give a little flip. 'This is the wilderness garden.' Flowers and plants in a multitude of colours danced up to their waists as they walked the hexagon paving stones, and once they were on the other side Julia and Eleni stood and stared.

'Wow, just wow!' Julia gave a little gasp. 'Can this place get any more magical?' The secluded woodland and ancient trees were the perfect sanctuary for the herd of sixteen fallow and red deer lolloping in front of their eyes.

'It's just something isn't it?' said Flynn. 'This undisturbed land provides refuge for birds, roosting bats, foxes, etc. I could sit out here and watch the wildlife all day.' He pointed over to numerous oak treehouses scattered around. 'Up there, such fantastic views.'

'I would have never known all this was even here,' exclaimed Eleni, watching the herd of deer. 'They are mesmerising.'

'There's something special about this place,' remarked Flynn, taking a glance at his watch. 'We can head back around the side of the lake.'

Julia turned and as her foot hit the tree stump in front of her, she tripped for the second time today. 'For God's sake,' she muttered. Bewildered and feeling a fool she was yanked to her feet by Flynn's strapping arms.

'I've never had a woman fall at my feet twice in less than five minutes.' His eyes sparkled and Julia wanted the ground to swallow her up, but she couldn't help thinking he was flirting with her a little.

She smiled and brushed herself down, yet was conscious

her face was burning a deep red colour. They began walking again and Julia caught Eleni watching her with amusement.

'Did you go weak at the knees?' Eleni whispered to Julia, who shot her a warning glance which Eleni knew only too well meant behave yourself.

'There's rocky ground up here. I'm just pointing it out in case you fancy falling for me for a third time,' joked Flynn, with a look of mischief on his face, leaving a tingling pulse racing through Julia's body which she couldn't control.

Julia gave a sarcastic smile while Eleni came to her rescue and began asking questions about the history of Starcross Manor. Flynn chatted amiably as they walked around the lake back towards the entrance and Julia took the opportunity to steal a sideward glance at him. He was probably in a relationship, men as handsome as him were never single. Julia bet he had settled down with a beautiful wife and no doubt had equally stunning children. Taking another look towards his wedding finger there was no evidence of a ring, not even a ring mark. She had to admit she was intrigued by him, even though a little wary. Here he was being the perfect host showing them around as though nothing had ever happened all those years ago.

They arrived back at the front of the manor house. 'This place is magnificent,' gushed Eleni. 'How's the inside coming on?'

Julia was curious to see what was going on inside too, and she put a foot on the stone steps leading to the grand entrance.

'I'm sorry ladies, inside isn't ready yet.'

Julia thought she'd noticed Flynn stiffen, but maybe she was mistaken.

'We don't mind,' pushed Eleni.

'Health and safety and all that, plus…' Flynn's tone now seemed a little matter of fact, he took another glance at his watch. 'I am waiting for a call around about now.'

Suddenly Julia felt disappointed, she was intrigued to take a look inside the manor house and took a last fleeting glance towards the entrance.

'But we must catch up again soon. Julia, it's been lovely to see you again after all this time,' Flynn seemed to soften again.

'You too,' she replied, looking straight into his eyes. 'Thank you for showing us around.'

Before Flynn could say any more his phone began to ring out. 'I must take this,' he said, looking towards Julia then back towards his phone, his eyes batting between the two like a slow game of tennis before he bounded up the steps and waved above his head.

The second he was out of sight Julia turned towards Eleni who was grinning like a Cheshire cat. 'What are you smirking at?'

'As if you didn't know.'

Julia knew exactly what she was going to say but ignored her and held out her hand. 'I'll drive back,' she said taking the keys off Eleni. 'I think it's safer that way.'

As Julia climbed behind the wheel Eleni slipped into the

passenger seat and was still smirking. 'Spit it out. I'm not having you look like that all afternoon.'

'I've only got one thing to say,' replied Eleni, pulling on her seatbelt. 'S-e-x-u-a-l c-h-e-m-i-s-t-r-y.' She strung out the words. 'Talk about electricity – you pair could light up the whole of Scotland with those sparks!'

'Don't be ridiculous,' argued Julia, but knowing there was some sort of feeling fizzing inside her. 'I know the kind of man he is.'

'He seemed genuinely lovely to me and you can't deny he is drop-dead gorgeous with the perkiest bum and that shirt clinging to every muscle! Not to mention that aftershave oozes class,' added Eleni, taking a swift glance towards Julia, who started the engine.

Still ignoring Eleni's comments, Julia turned the car around on the gravel carpark and gave a sideward glance back towards the entrance of Starcross Manor. Flynn was standing at the top of the stone steps with his phone to his ear. He saluted with an air of confidence and a twinkle in his eye that caused Julia's heart to race.

Damn, he'd caught her looking. She gave a little awkward salute back, leaving Eleni chuckling away. Ignoring the laughter coming from the passenger seat, Julia drove towards the entrance then headed back along the road towards the pub.

'He has got everything hasn't he?' Eleni continued. 'The looks, the money…'

Julia was fully aware how handsome Flynn was, and of his financial status. 'He has, but there's right ways of making money instead of ripping people off,' she replied, thinking back to her grandad's house.

It only took a couple of minutes to reach the Grouse and Haggis, and Julia steered the car into the carpark and switched off the engine.

'Retirement home did you say?' asked Eleni, unclipping her seatbelt and opening the car door.

'Yes, apparently so,' replied Julia, climbing out of the car. Flynn was still very much on her mind.

'All I can say is he was taken with you,' declared Eleni. 'He kept taking sneaky looks in your direction.'

'Don't be daft,' protested Julia, but she knew the second she'd set eyes on him that there was some sort of pull towards him, although she felt a little confused. Bad boys were always more attractive, weren't they? And considering their past, he'd surprised Julia by being so warm and hospitable, showing them around the grounds especially after Eleni nearly crashed into his car. He'd welcomed her like a long-lost friend. This wasn't the man she thought she'd remember so clearly from the past, and she wanted to discover more about Flynn.

As they walked towards the pub Eleni held open the door. 'And I've only got one thing to say.'

'I hope it's, I'm sorry,' suggested Julia, 'as you did very nearly crash my car.'

'More like, let's get a drink, we have your good news to celebrate.'

'And just so you know, the drinks are on you.'

'Okay boss!' chirped Eleni, with a salute.

Chapter Three

The second they stepped inside the pub Allie waved at Julia and Eleni from behind the bar. As usual Allie was thoroughly at home serving the regulars, leaning against the pumps with all her usual confidence on display. She was invincibly cheerful as ever, but as Julia weaved her way towards the bar with Eleni following close behind, she thought Allie looked tired.

Even though Allie was a natural behind the bar, she had her work cut out on days like this, and her words came out in a shout. 'How's your day going?'

'Apart from this one just tried to kill me.' Julia rolled her eyes towards Eleni.

'What? Why? How?' Allie asked confused, straightening the beer mats in front of them.

'Never offer to teach someone to drive.'

Allie chuckled. 'It's going well, then. You'll be in need of a stiff drink.'

'A bottle of pinot grigio and two glasses. We are celebrating.'

'You're celebrating she nearly killed you?' chuckled Allie, reaching for a bottle of wine from the fridge behind her.

Julia shook her head. 'Not quite. The planning permission for the B&B has finally been granted!'

'Oh, that's brilliant news Julia, I'm made up for you.'

'Thank you, me too,' replied Julia smiling. Everything was planned, Julia had numerous spreadsheets with all the costs estimated and how long each part of the building work should take. She couldn't wait to call the builder and negotiate a start date.

'Oh, and if you're hungry, Dad has the BBQ going in the pub garden. You know what he's like the second the sun comes out; he can't help himself.' Allie swiped Julia's cash card and gave it her back.

As they ventured outside Julia looked around for a vacant table. The setting was perfect, with a small terrace area filled with wrought-iron tables and chairs and glorious blooms tumbling from the planters in every corner. Fairy lights wrapped around the wooden trestle above them and there were three wooden steps down to the lawn area.

'This is the life,' said Julia, thankful that all her jobs at the B&B were done for today and she had no intention of venturing back anytime soon.

They settled on a wooden bench not far from the sizzle of the BBQ. Allie's dad, Fraser, was in his element and looked the part, wearing his wife Meredith's apron and poking at the coals vigorously. 'There's burgers ready,' he shouted triumphantly as Allie ferried out a large platter of bread buns and people began to form an orderly queue.

Julia relaxed and poured herself and Eleni a glass of wine. 'We can leave the car here, I'll pick it up in the morning.'

'Suits me,' replied Eleni, holding her glass up. 'Here's to you and new beginnings.'

They clinked glasses and both took a sip.

'I love days like this,' murmured Julia, but she knew it wouldn't be long before the temperature changed. Winter in Heartcross could be absolutely brutal, as everyone had discovered last year when the thawing snow had flooded Heartcross and the fierce storms had brought the bridge crashing down, leaving them all stranded. Julia glanced around the garden and, spotting Alfie, beckoned him over. 'Guess what I have?' she said, unable to hide the beam on her face.

Alfie smiled as he strolled over towards them. 'I know exactly what you have... planning permission. I get all the inside information, working in the council offices. Congratulations! When does all the chaos begin? Have you lined up your builder?'

'Hopefully as soon as possible, but I need to give Jack a ring – the builder you recommended.'

Jack Langdon was the eldest of three brothers working for the family business, established in the 90s, based in Glensheil. They'd come highly recommended by Alfie and when Julia checked out their history and reviews, no one had a bad word to say about them. She knew he'd be perfect for the job.

'Jack's here you know, I spotted him inside earlier. Go and have a chat with him,' encouraged Alfie, draining his pint and placing the empty glass on the table. 'I was just on my way home but congratulations again. Enjoy the rest of the afternoon.'

'Will do, thanks Alfie.'

'So what does this Jack Langdon look like?' enquired Eleni, watching the queue finally diminish at the side of Fraser. 'And I'm feeling a bit peckish, do you fancy a burger?'

Julia looked astounded. 'You're feeling peckish after that slab of cake we devoured before coming out?'

'Always room for more food, and it'll help to soak up the alcohol.'

Julia couldn't believe how much Eleni put away. One of the perks of cooking the Full Scottish breakfast every morning was that Eleni got to make one for herself, and the amount of cake she consumed was astronomical – yet she never put an ounce of weight on. Unlike Julia, who only had to look at anything remotely unhealthy and wham – she automatically put half a stone on.

'There's Jack.' Julie nodded towards the huddle of lads glugging lager and laughing heartily a few tables away from them. They watched as the lads lifted their pint glasses high in the air and cheered. 'It looks like they're having a good time.'

Jack Langdon looked like he should be on the front of a

surfer magazine, with his mop of curly hair and olive skin. He was deeply tanned and looked like he'd been on holiday for a month.

'How old is he? And he's going to be our builder? I approve.' Eleni was watching him closely. 'He will be a very welcome attraction around the place.'

'He's around twenty-five at a guess, and if he is going to be our builder, he doesn't need any distractions until my building work is completed,' joked Julia with a smile.

'Hmm, I'll do my best but no promises... Girlfriend?'

Julia shrugged. 'How would I know?'

'Because you village-type people know everything about everyone, always into each other's business.'

Julia swiped her arm playfully. 'Don't you be cheeky.'

'Oh, and don't look now, but here's your favourite villager...' Eleni tipped Julia a wink.

'Huh?'

Julia's head angled towards the entrance. In walked Flynn Carter with a confident swagger. He was now clean-shaven, wearing a Fred Perry T-shirt, navy blue shorts and flip flops.

'Nice legs,' stated Eleni, staring at his tanned legs and muscular calves, but Eleni didn't need to point them out, Julia had already noticed.

'There's only a certain type of man who can pull off wearing flip-flops and he's definitely one of them,' continued Eleni.

Julia watched as Flynn disappeared inside the pub and walked out moments later clutching a beer. He parked himself at an empty table not far from the BBQ and began scrolling through his phone.

'He's probably on Tinder looking to date and dump his next victim,' joked Eleni.

'It's not funny,' insisted Julia but whatever he was looking at on his phone, he was finding it mildly amusing, as his mouth hitched into a smile.

Julia couldn't help herself, she simultaneously kept flicking her eyes in his direction. 'Wait until I tell Anais he's turned up in the village. Out of all the villages in the country, he turns up here.'

'Did she ever see him after that day?' questioned Eleni. She too was staring over in his direction.

'No, she never set eyes on him again.'

Flynn looked up from his phone and caught Julia's eye, and the moment hung in the air. He acknowledged her with a lopsided grin, and again she felt a tiny flutter inside. Julia shifted in her seat. Damn, she thought, feeling a slight blush to her cheeks, he knew she was watching him.

'See, he's friendly, he seems alright to me,' said Eleni, noticing his smile.

'I'm definitely intrigued,' replied Julia. 'He certainly seems not quite the man I remember, from what I've seen so far, but I'm certainly keeping my wits about me. I'm nobody's fool.'

As the afternoon passed, Julia chatted to Eleni about her plans for the B&B. Everyone was in good spirits, enjoying the sunshine. Fraser patrolled the pub garden, chatting to the customers and making sure everyone was okay, when suddenly there was some sort of commotion. One of the hikers' dogs had managed to slip its lead and jumped up at a reveller's plate, swiping a hotdog and swallowing it in nearly one gulp. The hiker scooped up the dog and was apologetic and mortified, however the dog looked very pleased with itself, swinging its tail from side to side. Fraser hurried over with a fresh hotdog.

'There's a couple of burgers left – any takers... any more?' Fraser bellowed on his way back to flip the burgers over.

'Those burgers have our names on them. Come on,' said Eleni standing up. 'We best grab them before that dog goes in for seconds.'

Julia looked over towards Flynn, who wasn't sitting far from the BBQ. It would be rude not to pass the time of day with him.

'Maybe we should do the neighbourly thing and invite him over to join us, he won't know many people in the village yet,' suggested Eleni. 'And you can get to know him a little better.'

'Let's get those burgers,' said Julia, not rising to the bait and ignoring Eleni's suggestion even though she wanted to find out why Flynn was here in Heartcross.

'As my old granny said, life twists and turns in mysterious ways. People come into your life for a reason. There must be a reason he's turned back up in yours.'

'He hasn't turned up in my life, he's turned up in the village where I live. That's nothing to do with me.' But as they walked over towards Fraser, Julia's gaze once more drifted over towards Flynn. She noticed he'd taken another phone call and was chatting away once more.

'A burger, is it ladies?' asked Fraser, grabbing a serviette and opening up a bun. 'Onions?'

They nodded.

Just at that moment, the pesky dog escaped its owner again, and with its impeccable timing it tripped up Allie, who was carrying a tray full of drinks. Julia watched in slow motion as the drinks were hurled into the air, before spilling over the burning-hot coals of the BBQ.

Whoosh… Flames hurled high and out of control.

Fraser was waving his arms frantically. 'Water, we need water, a damp towel… anything.'

Out of the corner of her eye Julia was aware of a sudden movement. Eleni stepped back, and Julia squealed as a tidal wave of ice-cold water was thrown all over the BBQ… and her.

'What the hell do you think you are doing?' raged Julia, flinging her arms open wide as the water dripped from her face.

Flynn's face registered his alarm as he held the empty bucket. 'Putting the fire out.'

'Urghh,' Julia grumbled, swiping the water from her bare arms.

Eleni was doing her very best to stifle her laughter. She bent down and helped Allie pick up the glasses that had been thrown into the air; thankfully most of them had bounced along the grass and not shattered into thousands of pieces.

'I'm so sorry Dad, I tripped,' Allie looked genuinely shocked. 'That dog came from nowhere. I didn't see it. Is everyone okay?' She looked around for the dog who had caused the commotion, but he was now sitting down quietly next to his owner like it was nothing to do with him.

After checking Julia was okay Fraser looked down at the two soggy burgers left on the BBQ. 'I don't suppose...' he said turning towards Eleni and Julia. 'No, of course not. Too soggy and kind of cremated... if you are still hungry, it won't take too long to get the BBQ up and running again.'

Eleni looked towards Julia then towards Fraser. 'Why not, it'll give Julia time to dry out in the sun.'

'Are you alright?' asked Flynn, his voice soft and full of concern. 'I'm so sorry, I just heard a scream, saw flames and reacted.'

'Am I alright? You've just chucked a bucket of ice water over me.' Julia's eyebrows shot up. Feeling embarrassed. 'Look at the state of me,' said Julia, fully aware that everyone in the pub garden was staring in her direction. She exhaled and straightened her back.

Flynn took a cautious step back and looked at her.

Julia gave a brief headshake and was mortified: her old sodden T-shirt was drenched and clinging to her breasts.

'Stop looking at me,' she said with a twinge of irritation.

'But you just told me to look, and if it's any consolation you look pretty good to me,' he said, with a slight smile. But Julia was far from smiling. She huffed and was trying not to focus on his words, but couldn't help wondering if he was actually flirting with her.

Meredith hurried out then, holding a large towel that she draped over Julia's shoulders. 'Here, take this, at least you'll dry off quickly in this weather.'

'Thanks Meredith,' said Julia gratefully, clutching the towel tightly.

'Let me get you some drinks, it's the least I can do,' offered Flynn, this time looking hopefully over towards Eleni.

'Perfect,' she replied just in case Julia refused.

Fraser outstretched his hand. 'And thank you for thinking fast on your feet, those flames could have taken off my eyebrows.'

'It was nothing, and I am sorry about your soggy burgers.'

Fraser seemed to be chuckling away with Flynn as Julia traipsed back towards the table. She sat down and took a sip of her wine then immediately topped up her glass.

'It's a good job Flynn has offered to pay for more drinks, the rate you're throwing them back,' observed Eleni.

'Just look at the state of me. First I trip up not once but twice in front of him, and now he's flung a cold bucket of ice water over me.' Julia held Eleni's gaze and they both burst out laughing. 'You couldn't write it, could you?' Julia was shaking her head in disbelief.

'You shouldn't be allowed out without a government health warning stamped on you,' teased Eleni.

Just at that moment, Meredith appeared at the side of the table balancing a fresh bottle of wine and two new glasses, courtesy of Flynn.

'Thank you, Meredith,' said Julia, noticing Flynn was walking over towards them from the corner of her eye.

'Julia, I'm sorry again,' he said sounding sincere. 'Enjoy your drinks.'

He was just about to walk off when Eleni invited him to sit down. 'Come and join us; you can't know too many people here.'

He looked towards Julia, who gestured for him to sit down.

'Not many,' he admitted, looking pleased they'd invited him to sit with them. 'Thank you,' he slipped onto the bench opposite them.

'Can I get you a drink?' Meredith asked, still hovering by the table, and then promptly hurried to retrieve Flynn a cold beer.

'So tell me about Heartcross?' Flynn looked between Julia and Eleni. 'It seems such a relaxed place when dogs aren't pinching sausages off plates or I'm not throwing buckets of cold water over residents.' He gave Julia a wicked grin.

Julia shook her head in jest. 'You don't want to go falling out with the residents of Heartcross, you know. We are a very close community.'

She studied his face when Meredith reappeared with his drink. He seemed relaxed. There was a certain charm about him, and he was always polite. Julia began to question if this was the same man who had dumped Anais. She remembered back to how ugly that day had been, but the man sitting in front of her seemed to have a totally different personality. Maybe he was lulling everyone into a false sense of security?

As soon as Meredith disappeared back inside Julia carried on talking. 'Life in Heartcross is wonderful, and very busy this time of year.'

'You own the local B&B,' he queried. 'You must be full?'

'Always full,' answered Julia proudly. 'I love my job and as I'm the only accommodation in Heartcross, except for the camping site up at Foxglove Farm, then yes it's always extremely busy, which is good for me.'

Flynn took a swift look around the beer garden. It was packed full of people enjoying time with their family and friends. 'And is this the only pub in Heartcross?' he asked, taking a sip of his beer.

Eleni chipped in, 'It is, and it's always heaving, and everyone is great company. The food is amazing, the atmosphere always friendly and this is the place to come when the weather is scorching.'

'It certainly looks like the place to come,' agreed Flynn. 'And the company is definitely great,' he gave Julia a look that again nervously flipped her stomach.

'Well, the jury is still out on my part after having a bucket of ice-cold water thrown all over me.' But if the truth be told Julia felt very comfortable in his company, which surprised her after the past they'd shared.

With a huge beam on his face, Flynn dropped his head to his hands. 'There was a perfectly reasonable explanation, I didn't want you to be set on fire.'

Julia brought her hands up to her chest. 'He saved my life!' she joked.

Eleni was watching in amusement. 'You pair should join an amateur dramatics society,' she rolled her eyes and topped up her glass.

Julia felt as though they'd hit it off straight away. There was a chemistry between them that surely he felt too, but there was still that nagging feeling in the back of her mind. Flynn was a player, who'd jilted his bride on their wedding day. She didn't want to admit to herself she found him funny, charming, and she certainly wasn't going to put herself in the firing line to be hurt. She'd already witnessed what he was capable of doing.

'Anyway, now I've saved your life,' he chugged back his beer, 'I've got some errands to run, so hopefully I can save your life again someday soon.' He gave Julia a look that once more gave her a little skip in the pit of her stomach. Flynn stood up and popped his empty glass on Allie's tray as she walked past.

As soon as he was out of sight, Eleni swiped Julia's arm playfully. 'And the way he looks at you... smitten is what he is, mark my words.'

'Don't be ridiculous, he's only just met me again after all these years and our history is not exactly amicable.'

'The feeling I get is he wants to be very amicable.'

'Very funny,' replied Julia, noticing the huddle of boys in the corner begin to scatter in different directions. 'Jack's on the move, I want to grab him before he disappears.' Julia looked down at her T-shirt which thankfully was nearly dry.

As Jack walked past, Julia called over to him. 'Just the man I want.' She smiled.

'That's always good to hear, unless I owe you money,' he replied with a cheeky grin and hovered by the edge of the table. 'How are you? Enjoying the sunshine?'

'Very much so,' replied Julia. 'Let me introduce Eleni, who's working alongside me at the B&B.'

Jack held out his hand. 'Pleased to meet you.'

Eleni shook his hand. 'Likewise,' she replied, with a warm smile.

'The quote you gave me – how are you fixed to start work on the B&B as soon as possible?' she asked in a hopeful tone. 'The planning permission came through today.' Julia couldn't wait to get started. She was excited about the expansion to her new business and wanted all the rooms rented out by the spring.

'Julia, I'm so sorry, we're currently working up at Starcross Manor and have a number of other jobs pencilled in after that. It could possibly be Christmas time or just after? But I can definitely book you in for then? Ping me an email and I can add you to the diary.'

Julia sighed. 'And there's no chance starting at mine until before then?' She felt a tiny bit frustrated. She wanted everything to happen now, straight away.

'I can't commit, the job at Starcross Manor is already running over, which has a knock-on effect on everyone else waiting.'

'That may not be too bad,' reassured Eleni. 'There's still the possibility you could be up and running for springtime.'

'Yes, you're right.' Julia turned back towards Jack. 'We've just been up that neck of the woods. It's going to be a lovely place to retire to,' remarked Julia, thinking about the Manor House.

'Retire?' asked Jack, looking slightly puzzled.

'Starcross Manor... the rumour is it's being converted into a retirement home.'

'That's the thing about rumours: they aren't always true. Starcross Manor isn't a retirement home.'

Julia looked towards Eleni, then back towards Jack. 'What's it going to be then?'

'A five-star hotel.'

Those four words hung in the air.

For the second time today, Julia felt that time had slowed. She squished her eyebrows together and tilted her head to one side. 'A five-star hotel – it can't be. Everyone is saying it's a retirement home.' She needed clarification that she'd just heard Jack correctly.

'Well everyone is wrong. I should know, I'm the one working up there.' Jack looked over his shoulder to his friends who were leaving. 'Ping me that email Julia, and I'll be in touch,' he said, heading back over towards his friends.

'Eleni, I feel sick to my stomach,' declared Julia, as soon as Jack was out of earshot. Her mind was racing. A five-star hotel – surely not. Flynn Carter had just sat in front them asking about her B&B and hadn't even mentioned that Starcross Manor was going to be a hotel. What the hell was that going to mean for her own little business empire and the community of Heartcross? Why did no one know about this?

'Why?' asked Eleni, being slow on the uptake.

Julia could feel her heart pounding faster. 'What do you mean, why? A five-star hotel in the same village as my little B&B, how am I going to compete with that? I could go out of business in a matter of weeks.' The worry was etched all over Julia's face. 'Just think about it. What comes with a five-star hotel? Swimming pools, spas, restaurants, gyms, beauty treatments... the list is endless. Which would you prefer, a five-star hotel with all the trimmings or a room and a breakfast?'

'I've heard the breakfasts are amazing.' Eleni tried to lighten the situation, but Julia wasn't for smiling.

'That man has just sat with us and never thought to mention he was the competition.' Julia was wondering whether he'd purposely kept this from her. Why wouldn't you mention it? 'Eleni, think about it. If I go spending money on an extension and my business folds because of Flynn Carter's new hotel, I will have lost everything.'

'Julia, that's not going to happen.'

They both looked at each other.

'We don't know that for sure. I'm going to need to call a meeting. Just think about it. Starcross Manor is not just going to affect my business, but most of us in the community. The hotel will have a bar and a restaurant, surely that's going to have an effect on the pub, Bonnie's teashop and even Foxglove Farm. This could have the same effect on Isla's camping business too. Eleni, this is an absolute disaster.'

Julia pushed the glass of wine away from her. 'There doesn't seem to be much to celebrate any more. Flynn is a millionaire, he will have a huge marketing team behind him. He's going to put me out of business the second he opens those doors.' Julia swallowed down an emotional lump in her throat. She wasn't prepared to lose everything because Flynn Carter had chosen Heartcross to set up his next business venture. Julia made a promise to herself there and then: if this had any effect on her B&B, she would fight him to the bitter end.

Chapter Four

The next morning when Julia awoke, she brought her hand up to her jaw and rubbed her cheek. Bloody toothache again. Thankfully this morning she'd got her check-up at the dentist after breakfast. For the last couple of days Julia had been gargling with salt water to try and ease the pain but she needed to face facts, put on her big girl's pants and get her tooth properly checked out. Sitting up in bed, she glanced at the clock. Awake before her alarm sounded – absolutely typical when she could still be snuggled down under her duvet for another twenty minutes. Instead she resorted to swigging back a cold cup of tea from last night, to swill down a couple of paracetamols.

'Yuk,' she murmured to herself, wincing and shaking her head. It took Julia another couple of minutes to declare herself fully awake before swinging her legs out of bed and pulling on her dressing gown. As she padded down the private staircase, followed by Woody, she was amazed to hear movement already in the kitchen.

'You're here early?' asked Julia, causing Eleni to jump out of her skin as she spun round.

'Jeez, you shouldn't creep up on people you know,' said Eleni, putting a hand to her beating heart. 'You frightened me to death then.'

'Sorry, sorry,' said Julia, pouring a fresh cup of tea from the pot made on the table. 'But you aren't due for another half an hour at least.'

'Woken up by the dawn chorus, and with the sun shining through the gap in the curtains there was no chance I was drifting off again. So I cycled over, went for a quick run and here I am.'

Julia's eyebrows darted up involuntarily. 'Way too energetic for this time in the morning. I'd have just crawled back under the duvet anyway.'

'It's a great way to start the day, you should come with me one morning.'

'I'll think about,' mused Julia, knowing full well she was never going to think about it. She wasn't sure she even owned a pair of running trainers and there was no way she was jiggling her wobbly thighs around the village in a pair of tight black leggings, resembling the black puddings hanging up in the butcher's window... not a chance.

'And you look half dead, kind of yellow-looking too,' noticed Eleni, turning the sausages over and putting them in the bottom oven of the Aga to keep warm.

'I feel half dead, this toothache is becoming unbearable.

But thankfully I'm at the dentist just after breakfast so hopefully she'll put me out of my misery.'

'I can't stand the dentist... Obviously not literally the dentist, she seems a nice enough lady but going to the dentist... eurghh. I wonder what makes you decide you're going to be a dentist. I couldn't stand the thought of looking inside people's mouths all day long. It just doesn't do it for me.'

'Me neither.' Julia parked herself in the chair and hugged her mug of tea. Eleni was chatting about something, but Julia couldn't concentrate, her head was pounding, her toothache throbbing.

'Are you listening to me?' asked Eleni, knowing that Julia had wandered off into a little world of her own.

Julia didn't answer. She was staring into space, now clutching the side of her jaw again.

Eleni rolled her eyes then, with a slight smile hitched on her face. 'Anyway boss I want you to know before I tell anyone else. I'm pregnant, the baby is due in six months' time and I'll have to go on maternity leave, then if I could do a three-day week on my return that would be grand.'

At the mention of the word pregnant Julia soon catapulted back to planet Earth. 'What did you just say – you're pregnant?' She did a slow blink and placed her mug down on the table. 'Part-time?'

Eleni giggled. 'Oh, she's back on planet Earth,' teased Eleni, pulling a face. 'Of course I'm not pregnant, I just needed your attention... how many breakfasts do we need?' she stood waving the fish slice in the air.

'Phew! Even though that makes me sound like I'm not happy for you, it's just you brighten up this place... and aim for twelve cooked breakfasts this morning.'

'There's a compliment in there somewhere,' Eleni narrowed her eyes at Julia. 'And don't take this the wrong way and I know you have toothache, but you don't look very bright this morning. Did you get much sleep?'

Julia knew, apart from the toothache, the worry of Flynn Carter's brand-new hotel had kept her awake. Last night after Julia had climbed into bed, she'd logged on her laptop and spent nearly an hour trawling through internet posts about Flynn Carter. It seemed his business empire had expanded rapidly after his split with Anais.

'I'm just worried; how can I commit to extending this place knowing I could be throwing away my money? Once I've sorted out this toothache, I'm going to call a village meeting. Everyone needs to know that Starcross Manor is going to be a hotel. I just can't believe he showed us around the grounds of the manor and never told us it was going to be a hotel. Why the secrecy?' Julia felt confused. Sitting in the pub garden she'd felt a connection between her and Flynn. Why wouldn't he mention it when he asked her about the B&B? She just didn't understand.

Eleni posed the question to Julia that also had crossed her mind during the night. 'So this jilted friend of yours, Anais. Have you told her that Flynn's turned up in the village yet?'

Julia shook her head. 'I've been thinking about that but what's the point? She's moved on with her life. I'm not sure

what she will even think about it. I know it's a few years
ago but I really don't want to be upsetting her.'

Eleni nodded her agreement. 'You may be right.'

After the serving of breakfast was finished and
everything was cleared away Julia took the short drive to
the dentist in Glensheil. After registering her arrival with
the receptionist, she sat down in the bland-looking waiting
room, where everything was white except the TV screen
attached to the wall, which was flicking through adverts
from local businesses.

The receptionist popped her head around the door.
'Sorry, we are running approximately ten minutes behind,'
she said, looking straight at Julia.

'No problem,' replied Julia politely, but wishing they
would hurry up. The toothache was driving her insane and
the painkillers were wearing off. She really wasn't a fan of
the dentist and knowing that more than likely she needed a
tooth extraction, the queasy feeling in her stomach began to
escalate. Leaning forward and picking up a pile of well-
thumbed magazines from the table, she tried to block out
the ache in her mouth by flicking through the first celebrity
gossip mag. 'Who are these people?' she muttered under
her breath, not recognising anyone from the photos staring
back at her. Julia glanced at the date. 'Two years old,' she
mumbled again before tossing the magazine back on the
table.

Next in the pile was the magazine *Scottish Life*. 'This is
more like it,' she thought, noticing it was actually a recent
issue. Julia began to turn the pages in awe of the dream

kitchens, oldey worldey living rooms with soft furnishings to die for. In the past she'd used this magazine to help her style her own B&B. Julia loved interior design; she had a flair for style and soft furnishings and everyone who stayed at the B&B always complimented her on her bespoke furniture and luxury designs.

As she turned the page Julia stared. She couldn't believe it, there he was again – Flynn Carter, staring back at her. The headline: 'Business Tycoon Creates The Perfect Wedding Venue After Being Jilted'.

Julia felt her heart racing as her eyes quickly scanned the article. Wearing an expression of scepticism, she read and re-read the article, shaking her head in disbelief. Flynn Carter was telling the world that being jilted on *his* wedding day had given him the drive to focus on his business empire and create the picture-perfect five-star hotel to host the perfect wedding, so people could have their happy ever after, after *he'd* missed out. Julia's jaw dropped somewhere below her knees. This wasn't what had happened. The article described how Flynn Carter, the up and coming Scottish business tycoon, had been left heartbroken on his wedding day after being jilted by the love of his life, five years previously. He described how his weight had plummeted, how he had lain in bed for days after, with no motivation to get up, and how he'd isolated himself from his friends and family.

Mystified, Julia knew that wasn't the truth, so why had Flynn twisted the story? Was it to gain popularity, take advantage of the situation? Was he simply misleading everyone to entice more people to book his hotels for their weddings, increasing his profits? Julia was confused, she didn't know what to think. Taking her phone out of her bag, she was about to take a screenshot to send to Anais but then took a slow, steady breath. Even though she wanted to understand what was going on here, what was that going to achieve? Anais was happy now with her new family, and Julia would only be opening up old wounds. She remembered the beautiful wedding dress cut to shreds and how, alongside Mia, they had cancelled the whole wedding. He'd smashed Anais's heart into tiny pieces and walked away. And here he was, telling a totally different story in the magazine.

'This just doesn't ring true,' muttered Julia to the empty waiting room.

'Sorry, did you say something?' asked the receptionist now standing in the doorway, causing Julia to jump.

'I was just talking to myself, sorry,' replied Julia, feeling a little embarrassed.

The receptionist held the door open. 'We are ready for you now.'

Julia was still clutching the magazine as she stood up, then stuffed it safely into her bag. Still in disbelief at the article, she followed the receptionist down the corridor towards the room at the far end.

'How are things with you?' asked Charlotte the dentist, giving Julia a wide smile showing the most perfect set of pearly-white teeth.

'All good,' Julia answered, knowing that wasn't strictly true.

'Any problems?' asked Charlotte, ushering Julia towards the large chair in the middle of the room.

Julia brought her hand up to her jaw. 'Immense toothache. It comes and goes but at the minute it's back with a vengeance.'

'Let me take a look,' said Charlotte, passing Julia a pair of plastic glasses before lowering the chair. She pulled the overhead light towards Julia, who reluctantly opened her mouth as wide as she could.

Charlotte took a minute to poke and prod Julia's teeth and gums. 'You have an abscess, but there's good and bad news.'

'And the abscess isn't bad news?'

Charlotte shook her head. 'Afraid not.'

'Go on then, hit me with the bad news first.'

'You need a tooth extraction.'

Julia wasn't in the least bit surprised. 'And there's good news after that?'

'There is. Luckily for you my next patient has cancelled, so I can fit you in now instead of coming back, and I'll prescribe antibiotics for the infection.'

'Lucky me,' replied Julia, lacking enthusiasm. 'I suppose at least I don't need to come back.'

'Just relax, I'm going to numb your mouth and you won't feel a thing.'

Julia spent over thirty minutes in the dentist's chair with the bright light shining straight in her eyes. As she lay there her mind was fixed on Flynn and the article. If it was true that Starcross Manor was going to be a hotel, this was going to have an effect on all their livelihoods, and all the villagers needed to know. As soon as she got home, the first thing on her agenda would be to arrange a village meeting to share the information.

'Okay, you're all done,' came Charlotte's words at last. 'It'll take a few hours for the anaesthetic to wear off, so be careful, don't go chewing the inside of your cheek or your lips. Here's your antibiotics too.' Charlotte handed over a small white package. 'The instructions are on the label. Come back and see me in ten days.'

Julia nodded and headed towards the reception to pay, paid, then stepped outside. She rubbed her numb jaw and took a deep breath, gulping in the fresh country air. The weather was changing and dark clouds were beginning to gather in the sky, a far cry from the beautiful sunshine yesterday. As huge drops of water began to fall, Julia pulled out the umbrella from her bag and hurried towards the car. Feeling sorry for herself, all she wanted to do was to go home, curl up with a blanket and dribble in peace.

By the time she'd driven across the bridge into Heartcross, the rain had worsened. The radio was playing one of her favourite tunes but was drowned out by the frantic swish of the wipers. She flicked the indicator to turn left and saw a flurry of villagers racing along the High Street with their coats over their heads towards the pub, trying to keep the drenching to a minimum. Julia slowed the car down and swerved around the puddle at the edge of the kerb, then glanced to the right. That's when she spotted Flynn sheltering under the jutted-out roof of Hamish's shop doorway. He waved at her and she waved back – it was the polite thing to do.

But as soon as she got back to the B&B she threw her car keys down on the table and pulled the magazine out of her bag. Woody was fussing around her legs as she sat down on the kitchen sofa and re-read the article.

'All the beds are changed, fresh towels in every room, and I've emptied the bins and cleaned the bathrooms.' Eleni breezed into the kitchen and balanced the mop and bucket against the kitchen table, then looked towards Julia. 'You don't look too good. You okay?' She balanced on the arm of the sofa.

Julia whirled her finger near her mouth. 'One tooth extracted, I've got antibiotics and I can't feel my lips.'

'You poor thing, you won't want a cup of tea then?'

Julia shook her head. 'No thanks, I'd need a bib.' She touched her lips; even though they felt like they were inflated, she still couldn't feel a thing.

'And what have you got there?' Eleni pointed towards the magazine before handing Julia a tissue. 'You're dribbling.'

'Thanks,' she said, gratefully accepting the tissue and dabbing it against her lips. 'Take a look.'

Julia watched as Eleni slid into the armchair and began to read the article. She watched Eleni's expression as she raised an eyebrow and blew out a breath. As soon as she finished she locked eyes with Julia.

'I thought you said he was the one doing the jilting, not the actual jilted?'

Julia tapped the article. 'That just isn't what happened, and I'm perplexed why Flynn would twist the story like this.' She glanced towards the article again. 'Maybe, it is just a publicity stunt. All those people reading this, feeling sorry for him... the wedding he didn't have, but again that doesn't make any sense either. Flynn is a wealthy businessman, he doesn't need to put a spin on anything, his hotels will book because they are exquisite five-star hotels. It's just so strange.'

Once again Julia thought back to the day, wondering whether she'd remembered it all wrong, but after going over it in her mind she knew her memory wasn't failing.

'He seemed such a genuine man, sitting in the pub garden with us yesterday. I couldn't imagine him being this underhand. He doesn't need to lie,' added Eleni.

Julia knew that Eleni was right, that's why it was all so weird. 'However,' she replied thinking about her grandfather's house, 'he did take advantage of me over my grandfather's property, knowing the property market had crashed so he could use it to his advantage.'

'But I suppose that's business. Wouldn't we all try and get something for the best price we could?' replied Eleni.

'The more I think about it, the more I feel confused,' admitted Julia, still turning it all over in her mind. 'But the fact is, Starcross Manor is going to be a hotel and I think the villagers should be aware of the impact this may have on their very own businesses.'

Eleni agreed, 'Yes, they do need to know.'

'A village meeting it is. Here, or over at Bonnie's teashop?'

'We have guests milling around here and we don't really want them getting wind there's a brand-new five-star hotel opening up in Heartcross. Ask Rona and Felicity, I'm sure they'll let you use the teashop after opening hours.'

Eleni was right. Julia began to text Rona to ask whether the teashop was available. Almost instantly the reply came back. 'It's free tomorrow night.' Julia tilted her phone towards Eleni.

'Perfect.'

Immediately, Julia posted the details of the meeting in the community group on Facebook and sent out the same post in the village WhatsApp group. 'Hopefully most people will be able to attend. Maybe I'm worrying over nothing but I'm feeling a little tearful,' admitted Julia, leaning across and placing the phone on the coffee table.

'Of course you're feeling emotional, this place is your life, and you've poured your heart and soul into it. You need clarity: will the hotel have an effect on your business? Is it worth parting with your money into the extension?'

Julia blew out a breath. 'That's exactly what I'm thinking. I just need to know what everyone else thinks and we can take it from there. Maybe I'm worrying about nothing.' Julia dabbed the dribble from her lips once more. 'But what I need right now is to sleep this off, I'm not feeling the best at the moment.'

'You snuggle up there, everything is in order and there's

no new guests arriving until tomorrow. I'll pop back later and check in on you.'

'Thanks Eleni, you are a superstar.'

Once Eleni had left, Julia laid her head on the cushion and pulled the grey velvet throw over her and snuggled down. Woody jumped onto the sofa next to her and rested his head on her thigh. Feeling wary of Flynn's motives, Julia closed her eyes. She knew once the villagers knew about the hotel she'd feel like she had some support, but she also knew it would be difficult to compete with the likes of Flynn. He had money and clout; all Julia had was a small business, although with a good reputation.

A few hours later, Julia woke up to muffled shouting filtering from the hallway. She stretched and glanced at the clock; she'd been dozing for the whole afternoon. Eleni bounded into the kitchen and plonked herself down on the chair opposite. 'I've just shouted you, have you been asleep all this time?' she asked grinning. 'How's the mouth feeling?'

'Gappy,' Julia replied, sitting up and stretching out her arms. Woody opened an eye, but he wasn't for moving anytime soon. 'There's a big hole in the back of my mouth, but my lips seem to be back to normal,' she replied, prodding them with her finger.

'Are you hungry?' asked Eleni, looking over towards the crusty bread on the side.

'Not really, but I could do with a cup of tea. I think I'll be able to manage one now.'

'Do you mind if I grab some bread? I've worked up an appetite.'

'Mmm, I was just about to ask what's with the attire,' said Julia, noticing Eleni was overdressed for a normal weekday afternoon in a velour tracksuit with a push-up bra underneath the hoody which was zipped down dangerously low.

'A lunch date,' she said with wink. 'I think I'm in love.' Eleni made a heart sign with her hands and grinned.

Julia's eyes shot up. 'Sounds intriguing! You are seriously a fast worker. Who's the victim? I mean the new love of your life.' She gave a little chuckle.

'Don't be cheeky! It's Jack... Jack Langdon.'

'Blimey! Builder Jack? That is fast work. How did that come about? You didn't even know him yesterday.'

'That's the joys of social media. I slid into his DMs. I have no shame.'

'I'm in no doubt looking at that outfit,' joked Julia. 'Switch on that kettle will you.'

Eleni did as she was asked then sliced off a piece of bread and smothered it in butter and strawberry jam.

'And where have you been on this date?'

'The matinee at the cinema.'

'And how was the film?'

Eleni shrugged, Julia cocked an eyebrow and they both burst out laughing.

'Don't look at me like that. You have to admit he's hot.'

'What I want to know is, why Jack Langdon is sneaking off to the cinema with you? Why isn't he working?'

'Blame the weather,' replied Eleni, handing Julia a cup of tea. 'It was too dangerous on site due to the storm, so I took full advantage. It wasn't all pleasure you know, for a short time I was playing the detective.'

'Come again?' Julia couldn't help but notice that Eleni was looking rather pleased with herself. 'Detective?' she asked, giving a little wave to get her attention as Eleni sat up and began rummaging around in her bag.

Eleni plonked herself down in the chair and slid her legs over the arm of the chair as she tucked into her bread. 'I've got this from Jack's van and sneaked it into my bag. Something you might be interested in.' Eleni placed a leaflet in Julia's outstretched hand.

Julia pulled in a breath. 'A brochure for Starcross Manor.' The colour drained from Julia's face.

'Jack said the west wing is finished, but there's still a lot to do. Flynn is looking to open in the next couple of months. Jack confirmed he's been working up there for months already.'

'Starcross Manor, Spa Resort, Heartcross. No Reservation Costs. 24/7 Customer Service. Great Availability. Low Rates,' Julia read out loud. She opened up the pamphlet. 'State-of-the-art gym facilities at Starcross Manor will impress you from the moment you arrive...'

'Luckily for us our guests are hikers and businesspeople, they won't have time to spend in the gym,' Eleni was trying to smooth the way a little but Julia read on.

'Personal training accompanied by guidance can be enjoyed in the always-friendly, relaxed atmosphere.'

'Who books a weekend break to spend it with a personal trainer?' Eleni was doing her best to be positive.

'Spa days... an extensive range of gorgeous treatments followed by a swim in the tranquil pools and exquisite sensory showers,' continued Julia.

'Okay, we could get a hot tub in the back garden,' suggested Eleni with a shrug.

Julia rolled her eyes. 'Oh and there's a wonderful choice of dining options too, the sumptuous evening meals served in the stunning ballroom. Innovative dishes prepared by world-famous chefs with ingredients sourced from all over the world, or you could try the Starcross Gallery which offers a superb selection of lighter bites – but be sure to leave room for a traditional Afternoon Tea. Starcross Manor provides the most elegant backdrop of all.' Julia paused for breath.

'Well, we support our community, we've always sourced our meat and dairy from Foxglove Farm,' promoted Eleni proudly.

'They hire out function rooms that could have a big impact on the village hall, too.' Feeling worried, Julia put the brochure on the table. She knew she couldn't compete with any of that. 'I'm actually doomed.'

'Let's not panic, let's see what the others think at the meeting.'

Julia took a breath. 'Did you tell Jack about the meeting?'

'Of course not, I know where my loyalties lie, but he did speak about Flynn in the highest regard. Said Flynn was a decent, genuine bloke, always goes out on a limb for the workers, in fact the best bloke he's ever worked for.'

'Really?'

'Really. Jack said one of the scaffolders recently had an accident and Flynn took care of everything through some sort of private medical care, and even though he was self-employed, Flynn paid his wages in full.'

Julia couldn't help but think that was the decent thing to do, not many people would have gone to those lengths. 'Are you seeing Jack again?' quizzed Julia, thinking it would be good to have someone on the inside who was working up at Starcross Manor.

'I know exactly what you are thinking,' Eleni cocked an eyebrow. 'And the answer is no!' Eleni reached forward and took the brochure from Julia. 'I shouldn't have even taken this from his van. If he finds out…'

'Yes, you're right. Sorry, I wasn't thinking straight.' Julia knew that, even though it was very early days, she didn't want to rock the boat for Eleni if she really saw potential in Jack; she deserved happiness after her last disastrous relationship hadn't ended well.

Standing up and rubbing her jaw, Julia was relieved to have full feeling back in her lips, even though there was still a dull ache coming from the inside of her mouth. She poured a glass of water and swilled down another painkiller. 'Your phone just pinged,' she pointed out to Eleni, who was oblivious, taking another look over the brochure.

A wide smiled hitched on Eleni's face. 'It's Jack, inviting me to the pub tonight.'

'Two dates in one day, he must be keen. It's alright for some.'

Julia relished her independence after one disastrous relationship after another, and often she was the envy of her friends, who indicated they'd love to be in her situation, with no ties. Julia loved her own company, she could do what she wanted when she wanted, but sometimes she missed that special someone to share the exciting things in life with.

'Come to the pub with us? Isla and Allie are bound to be about, and no doubt a few others will be in there.'

'Thanks for the offer but I'm going to have an early night. Boring, I know.'

'You have an early night and things will look clearer in the morning,' said Eleni brightly, picking up her bag and ruffling the top of Woody's head. 'See you tomorrow, bright and early.'

Julia stood in the doorway and watched Eleni wheel her bike down the path. As soon as she disappeared out of sight, Julia stepped back inside and stretched her mouth like a hungry baby bird. Her stomach began rumbling as she opened the cupboard, looking for food.

All she could manage was a can of soup, and as she began to eat Julia checked her phone. So far, the majority of the villagers had responded and were intrigued to know what the meeting was about. Reaching over to the far side of the table, she pulled her notepad from the side of her laptop bag and began noting down points she wanted the community to think about. She was thankful she was able to share her concerns with her friends; Heartcross was the best community and they always had each other, and no matter what, Julia would fight for her B&B. Her little business was her life, and she wasn't going to let it go under anytime soon.

Chapter Five

The next morning, Julia lay on her bed with her laptop open, with thirty minutes to spare before she needed to get up and head downstairs. She'd been playing around with interior design software for the new extension, but as her mind wandered she began to check her emails. There wasn't much of interest, but she did have a few booking enquiries for spring next year, which she was going to jump on as soon as the breakfast rush was over. Any secure bookings with the uncertainty hanging over her head were an added bonus, but thankfully after tonight's meeting she would have everyone's point of view, which would help to settle her anxieties about the situation. Next Julia moved on to Facebook and scrolled through her home page. As usual it portrayed a portfolio of happy marriages, talented children and wonderful-looking holidays. She noticed Anais had uploaded an album of photographs of her latest family holiday in Dubai. She looked stunning, holding a glass of wine, wearing the perfect smile, photographed alongside her children and husband. Julia was thankful she hadn't contacted Anais with the news Flynn had rocked up in her tiny village. It wasn't going to achieve anything.

The next post she saw was from her cousin, Callie. Callie was two years younger than Julia and lived in Devon with the love of her life, Dan, who was a surf dude. Their carefree life looked fantastic and Callie often posted photos of her and Dan riding the waves on their surfboards, followed by cream teas in the quaint coffee houses. Julia missed Callie, but now with Eleni's extra hands helping out at the B&B she was determined to make a firm plan to visit her soon. And she had everything crossed that Callie would be able to get some time off work to visit Julia for her upcoming fortieth birthday celebrations.

Julia continued to scroll through the latest updates on her homepage when curiosity got the better of her. She typed in Flynn Carter's name and hit search. Immediately, his photo appeared, taking her by surprise. Either he'd resurrected his old account or he'd created a new one after the wedding fiasco. Immediately Julia was drawn to his profile photo. There was no denying he sailed the fine line between handsome and downright sexy. His privacy settings were tight, his photos locked down, his friends list hidden. There was nothing Julia could find out about his personal life at all.

'Damn, damn, damn,' Julia exclaimed. With just one slip Julia had only gone and sent Flynn Carter a friend request on Facebook. 'Oh my God.' With her heart hammering against her chest and a shaky hand it took only a matter of seconds to delete the request. For one thing she didn't want him thinking she'd gone looking for him, and secondly if Anais spotted him in her friends list, she didn't want her to think she'd been disloyal. Hopefully Flynn wouldn't notice if she'd managed to delete it so quickly.

Her panicky thoughts were interrupted by Eleni shouting up the stairs. 'Are you awake? I'm here!'

'Coming!' hollered Julia, jumping off the bed and quickly grabbing a bobble to tie up her hair.

When Julia appeared downstairs, Eleni was already setting out the tables in the dining room: the crisp pristine white linen cloths, shiny cutlery laid, and a jug of fresh orange juice stood in the middle of each table. 'How are you feeling this morning? Is that toothache of yours any better?' asked Eleni, spinning round to see Julia standing in the doorway with Woody dancing on his paws waiting to be let out in the garden.

'It must be, because I haven't given it a thought,' replied Julia, feeling relieved that the pain had finally subsided. 'I'll just let Woody out then I'll check what arrivals we have today. I think the guests in bedroom four are due to leave by 10am.'

'I'll make that room my first priority after breakfast.'

'Fabulous, thanks.' Woody bounded ahead into the kitchen and began frantically scratching at the back door. 'Hold on Woody, let me get the keys.' Julia grabbed them from the dresser whilst wondering what the hell had got into him. Woody was now barking and jumping up at the handle. Turning the key in the lock Julia finally opened the door and was startled to see Alfie staring back at her.

'You gave me the fright of my life.' Julia brought her hand up to her thumping chest.

'Sorry, sorry, I don't normally lurk around people's back doors. Honestly!'

'That's good to hear,' Julia smiled. 'What can I do for you? I'm assuming Polly hasn't chucked you out and you don't need a bed for a night?'

Alfie gave a little chuckle. 'No, I'm just a little curious about the village meeting tonight.'

Julia opened the door wide and Alfie stepped inside. 'What do you know about Flynn Carter?'

'Not much, to be honest, even though some of the contractors I know have worked for him. They said he's a decent guy. Apart from that, all I know is he's a property tycoon, worth millions allegedly,' replied Alfie.

'And did you know Starcross Manor was going to be a hotel?'

Alfie raised an eyebrow. 'A hotel? No, all I knew it was a sealed-bid auction.'

'What's a sealed-bid auction?' interrupted Eleni, tying her apron around her waist.

'It's a type of auction in which bids are not viewed until the auction date. The bids are literally sealed, often physically in an envelope and they are all opened at the same time and the highest bid wins. From what I heard... off the record of course... Carter paid thousands above the actual worth, which means by hook or by crook he wanted

Starcross Manor. He obviously knew the potential of the place,' revealed Alfie, checking his watch. 'But turning Starcross Manor into a hotel he would have had to jump through hoops. It's not my department but I can check if everything has gone through for you when I get to the office.'

'Would you?' asked Julia gratefully, thinking if it hadn't gone through it may give them some bargaining power somehow.

'Of course, I'll ping you over a text when I get to work. Is this what the meeting is about?'

'Yes, I'm worried Alfie, that the hotel will put this place out of business. I can't compete with a five-star hotel.'

He nodded his understanding. 'I see your point.'

'Thanks Alfie.'

Julia closed the door behind him and looked pensive. 'Maybe, if all the regulations aren't in place there may be something we can do.'

Eleni laid out the sausages in rows in the large aluminium tray and slid them into the Aga. 'Let's not worry about anything now, breakfast is nearly ready and the meeting will be here before we know it.' Eleni paused. 'I know I've just said let's not worry about it, but do you think I need to look for another job?' she probed, stirring the baked beans in the pan on the stove.

It was like Eleni could read her mind, because that very thought had been worrying Julia too. If things became tough and Julia lost business she wouldn't be able to afford to keep Eleni on. But Julia needed to stay positive. 'It will be okay, because I'll make it okay. If there's one thing I know about Heartcross it's that our community are always supportive of each other. If that hotel put me out of business they'd run Flynn out of town first.'

Eleni gave a chuckle. 'I've got visions of Drew and Fergus chasing Flynn across the bridge into Glensheil. "Stay off our patch and don't come back!"'

After tying on her pristine white apron around her waist Julia was about to join Eleni when her phone pinged. Quickly glancing at the screen she saw it was a text from Alfie. Her eyes quickly scanned the message, revealing information that Julia didn't want to read:

'Flynn had everything in place from fire regulations, insurances to TV and music license etc.'

For Julia, tonight couldn't come quick enough.

Three hours later, after breakfast was served, the dishes loaded in the dishwasher and the bedrooms spick and span, Julia found Eleni sitting outside sketching at an easel in front of her. Julia watched her holding up her pencil in the air, then watched as she altered the branches of the willow tree on the drawing in front of her. She blew away the eraser debris then sat back.

Julia admired the sketch. 'You have a real talent, you know.'

Eleni looked up and shielded the sun from her eyes. 'My grandfather was an artist.'

'And that's where you've got your talent from,' said Julia, still admiring her work.

'I usually draw places I want to visit, my bucket list is getting larger by the minute.'

'And where is next on the bucket list?'

'New York City, maybe, if I play my cards right.' Eleni gave a little smile. 'Oh and before I forget, whilst you were in the shower, we've had a cancellation. Mr Jones, his business trip was postponed at the last minute, which means we have a spare room if we get any enquiries.'

'Oh bugger,' replied Julia. 'At least there will be the cancellation fee.' Woody circled around a couple of times and lay down at Julia's side but as soon as he spotted a squirrel running across the garden he was off, lolloping across the grass. He looked defeated as the squirrel disappeared up the old oak tree, and mooched about at the edge of the brook.

'Do you hear that?' asked Julia.

Eleni sat up straight. 'I can't hear anything.'

'Exactly! I'm going to enjoy five minutes before I head over to the town.' She smiled, clasping her hands across her stomach and tilting her face up towards the sun.

The peace and quiet was short lived. 'Service!' The old-fashioned bell in the reception area was ringing out. 'Service! Anyone there?'

Julia sat bolt upright in the chair. 'Who's that? I don't recognise the voice.'

The bell rang a second time as they hurried up the hallway. Eleni stopped dead as she saw the man standing at the desk, leaving Julia bumping straight into her. 'What are you doing?' she exclaimed, smoothing down her top.

'Oh my God,' Eleni's mouth dropped open. 'Andrew Glossop, I'm a huge fan of yours.' Eleni side-stepped past Julia and outstretched her hand. 'Welcome, welcome, do you need a room?'

'Andrew Glossop...' Julia mused, as she scrunched up her forehead. He was striking, the kind of face that stopped you in your tracks, with his blond tousled hair, his eyes deep ocean blue, and a prominent jaw.

'Oh my Gosh, Andrew Glossop, celebrity chef off the TV. Hi, I'm Julia, owner of the B&B,' she said feeling a little starstruck. 'I love your programme, the road-trip around Italy was brilliant.'

Andrew was looking amused. 'Thank you, it was a fun programme to make. Have you by any chance got a spare room just for a couple of nights at most?' he asked looking hopeful.

'Yes!' They both enthused in unison then looked at each other and smiled.

Julia stepped behind the reception desk to take down some details. She couldn't quite believe that Andrew Glossop was wanting a room in her very own little B&B. 'Breathe,' she told herself, feeling her hands shaking as she began to load up the booking page in front of her on the computer.

'I just need to take down a few details and payment, if that's okay?'

'It is, thank you. I didn't know if you'd have any room at such late notice.'

'Luckily, we've had a cancellation. Can you get the key

for room four please?' Julia put on her posh voice and Eleni raised an eyebrow.

'I can,' she replied, opening up the key cupboard at the back of the reception area.

'It's a lovely quaint place you have here,' noticed Andrew, looking round before handing over his credit card.

'Thank you,' replied Julia, still not quite believing that Andrew was standing in front of her. She was dying to ask what brought him to Heartcross, but the first rule was never to pry into a guest's business unless they volunteered the information. But Eleni had clearly forgotten this when she blurted, 'Why are you here? What are you doing in Heartcross?'

Andrew willingly answered. 'I'm working, I have a new job here for a short while,' he said, slipping his credit card back into his wallet. 'And I'm so glad I was talked into it... those mountains and the scenery are breath-taking. It's a little different from London.'

'A job? Here in Heartcross?' quizzed Julia. What job could Andrew Glossop be doing here in Heartcross?

But before Andrew could answer, the B&B door swung open and in walked a smiley Flynn Carter.

A surprised Julia was taken aback. Flynn's hazel eyes sparkled as he greeted Andrew like a long-lost friend.

'Andrew!' Flynn stepped towards him, his greeting over-familiar as they thumped each on the back. 'I'm glad you've found it. Was there any room at the inn?' Flynn gave Julia a wide beam.

Goodness, he was attractive with his huge hazel eyes,

flawless olive skin and a mass of auburn hair. His crisp white short-sleeve shirt complimented his tan perfectly, thought Julia.

'Yes, we have a room,' Eleni stepped in. 'So you two know each other?' Eleni asked the question that Julia was dying to know the answer to.

'We do! And when Flynn persuaded me to become the head chef...'

'You didn't need much persuading,' interrupted Flynn.

'You're right, I needed a change and you sold me Heartcross.'

'Head chef...?' quizzed Julia.

'My right-hand man.' Flynn rested a hand on Andrew's shoulder. 'This Michelin Star genius is going to run the main restaurant up at Starcross Manor and we are interviewing for staff tomorrow.' Flynn looked pleased with himself. 'We are going to put this place on the map.'

Julia realised at this point Flynn was being honest, he wasn't hiding the fact Starcross Manor was going to be a hotel because she knew you certainly weren't going to need a Michelin Star chef for a retirement home. 'Congratulations!' remarked Julia, trying to take it all in.

'That's brilliant news, so where will you be staying on a permanent basis?' probed Eleni, handing the room key over to Andrew.

'I'm around for approximately six months unless I get talked into staying longer. I've got a room up at the manor house which will be ready in a couple of days, it's being decorated today then I'll be living in.'

'Nice work if you can get it,' chipped in Eleni.

'It is.' Andrew picked up his holdall then looked towards Flynn. 'This was a good choice by you.'

'I told you, and it's walking distance to the Manor. It's a great location and a great B&B,' Flynn looked towards Julia with a warm smile. 'Great place you have here.'

'It most certainly is all of those things, but I'm a little biased.' Julia was completely surprised that Flynn had recommended the B&B – surely these weren't the actions of a man who wanted to put her out of business. It really was a nice thing to do and Julia was beginning to wonder whether she'd over-reacted and got the whole situation wrong.

'The weather is gorgeous out there, any plans for this evening? Maybe you could both join us for a drink?' Flynn looked between Julia and Eleni.

It was safe to say Julia was not expecting this invitation. Flynn was being warm and friendly and her plans for the evening involved telling the village that everyone needed to be wary of this man. Maybe she should have gone to chat with Flynn first before calling the meeting and now she was feeling a tad guilty about it all.

'That would have been lovely, but we have plans this evening,' she replied, stepping out from behind the reception desk. She touched Andrew's arm. 'Would you like to follow me? I'll show you to your room.'

Julia led them down the winding hallway. She glanced over her shoulder to see that Flynn was following them. He stopped now and again to admire the walls that displayed intricate artwork.

'This artwork is amazing, you've kitted this place out with such style.' Flynn gave Julia his nod of approval.

'She's amazing, isn't she?' chipped in Eleni. 'Julia has a flair for interior design.'

'I agree, this whole place has such a good feel about it,' continued Flynn.

Julia felt a slight blush to her cheeks – not only was he recommending her B&B, he was now complimenting her on her interior design. She was feeling addled yet proud that Flynn had noticed.

'Aww, behave,' she replied, waving off the compliment. This just didn't seem to be the same man she thought she knew.

They continued to follow her down the small steps that led to a cosy reading corner – a pew, arrayed with soft furnishings, overlooking the gardens and back patio. She paused outside the communal sitting room. 'This room is for all guests to use at any time. Feel free to open the patio doors onto the garden. Usually guests gather here between 7 and 8pm, for an hour of interesting conversation, finding out where people have come from and what they do for a living, but I kind of think everyone may recognise you.' Julia turned towards Flynn. 'I'll show Andrew to his room, there's tea and coffee over there if you wish to grab a drink. Eleni will show you.'

'Thank you,' replied Flynn stepping into the sitting room.

Andrew followed Julia up another small flight of stairs.

'Any plans for the rest of the afternoon?' asked Julia, putting the key in the lock.

'We are going to head over to Starcross Manor so I can inspect my new kitchen and then maybe grab some food in the local pub,' he answered, stepping into the room and placing his holdall on top of the bed.

'Sounds like a perfect afternoon. Here you are, room four.'

Bedroom four was a simple rustic room featuring a beautiful four-poster bed, the white walls and minimal decoration allowing it to stand out. A goose-down duvet with Egyptian cotton linen added elegance and charm, and was dressed with pale blue scatter cushions.

'This is a magnificent room, and what a view.' Andrew stepped across the oak-beam floor towards the window and stared out across the acres of lush grasslands. The beauty of the mountains standing proudly in the distance. 'I really wasn't expecting this. How many rooms do you have here?'

Thinking fast on her feet, Julia turned the question around. 'Not as many as Starcross Manor – that would maybe be around sixty?' Julia knew she was fishing for information.

'And the rest,' revealed Andrew, still looking at the scenery. '110 rooms in total,' Andrew said as he pulled his ringing phone out of his pocket and glanced at the display. 'Sorry, I need to take this.'

'Of course,' Julia nodded and her heart sank as she closed the door behind her. 110 bedrooms, how was she ever going to compete with that? She could hear Andrew chatting away as she took the staircase back towards where she'd left Eleni and Flynn, but they were nowhere to be seen. Stepping out onto the patio Julia was surprised to see Flynn sat next to Eleni, looking through her sketch pad. Eleni was smiling and they were locked in conversation.

'What have I missed?' asked Julia, feeling a little left out, pulling out a chair and sitting down.

Eleni looked up. 'Flynn thinks some of my sketches are amazing and I should transfer them onto canvas. He thinks I might be able to sell them.'

'You are very talented,' agreed Julia.

'I would like to think I'm well up on my art,' admitted Flynn, holding Julia's gaze. 'And you are talented, Eleni.'

Eleni was beaming in pride and shut the sketch pad. 'I might just think about that.'

'You must, you can't let that talent go to waste. Maybe you could think about selling them in the shop up at Starcross Manor?'

'Shop? What type of shop?' Julia questioned.

'A giftshop-cum-newsagent. Kind of like what you'd get in a motorway service station.'

Julia turned his words over in her mind, a separate shop within the hotel complex would have a massive effect on Hamish's newsagent's.

Flynn turned back towards Eleni. 'I am being serious, put them onto canvas and there's a possibility I might even buy some to hang on the walls up at Starcross Manor.'

'I will, I'll think about it.' Eleni was gushing. 'Thank you.'

Julia could see the excitement on Eleni's face. On one hand she was happy for Eleni if she managed to sell her artwork, and the hotel would have lots of passing trade, but on the other hand, was this just Flynn trying to get everyone on side? She was just a little wary of his sentiment.

'I'm all set,' Andrew appeared and was walking towards them while Flynn stood up and admired the view from the garden.

They watched Woody, who was now paddling in the brook – but as soon as he spotted a newbie in the garden he began racing towards Flynn and Andrew. With his tail wagging he launched his wet paws all over Flynn's shorts.

'A man's best friend,' remarked Flynn, giving Woody a fuss.

'I'm so sorry, Woody get down... get down,' Julia repeated, but Woody took no notice whatsoever.

'Don't worry, it's only water. I think he likes me.'

Flynn looked up towards the back of the B&B. 'Great spot you have here, lots of land. I bet business is good.' He swung a glance towards the mountainous terrain. 'It's estimated 150,000 climb Ben Nevis each year. Heartcross Mountain must be similar figures, which leaves a hell of a lot of hikers traipsing through the village.'

Julia knew since Heartcross had been catapulted into the news, after the bridge had collapsed, that tourism had increased tenfold. She knew that at the moment, her little business was booming, but with 110 bedrooms becoming available soon up at Starcross Manor that could change overnight.

'Yes, there's always hikers, it's what makes this place so special, and some come back year after year.'

'What do you offer here? Hot tub? Bar?' Flynn snagged a glance around at the garden.

'Old-fashioned bed and breakfast, no frills, but yes we do have a small bar.'

'And planning permission granted too. You must feel excited about your plans.'

Julia was taken back that he knew this information. 'You have done your homework and yes, I'm very excited.' Julia felt a little nervous that he been checking out her business.

'It's a good idea, more bedrooms to increase profit?' he continued. 'It looks like a little goldmine this place.'

Julia nodded. 'My own little business empire.'

'I love a woman with ambition,' replied Flynn. His deep hazel eyes searching hers, he held Julia's gaze.

There was something about the way he was looking at her that caused her to blush uncontrollably. How did he manage to do that? She was wary of his intentions, yet he easily caused her stomach to flip.

'Right, come on,' Flynn continued as he turned towards Andrew. 'Let's go and show you your new kitchen empire.'

Eleni was still beaming at Flynn's praise as the two men left. 'He loves my sketches! And can you believe THE Andrew Glossop is staying at your B&B? You need a photograph, post it on your Instagram, that will pull in a few guests.' Eleni sat back in her chair. 'This will be good for you, Julia.'

But Julia wasn't listening, she was in her own little world. All she could think about was why would Flynn be checking up on her B&B?

'And how good was that of Flynn to offer to sell my paintings in his shop? And to see them hanging on the walls at the manor house, that's just... that's just amazing,' gushed Eleni, her voice bubbly. 'I can picture them now, hanging along the massive hallways at Starcross Manor. Maybe I could even open up my own gallery one day.'

Julia looked up and noticed the sparkle in Eleni's eyes. She was fit to burst and why shouldn't she enjoy any praise and success with her drawings? After all she was talented, but Julia's feelings of confusion were still there. Was Flynn actually being genuine? Of course she wanted to be happy for Eleni, encourage her success, but Flynn hadn't been genuine in the past. Was this a ploy by Flynn to get Eleni on side, or was Julia just reading too much into the situation?

'Your drawings are amazing, you should feel really proud of yourself, I always said you had an amazing talent but...'

'But what?' interrupted Eleni, sensing something was bothering Julia.

Julia exhaled; she didn't quite know how to say exactly what she was thinking without sounding selfish. 'Flynn makes me nervous. He's gorgeous, polite, says all the right things and acts the right way, but in the past he hasn't operated this way. He was ruthless, uncaring...' Julia blew out a breath. 'I just don't know what to think. I actually think I'm going a little mad but he's right, your sketches are amazing, there's nothing stopping you painting on canvas, putting them for sale in Hamish's shop or selling them online. You could even sell them here in the B&B.'

'I think we can only take Flynn at face value,' Eleni looked across at Julia. 'He seems genuine enough to me.'

Julia was beginning to admit to herself that she thought Eleni was right. He hadn't actually stepped a foot out of place since his arrival, but there was still that slight niggle in the back of her mind. All she could do was gauge the rest of the villagers' reaction tonight at the meeting.

Chapter Six

A couple of hours later Julia checked her appearance in the mirror numerous times. Discarding numerous outfits, she'd finally opted for a navy blue tunic with a tiny pink rosebud pattern, and with its sheer long sleeves and keyhole neckline, it was a flattering fit accompanied by a pair of navy blue leggings and flat ballet pumps. Pulling a brush through her hair, Julia dabbed on her lip-gloss and declared herself ready.

Eleni was waiting downstairs in the private quarters and was messing about on her phone when Julia appeared in the doorway.

'You look nice,' Eleni looked her up and down then slipped her phone into her bag.

'Thanks. Are we ready?' asked Julia, taking one last look in the mirror and smoothing her hair down.

'Ready,' Eleni saluted. 'Let's go and find out what the rest of the community think.'

Julia chucked Woody a chew, who immediately settled down on his bed, before she grabbed her bag from the kitchen table.

Locking the door behind them, they set off. All Julia could think about was if she had gone about this the wrong way. Maybe she should have chatted with Flynn first to see how he thought the hotel was going to fit into the community? But it was too late now, the meeting had been arranged and it wouldn't be long before she knew what everyone else thought.

'What are you thinking?' asked Eleni, noticing that Julia had gone quiet.

'I'm obviously worried about all the businesses in Heartcross, but my opinion of Flynn seems to be changing. He just seems down-to-earth and very friendly for someone that is intentionally trying to put someone out of business. I've just no idea what he's thinking.'

As they turned onto Love Heart Lane, and with Bonnie's teashop in sight, the church bells chimed seven o'clock in the background. Julia could already see that the teashop was packed to the rafters, everyone was sitting around the tables, no doubt waiting patiently to discover what this emergency meeting was about. As soon as Julia stepped inside all she could hear were the villagers talking excitedly.

'It is him, he's sitting in my pub eating my food. I couldn't quite believe it when he chose my pub to walk into.' Meredith was fit to burst.

Julia knew that they'd spotted Andrew Glossop in the village.

'So where is he staying?' asked Isla over the chatter, 'because he's not staying in one of my vans.'

'Heartcross is becoming the celebrity capital of Scotland. Andrew Glossop is one of my favourites, we watch all his programmes, don't we Mum?' Felicity turned towards Rona who was hanging on to every word.

'I hope he pays us a visit, can you imagine, him giving us a magic handshake after sampling one of my cakes?' She swooned.

'I think you are thinking of Paul Hollywood, Mum,' Felicity gave a little chuckle.

Julia stood in front of them all and cleared her throat. Everyone's head turned in her direction. The teashop fell silent as everyone waited for Julia to speak.

Eleni slipped into a chair next to Aggie and Julia looked out over a sea of faces.

'Come on, what's all this about?' asked Fergus. 'The last emergency meeting we had was when the bridge collapsed. What's so urgent, Jules?'

Julia took a breath. 'Thanks for coming everyone. I'm just sharing some information with you all that I discovered this week. Starcross Manor is not going to be retirement homes,' Julia watched their reactions closely as her words sunk in. 'It's actually going to be a five-star hotel.'

There was an undercurrent of muttering around the room.

'Are you sure?' Isla looked towards Alfie for confirmation, who was sitting next to Polly at the back of the room.

Alfie nodded. 'Julia's right. It's going to be exactly that, an all-singing, all-dancing five-star hotel.'

'But I don't get it, why the meeting?' Isla looked as puzzled as everyone else in the room.

'I'm concerned about the impact it's going to have on the village and our businesses, but not only that. I know the developer, Flynn Carter, from the past. I found him to be... untrustworthy and he didn't exactly always play fair.' Julia wasn't out to give a character assassination, but she also knew what this man was capable of.

'I knew there was a look about him,' remarked Aggie looking at Rona. 'I said his eyes were too close together. That's a sign of a distrustful man. Mark my words.'

'Andrew Glossop,' Julia raised her voice. 'Andrew Glossop is also the new Michelin Star chef up at the manor house. To my knowledge there will be numerous restaurants including fine dining, comfort food, afternoon teas...' Julia took a breath. 'I'm worried that these restaurants will take away your trade.' She looked towards Meredith and Rona. 'With a celebrity chef on board tourists will flock to the manor house.'

'Interesting,' replied Rona mulling over the information she'd just heard. 'Afternoon teas will certainly have a big impact on our afternoon trade. I'm not liking this Flynn Carter much.'

'Not only will there be a spa, swimming pool, gym...' Julia reeled off the list. 'There's also going to be a shop... imagine a motorway service station type of shop, one that sells everything from batteries to refreshments, from newspapers to cuddly toys – this will have a huge impact on you Hamish. The guests staying at that hotel will have everything at their fingertips.'

Julia noticed the colour drain from Hamish's face. 'Have you got this on good authority?' he asked her.

'Yes,' confirmed Julia, thinking back to her earlier conversation with Flynn. 'Straight from the horse's mouth and then there's my business too. I can't compete with the amenities of a five-star hotel and I'm worried I'm going to lose business.'

'That's possibly the same for me too,' exclaimed Isla, speaking up.

Almost immediately there was a barrage of questions put forward from the residents of Heartcross. 'Can this actually happen?' Drew directed his question at Alfie, trying to get a handle on it all.

All heads swung towards Alfie. 'I'm afraid so. All his licences are in place and Flynn has everything covered.'

Hamish looked forlorn. 'So what we are saying here is this man can waltz into Heartcross, build a hotel, increase traffic through our village and the only person that is going to benefit from this is Flynn Carter? Leaving all our businesses struggling?'

'I'm afraid that could possibly be the case Hamish,' answered Julia.

The room fell silent, everyone looked suitably horrified.

'The Boathouse is due to open soon and I know this for a fact because Flynn was in the pub when we were talking about Allie's fundraiser and her farewell drinks... just a quick reminder whilst you are all here, that's tomorrow night in the pub alongside the airing of Rory's TV show.'

Tomorrow, Allie was swapping the idyllic countryside for the bright lights of the city of Glasgow. She'd landed a job as a photographer on a national newspaper for six months whilst her fiancé was working for a lion sanctuary over in Africa alongside Zach Hudson, already a TV superstar. Allie and Rory had inherited Clover Cottage, and its acres of land, which was currently being renovated. Within the grounds a new state-of-the-art vet's surgery was being built for Rory whilst Allie was opening up a centre for disadvantaged kids focusing on photography.

'We will all be there.' Julia smiled warmly towards Allie.

'Flynn has actually donated a prize for the fundraiser,' added Meredith.

Fergus waved his hand to speak. 'What are we going to do about it?'

'I'm suggesting that if you have got the same concerns as I have then maybe someone should talk to Flynn. Voice our worries, ask him how his hotel fits into the community, because the last thing we need is a him-and-us situation. If I'm being honest with you all, with his money and clout I think it will be our little businesses that come off worse.'

'What do we know about this man? Is he a decent bloke? You said he's been untrustworthy in the past,' shouted out Drew.

Julia was in a dilemma. The old Flynn she knew seemed worlds away from the Flynn that she'd met recently. But what if he was just playing a very good game to lull everyone into a false sense of security before whipping their business from under them? Since he'd arrived, Flynn hadn't put a foot wrong, and actually seemed like a nice guy. Julia could feel Eleni's eyes on her, and she knew Jack thought he was a decent, genuine guy. If Julia had been asked to answer Drew's question on the day Flynn had stepped back into Heartcross it would be a different answer to what she was about to say now. Flynn was charismatic, she'd felt comfortable in his company, but there was still that niggle about him in the back of her mind.

'All we can do is elect a spokesperson and address our concerns,' replied Julia.

Drew threw his hands up in the air. 'Well with the B&B in the firing line, would you be prepared to talk to him on behalf of us all?' Drew looked over the sea of faces and everyone was nodding in agreement.

All eyes were on Julia who nodded. 'Okay, I'll talk to him,' she agreed, taking out her notepad and pen from her bag. 'Let me write down everything you want me to ask.'

For the next five minutes the residents fired numerous questions at Julia which she jotted down. 'Okay, I think I have everything now,' she confirmed.

As Felicity began to pass round plates of biscuits Rona touched Julia's arm. 'Try not worry about your B&B, whatever happens we all stick together.' Rona put on her best encouraging smile and gave Julia's hand a little squeeze.

'Thank you. I am really worried, but I'll talk to Flynn tomorrow after breakfast.'

'Good plan and once we have more information we can take it from there.'

Julia felt a sense of relief, this was what living in Heartcross was all about, friends being there for each other no matter what. This was a special community and hopefully Flynn could see how anxious everyone was about the impact the hotel would have on their business.

Chapter Seven

I t was just after 11am when Julia climbed into her car armed with the list of questions from last night's meeting. She'd been clock-watching all morning, willing the chores to be done so she could go and chat to Flynn, who'd been on her mind all morning. The community had elected her as spokeswoman, and she was on her way to find out his view on how the hotel would affect the residents of Heartcross, and more importantly the effect on her own B&B.

As she arrived the carpark was full of vehicles, and Julia pulled up next to a white transit van before jumping out and making her way up the stone steps towards the entrance. She felt nervous, but Flynn hadn't shown any signs of being difficult since he'd arrived, so she had everything crossed it was going to stay that way. After rehearsing the conversation over in her mind, she was surprised to find a group of builders hanging around in the lavish foyer. This was the first time she'd set foot inside Starcross Manor, and she had to do everything in her power not to gasp out loud. This place was out of this world, it looked regal with its crystal chandelier hanging from the ceiling and the slate marble floor that stretched to a grand arching stairway. A balcony circled the entrance hall, which seemed bigger than the whole of Julia's B&B – this place was huge!

For a second, she hovered, then heard Flynn's raised voice filtering from a room just off the reception. Realising there was something going on and that maybe this wasn't the best time to discuss things with Flynn, Julia was just about to slip back out the door when Jack caught her eye.

Julia whispered, 'Hey, what's happening? Everyone seems...' she was trying to put her finger on it, 'stressed.'

'That's an understatement,' Jack lowered his voice and moved backwards from the rest of the builders. He was just about to share with Julia what was going on when once again Flynn's tense voice could be heard. Then the door flung open and Flynn strolled into the foyer and hung up his phone. He looked frazzled, shaking his head in disbelief and threw his arms up in the air. 'Down tools. You may as well all leave. There will be no materials arriving today.'

All the builders began muttering amongst themselves. Jack spoke up. 'Why have the contractors cancelled?'

'Your guess is as good as mine, but if we don't get the building materials here soon, this place won't be finished in time for the very first wedding booking and it will have to be cancelled,' replied Flynn, looking increasingly flustered.

'The only thing I can do is make sure you all get paid today and I'll keep you updated,' he nodded towards Jack. 'I'll ring you as soon as I know something.'

Julia, who was standing behind Jack and shielded from the group of builders, wasn't visible to Flynn. She remained quiet, but her head was whirling. Flynn sounded frantic. Why would the contractors cancel if they'd been working up at Starcross Manor for months? Julia gulped down a feeling of dread – surely this wasn't anything to do with the meeting last night? She knew Hamish was far from happy, but he wasn't the type of man to sabotage the building work… was he?

Jack touched Julia's arm. 'We are going to get off, there's nothing we can do here today without the materials.'

She nodded and stepped to the side whilst the disgruntled builders began to vacate the manor house. Flynn began scrolling through his phone and hadn't noticed Julia until she stepped forward and he glanced up in surprise. 'Hey, what are you doing here?'

'It doesn't look like a good time,' she pointed to the last of the workmen disappearing through the door.

Flynn exhaled. 'You wouldn't believe my morning.'

'Honestly, I'll just go. I don't want to add to your stress.' Julia was just about to turn around when Flynn spoke again.

'I'm sure you couldn't add to my stress. I need a strong coffee… care to join me?'

Julia hesitated for a second then agreed. 'As long as you're sure.'

She followed Flynn into an office just off the foyer. His desk was littered with papers, the walls covered with charts and figures. He switched on the coffee machine and pulled out a chair for Julia who sat down.

'So, it's not the best morning then?' prompted Julia, placing her bag on the floor next to her feet wondering what was going on.

Flynn shook his head. 'I'm at a loss, I've no idea what's happening. I've woken up this morning and all hell has broken loose.'

Julia noticed his rapid blinking, his wandering gaze, his voice was shaky. As the coffee machine began to beep he stood up and Julia cast an eye over the papers on his desk. There was a photo of a couple, a room plan, and photos of ice sculptures.

'Sugar?' Flynn asked, looking towards Julia.

'Just one please. What are these for?' she asked pointing to photos.

Flynn placed the cup of coffee down in front of her. 'Those are ice sculptures for the wedding of the century, which has just become my worst nightmare.'

'Huh?' asked Julia, cupping her hands around the cup.

Flynn let out a hard sigh. 'The renovation of this place was going like clockwork, the building work almost complete with the grand ballroom still left to do, this...' he tapped the photograph, 'this is the first couple to get married here at Starcross Manor in the grand ballroom. They've paid thousands for this wedding, every detail planned like a military operation. They even leave the reception to go on their honeymoon via a hot air balloon, we've even had dummy runs and now the whole thing may need to be cancelled or postponed, leaving me refunding thousands. It will be such bad press.'

'Why?' asked Julia, but her gut feeling knew exactly what Flynn was going to say.

'The contractors providing all the materials for the ballroom pulled out this morning, Jack and the lads should have been working on that for the next two weeks ready for the grand opening, followed by the wedding the week after. I just don't understand it. I've been on the phone all morning trying to get answers, but no one is telling me why they've cancelled. It's like some sort of weird conspiracy.' Flynn was talking fast, his words tripping over each other. 'And now I really don't know what to do. I've been ringing around trying to get other suppliers, but they are already booked up and some haven't even returned my call. The ballroom was going to be magnificent, some of the walls cladded with gold. The design of that room took nearly eight months to complete and now...' he threw his hands up and leant back on his chair. 'It feels like someone is out to sabotage me, but I really have no idea why. I'm probably just over-thinking it.' He took a sip of his drink and looked straight at Julia. 'I am going to have to phone the happy couple and let them know we've hit a problem. It's not a phone call I'm looking forward to. They had their heart set on everything just being perfect.'

Julia was rendered speechless, her mind in overdrive. Flynn looked worried sick, and all she could think about was last night's meeting and that this was something to do with her. She knew she was worried about her little business going under, but she wouldn't deliberately go out to sabotage anyone's business or weddings, she wasn't a monster.

'Julia, I just don't know what to do. It just seems strange,' carried on Flynn. For a second he tapped frantically on his computer then turned back towards her. 'First thing this morning…' he took a breath to steady his shaky voice. 'I nipped to the teashop, and I brushed it off at the time, but if I'm being honest they didn't seem as friendly towards me as usual. And then I walked into the village shop and, Hamish is it? He seemed very standoffish. Maybe it's just my imagination but something doesn't feel right. You've lived here a long time, do you know anything?' Flynn's eyes went to hers.

Julia could see Flynn was desperate for answers, but Julia didn't know what to say. Surely the villagers hadn't taken matters into their own hands in just a matter of hours? This was the perfect opportunity to come clean and tell Flynn about the meeting and the villagers' concerns but she didn't want to add more fuel to the fire. Her first thoughts were to uncover if anyone had deliberately gone out of their way to put a spanner in the works.

Julia swerved the question but seeing Flynn this way, she wanted to help. 'I know Alfie deals with a lot of contractors in this area, he knows everyone in the industry. Let me check with him, if he knows anything.'

'Would you?' Flynn's voice lifted. 'My gut is telling me

something isn't quite right, but I can't put my finger on it.' He picked up the file on his desk. 'Over 300 guests at this wedding, it's not going to be the same if they have to get married in the bar.' Looking deflated, he placed the file back on his desk. 'It's just a disaster. And why are you here?' he asked.

Julia thought quickly. 'I just needed a quick word with Jack,' she replied.

He nodded. 'And Julia, thanks for listening,' he said sincerely.

Julia stood up. 'I'll check to see if Alfie knows anything and I'll get back to you.'

As soon as Julia left the office, once more she could hear Flynn frantically on the phone searching for answers. Her gut feeling suggested her meeting last night was most probably behind all this. She wished now that she'd come to chat with Flynn first about the impact of the hotel so that she had answers for the villagers, but she couldn't think who would have taken matters into their own hands. Now, everything seemed to be spiralling out of control. Julia didn't want anyone's wedding cancelled or postponed – that would cause so much upset. She felt so guilty, but all she could do was get back to the village and see if anyone knew what was going on up at Starcross Manor.

Chapter Eight

L ater that evening Julia and Eleni walked along the High Street towards the pub. The heat of the day had ebbed to a comforting warmth and the village was alive with dog walkers, children playing on the green and the straggling hikers heading down from the mountain top. The tables outside the pub were already littered with thirsty revellers, and as they stepped inside the Grouse and Haggis it was packed to the rafters. There was an excitement about the place, a buzz in the air. Tonight was the night Rory's TV show would be aired to the nation. Julia noticed the tables in the dining area had been pushed to one side and the chairs lined up in rows in front of the TV screen. Over in the far corner there was a magnificent-looking buffet laid out, too. Julia tried to see past the bobbing heads, the bar was three deep and already she was engulfed by the sweltering heat. 'My God, it's warm in here,' she muttered under her breath.

'Apparently, according to the news, tomorrow is going to be the hottest day on record,' shared Eleni.

'I'll look forward to that when we are stripping down beds and cleaning rooms. Today felt like a killer, it's going to be worse tomorrow,' replied Julia, waving across the room at Felicity and Isla who'd found a spot on the other side of the pub.

'What would you like to drink?' asked Eleni, confidently pushing her way to the bar.

'Gin and tonic, thanks. I'll go and grab a seat with the girls,' Julia began to weave her way over towards Felicity and Isla who were flicking through Rory's latest Instagram posts. The photos were magnificent. Rory and Zach were currently working within the rehabilitation centre and Rory was caring for the sick, injured, abandoned, and orphaned lions alongside a professional veterinary team.

'Rory looks like he's having an amazing time,' Isla swung the phone towards Julia as she pulled out a chair. 'I wonder if he gets to watch the programme tonight on TV?'

'I believe Stuart was the star of show, always interrupting Rory, that's what Allie was saying,' Felicity gave a little chuckle. 'And where is Allie? It's going to be funny not having her around.'

'I've not seen her yet tonight, maybe she's still packing,' answered Isla, looking up as Jack approached the table.

'Hi Julia, is Eleni with you?' he asked, giving Julia a warm smile.

Julia nodded towards the bar. 'She's over at the bar.'

'Thank you,' he replied, and headed off in her direction.

'Are they dating?' remarked Isla, as soon as Jack was out of earshot. 'Mmm, now he's a catch and a half.'

'A couple of dates,' replied Julia, thinking they did make a stunning-looking couple.

They watched as Jack slipped his arms around Eleni's waist causing her to jump. She immediately looked over her shoulder and kissed him on the lips.

'Love's young dream,' continued Isla, bringing her hand up to her heart. 'Remember those days? The first flush of love is so romantic, then it becomes all mundane, the washing of dirty socks and the sweeping of cut toenails from the bathroom floor.'

'Eww, haven't you just killed the mood,' chuckled Felicity, taking a swig of her drink.

After Eleni had bought the drinks, Jack had pulled her over to one side. He was leaning in close talking to her. Looking slightly troubled, he kept glancing towards the door of the pub.

'That suddenly looks all very serious,' remarked Isla. 'I wonder what that's all about?'

Julia suspected she knew exactly what it was about. She'd tried to reach Alfie all afternoon and left numerous messages but he'd been tied up in meetings. There was no getting away from her worries that the hotel was going to cause her business to go under, but she couldn't live with herself if people's weddings were cancelled after so much planning and expense.

As soon as the conversation was over, Jack pressed a kiss

to Eleni's cheek and she walked over to join them at the table.

'That all looked very cloak and dagger,' prompted Julia, wanting to know if it was about Flynn as she suspected.

'That was an interesting conversation to say the least. Wait until I tell you this,' her eyes were wide, and she took a swift glance over her shoulder to make sure no one was in earshot. All the girls leaned inwards waiting for Eleni to spill the beans.

'Flynn Carter is having a few problems up at Starcross Manor, apparently some of his building suppliers cancelled on him today and people in the village are giving him the cold shoulder.'

Julia looked round at everyone and divulged that she'd gone to visit him late morning to share their worries about the hotel and she'd found him in a state.

'Really, that's awful isn't it?' said Felicity, looking directly at Isla.

'Yes, awful,' echoed Isla.

'Awful,' repeated Felicity.

Julia clocked the look between them. 'Hmm, what do you know about this?' Julia kept her voice low. 'What have you done?'

'Me, I know nothing,' Felicity replied, in a spy-like voice and brought her hand up to her chest in mock protest. 'However…' she took another look to see who was in close proximity before leaning forward once more. 'Last night after you left the teashop, conversation regarding Flynn Carter carried on. Hamish is out for blood. The village shop has been his livelihood for years and he's not about to be forced into retirement before he's ready.'

'To be honest, Mum isn't too happy either,' admitted Felicity. 'Afternoon teas are a big part of our income. And we agree with you that your B&B will most probably be affected. And think about this place – having a celebrity chef up at the manor, who is going to want to eat in the pub when they can get their food prepared by Andrew Glossop?'

'What have you all done?' asked Julia.

'Nothing directly, but Hamish hinted Flynn may hit a few problems with his suppliers.' Felicity was suddenly a little shifty.

'Come on, this isn't like us, we need to play fair and keep our dignity. I thought the plan was I'd speak to Flynn and we can see how the land lies.'

'This man may put your B&B out of business, and you want to play fair?' Isla raised an eyebrow. Julia was surprised by Isla's reaction, knowing she was always the level-headed one. 'We know he's untrustworthy – look at the way he swindled you out of some of your grandfather's inheritance,' carried on Isla.

Julia knew that Isla had a point and she was still wary of Flynn, but since he'd arrived, he seemed like a down-to-earth, genuine bloke, despite his millions in the bank.

'He was frantic this morning, the contractors didn't deliver the materials for the ballroom, which means if that's not finished on time, he will need to cancel the first wedding at Starcross. It doesn't sit with me that someone's special day is going to be ruined because we've interfered.'

'He ruined your friend's wedding day,' Eleni cocked an eyebrow.

'Two wrongs don't make a right, though, do they?' said Julia, giving food for thought. They all sat quietly for a moment before Julia broke the silence. 'And anyway surely Hamish doesn't hold that much clout that he can go cancelling contractors. They need to earn a living too.'

Isla and Felicity looked at each other again.

'Now what aren't you telling me?' urged Julia.

'Hamish did some digging, and it turns out his godson is the main contractor. Of course, he's going to put Hamish first.'

'What did you say to Jack?' probed Julia, looking towards Eleni.

'I didn't tell him anything because I've only just discovered all this, just like you,' she replied, before taking a sip of her drink.

Julia knew it wouldn't be long before Flynn began to discover what was going on too. Even though the community weren't happy, she needed to talk to him and explain what was going on. She didn't like the fact the hotel threatened her business, but there was a right way to go about things.

Their conversation was interrupted by the sound of applause. They looked over to see Allie walking into the pub from the living quarters.

'Glasgow! What a fabulous opportunity for her,' exclaimed Julia, joining in the applause.

'Allie!' Felicity beckoned her over.

Allie was wearing a huge smile as she weaved her way towards them. 'Can you believe this is my last night in Heartcross, well for a while anyway... little old me is venturing out in the big wide world.'

No one could quite believe that Allie had accepted the job on a newspaper 173 miles from home, as Allie had always been a home bird, but when Rory wanted to follow his dream of working in Africa, it began to make her think about her own passions for life.

Immediately, Isla and Felicity stood up and squealed. They both wrapped their arms around their oldest friend and hugged Allie as tightly as they could. 'Let me breathe,' she laughed. 'Please let me breathe!'

Felicity stood back and held Allie's hands. 'We will miss you!' Felicity came over all emotional whilst Isla blinked back the tears.

'Don't cry, I'll be back before you know it.'

'That's why we're crying!' teased Isla, pulling Allie in for another hug.

'Cheeky!' Allie swiped Isla playfully. 'And I'll be back soon as there's a special birthday coming up, I wouldn't miss the odd cocktail or two for the world.' Allie looked towards Julia.

'And what's all this I heard on the grapevine, the village has taken matters into their own hands? Hamish mentioned something this morning in the village shop then Flynn popped in to see Mum.' Allie looked around the table.

'What do you mean?' asked Julia, wondering what he would want with Meredith.

'Apparently the Boathouse is due to open in a couple of weeks and the supplier for all the food and beverages has cancelled on him. He was asking Mum could we possibly help him out with the drinks.' Allie raised an eyebrow. 'People aren't happy he's taking over the community.'

Julia knew this was getting out of hand. Flynn Carter was an influential man, a millionaire. If the villagers began taking matters into their own hands, Julia knew that in the long run they surely would come off worse. The sooner she could have a chat with him the better.

Julia snagged a glance around the room, but she couldn't see Flynn. Maybe, after the day he'd had, he'd decided to stay away. 'It's absolutely heaving in here now,' she said, noticing Hamish looking quite riled in the corner of the room with his animated body language, in discussion with Drew. Perhaps in a minute she'd slip over to him and have a chat about what was going on, and what Hamish was trying to achieve, because Julia had a feeling that World War Three could erupt anytime, and that wasn't going to help anyone.

'The pub is packed, because we are all making sure we get rid of Allie!' teased Felicity, tipping Allie a wink.

'Don't wind me up! Honestly, one second, I'm excited, the next I'm teary, then scared. I don't want to leave Mum and Dad, and this place is my home, not to mention it feels weird not to have Rory by my side. I'm doing it all by myself. I feel like a proper grown-up now.'

'Breathe!' everyone said in unison then laughed.

'I know, I know! But look at this place, it's busy all the time.' Allie nodded towards her mum and dad who had their work cut out behind the bar.

'I've noticed the whole village seems busier this summer. Heart Mountain is attracting thousands more tourists since the bridge collapse, and with Rory's TV show I bet Stuart has had a new influx of clients,' chipped in Felicity.

'You shouldn't joke about that, Stuart told Mum that people just randomly walk past the surgery and take photos, the clients on their books have tripled and he's counting the days until Rory's return. He's finding all this fame stuff very bizarre, and my guess is when this TV show airs tonight Stuart is going to be famous in his own right. Remember, I watched it being filmed, and he was hilarious,' reported Allie with a grin.

'We were just looking at Rory's Instagram, it's amazing. Every morning I check,' admitted Isla. 'And how's the renovations going up at Clover Cottage? Will the new surgery be ready to open by the time Rory comes back?'

Allie shook her head. 'We are looking at approximately six months, Stuart would like the original surgery closed by Christmas. There's going to be a short crossover period I think. We are definitely going to need a bigger surgery with Rory's new-found fame, not to mention more staff, especially with the animal hospital too.'

'It all sounds amazing, you've got so much to look forward to,' exclaimed Julia, feeling a little jealous that her expansion of her own little business empire may have to be put on hold until she knew the state of play with future bookings.

'I know, and with the new job my whole world is going to be so much different, and when I get back I'll be opening up the new photography centre, too, for the disadvantaged kids. In fact the raffle is being drawn tonight, we've already raised a good sum of money to put towards the new equipment.'

'I've donated an overnight stay in one of my vans... take an alpaca for a walk and free fresh eggs for a month,' declared Isla.

'And we've donated a free cream tea plus guest,' added Felicity.

'I can add a free overnight at the B&B if that helps?' said Julia, thinking aloud.

'And I could donate one of my sketches,' chipped in Eleni.

'Sketches?' queried Allie.

'You should see Eleni's sketches, they are amazing! One day this girl will have those sketches in art galleries all around the world – and before you become famous, I best take one off your hands,' exclaimed Julia, 'or else!'

'I can't wait to see them,' chirped Allie, who looked over towards her mum. 'I'm needed behind the bar. I best help out before I get sacked,' she gave a little chuckle. 'The raffle ticket books are doing the rounds. The draw will take place just after the TV programme,' informed Allie. 'I'm coming!' she shouted towards her mum who was giving her that look to get back behind the bar pronto.

Julia noticed that people were already parking themselves on the chairs in front of the TV. It was going to be strange watching Rory on the TV and not seeing him in the flesh, every one missed his presence. He was part of this village, a familiar face and once the programme aired alongside the famous Zach Hudson, Rory's face was no doubt going to be recognised in every house in Scotland. Julia was genuinely happy for him. Rory was as honest as the day is long, a faithful partner, a guy who supported his parents. He deserved it all.

The four friends chatted as Julia looked around the busy room. Suddenly she spotted Flynn walking into the pub via the back entrance, looking more distressed then he had this morning. He was in search of someone as his eyes flitted madly around the room and the second he caught Julia's eye he began strolling towards her.

'Julia, there you are, is it possible to have a word?' He sounded earnest.

All eyes were on Julia as she stood up and pushed her chair under the table. 'Of course,' she said feeling a little nervous. He stretched out his arm and led her to the corner of the room, but before she could ask what this was all about, Flynn began to speak.

'I just want to thank you for listening to me this morning and wondered if you'd managed to find out anything more? Things are going from bad to worse and suppliers have pulled out from the Boathouse too.' Flynn was clearly very frazzled. 'I just don't know what's happening.'

This was Julia's cue to come clean, she could see Flynn was mystified and worried, and she didn't want to cause anyone stress and upset.

'Flynn, it's the hotel.'

Flynn raised an eyebrow. 'The hotel?'

'We are all worried about how it's going to fit into Heartcross. It's going to have an impact on all our businesses... including mine.'

'Julia, I don't understand. The hotel will bring in more tourists to the area – that will benefit everyone's business.'

'How's it going to benefit me when I can't compete with what you have to offer? I'm simply a B&B, I don't have spas or swimming pools. How can I even think about building an extension when I don't even know if I'll have guests wanting to book...'

Flynn was listening intently to Julia. 'Why didn't you come and talk to me about this?'

Julia knew now that that would have been the sensible thing to do and she didn't want to get into a conversation about it, but she was still wary of Flynn, even though since he'd arrived in the village he'd acted with decency.

'It was a shock at first; everyone thought Starcross Manor was going to be converted into retirement flats and then when we discovered it was going to be a hotel... well, everyone has concerns.'

'I didn't try and hide it from anyone.'

'But the community didn't know, somehow everyone

missed the memo. And I do apologise, I should have come to talk to you sooner.' Julia knew all she'd done was make life more difficult for him, but it was still her business that could be affected and she might end up with nothing.

A sudden movement caught Julia's eye, and she looked over Flynn's shoulder to witness Hamish striding towards them, his hands flailing in the air, his face reddened. This really didn't look good.

'The man who wants to take over Heartcross.' Hamish's tone was sharp, and Flynn looked at him in surprise. 'Thought you'd stroll into our village and put us all out of business, did you?'

Julia was stunned, all the time she'd known Hamish she'd never known him to have a cross word with anyone. He was such a gentle soul and to react like this meant he must be riled, it was so out of character for him.

'I'm not here to put anyone out of business,' Flynn replied in a calm manner, conscious there were numerous people now looking over in his direction.

Hamish raised his voice as he continued, 'You would say that though, wouldn't you? Do you know how long I've owned that village shop? And you think you can waltz in here and open up another shop within arm's reach.' Hamish was physically shaking with anger. 'You are not going to put me out of business. Serves you right, now all your contractors are pulling out.' Hamish's face was crimson with anger.

Flynn narrowed his eyes. 'Do you know something

about that, Hamish? Has that got something to do with you?'

'If it wasn't for Julia calling the village meeting and warning us about how untrustworthy you are, you might have got away with it. But we won't stand for it. This community sticks together.'

Julia swallowed. Flynn wasn't listening to Hamish any more, he was staring open mouthed at her.

'You called a meeting? Untrustworthy?'

Julia wanted the ground to swallow her up. Shaking his head in disbelief, Flynn was still staring at her in bewilderment. 'You're the one who's caused all this? And there I was, telling you this morning about how the ballroom wouldn't be completed on time and how someone's wedding was going to be affected... and all the time you knew... unbelievable.'

Julia was mortified, the anguish surging through her body. This sounded a lot worse than it actually was. She'd only just discovered that Hamish was behind the cancelled contractors and had taken matters into his own hands. 'I... I—'

Flynn put his hand up. 'Julia just stop there.' He looked furious. 'I don't want to hear any more. I'll leave you all to enjoy your evening.' And with that Flynn looked away from Julia and stormed towards the front door of the pub.

'Ashamed is what you should be,' were the last words Hamish shouted before the door swung shut behind Flynn.

Julia felt dreadful, Flynn had come to the pub to thank her and now it had ended like this. 'Hamish, what have you done? This was the wrong way to go about it all. This could make the whole situation worse. Flynn won't care at all about supporting our businesses if we alienate him. I know you're worried Hamish but,' Julia blew out a breath. This wasn't how she'd expected the evening to pan out. Flynn would be gunning for and her little B&B. Hamish's hot-headed reaction could have a devastating effect on everyone. 'I need to go and try and rectify the situation.'

Looking a little sheepish, Hamish had now calmed down a little. Julia was just about to go after Flynn to try and clear the air when, right on cue, Fraser blew into a microphone that was set up at the side of the TV. 'Attention everyone.' Immediately the pub hushed, and Fraser continued. 'The show is about to be aired in five minutes, please come and take your seats.' He waved everyone over. 'Hurry!'

The timing couldn't be worse, Julia couldn't go running after Flynn right at this moment. Rory's TV show was about to air any second. 'Hamish, what possessed you?'

'That business is my life and I'm not prepared to go down without a fight.'

Julia fully understood the way Hamish was feeling, that's exactly how she felt about her business. 'But there's ways to go about it. We need to sort this out,' she said, wondering what the hell she was going to do now and worried about how Flynn was going to react to it all. Only time would tell.

Walking back to the table, all eyes were on Julia as she sat back down.

'What the hell just happened there?' asked a wide-eyed Eleni, who'd watched the showdown from afar. 'Flynn didn't look too happy.'

'He's far from happy. Flynn asked this morning whether I knew what was going on and at the time I didn't, but now Hamish has just told Flynn that it was me who organised the meeting and told everyone how untrustworthy I thought he was...'

'Yikes! Who needs enemies,' chipped in Eleni.

'I've probably got a new enemy now,' replied Julia feeling deflated as Martha and Aggie appeared at the side of the table.

'Good evening ladies, who would like raffle tickets?'

Everyone delved into their purses for change. Martha ripped off numerous strips of coloured tickets and handed them over whilst Aggie placed all the money in a clear plastic box.

'There's some great prizes and lots of money already raised, any more for any more?' asked Aggie shaking the box.

'I think we are done, thank you,' smiled Isla. 'Rory's show should be starting soon. Allie said she'd saved us all the front row, so shall we move over there?' Isla nodded towards the TV.

'Good plan,' Felicity said, standing up before turning towards Julia. 'You've gone quiet. Don't think about it now. Just enjoy the show and we can sort it out later.'

Julia nodded, knowing her mood had slumped. She felt awful about the situation. With a nauseous feeling in her stomach she followed the others to the chairs in front of the TV. 'And there will be no bar service until the interval because we would like to watch our future son-in-law on TV too,' added Fraser.

Stuart and Alana took pride of place next to Allie. They were so proud of their son, and Rory rang them numerous times throughout the week to update them on his African adventure. As everyone took their seats Fraser switched on the TV. The second Rory's face flashed across the screen Allie gave out a little squeal causing everyone to laugh. 'OMG, and there's me,' she said pointing, then covered her face up. 'Do I really sound like that?' she exclaimed, feeling embarrassed.

The TV show was entertaining and hilarious in places, especially the times Stuart had interrupted the filming, but the producer had not edited those parts out, leaving everyone in stitches. He was simply hilarious. No one moved from their seat for the whole half an hour and as soon as the credits rolled, the whole pub let out a rapturous applause.

For a short time, the show had taken Julia's mind off Flynn. 'That was brilliant, so entertaining,' she exclaimed, tapping Allie on the shoulder. 'Rory the supervet, and you are a natural on screen. I can't wait for the next episode.'

'Mmm, I'm not sure about me being a natural but it was definitely fun to film, and I have to admit it seemed strange seeing Rory, it was like he was in the room. He was brilliant, wasn't he?' Allie was beaming and the room let out another cheer. She made her way over to the TV screen and picked up the microphone. 'Thank you all for coming! How brilliant was that? I think it's safe to say that was very entertaining and I'm very proud of Rory.' Allie flapped a hand in her face and took a breath. 'I've come over all emotional. Rory will be chuffed to know we are all out in force tonight supporting him while he's off saving the lions.' Allie laid the microphone down on the table and began clapping alongside everyone else. Fraser and Meredith joined their daughter at the front of the room and hugged Allie.

After a few seconds Fraser picked up the microphone. 'I think tonight we are all a little emotional.' He was looking towards his daughter with such admiration. 'Not only do we all miss Rory, in fact it's safe to say since he left for Africa our profits have dropped.'

Allie gave a small chuckle.

Fraser continued, 'And tonight we are all gathered here with all our friends to say goodbye to Allie too. Even though she is leaving us short-staffed and I have to do the early morning shifts, we wish her all the best and will miss her.'

Tears began streaming down Allie's face and Julia quickly delved into her bag and passed her a pack of tissues.

'We wish you so much luck in your new job and we are proud of you and Rory,' echoed Meredith, taking the microphone from Fraser. 'Not only is Allie off to work for the newspaper, tonight she's fund-raising to open the James Kerr Centre for Disadvantaged Children. The centre will be based in the grounds at Clover Cottage and will look to open spring next year.' Meredith looked over the sea of people and waved towards Martha and Aggie, who were sitting at the bar folding the last of the raffle tickets and throwing them into a bucket. 'Aggie... Martha... are we ready to do the draw?'

Martha gave Meredith a nod of the head and made her way over towards Meredith, carrying the bucket. 'Get your tickets ready, there are some fantastic prizes to be won.'

A ripple of excitement filled the room whilst everyone clutched what they hoped was one of the winning tickets. Julia couldn't help but think what an inspiration Allie was. She'd dabbled in photography since her school days and here she was now, off to Glasgow to work on a national paper.

Fraser took the microphone and hushed everyone while Meredith shook the bucket of tickets with both hands. 'Allie, will you do us the honour of pulling out the first ticket,' she asked, holding the bucket up high whilst Allie delved in. She pulled out the first ticket and handed it over to her dad.

'It's a pink ticket,' bellowed Fraser down the microphone causing it to whistle loudly. 'Sorry!' he apologised moving it away from his mouth.

There were lots of ooohs and aaahs filtering around the room from all the people that were clutching their pink tickets.

'The first prize is a month's supply of eggs donated by

the wonderful Drew and Isla of Foxglove Farm, and the winning ticket is pink... 242.'

There was a rustle of tickets and a murmur of voices.

'No way! Allie draw again,' hollered Drew. 'I don't need to win my own eggs,' he said, rolling his eyes. 'I never win anything then I win my own prize... typical.'

Fraser shook his head in jest and Allie dived into the bucket again pulling out another ticket.

'Here goes, this time it's blue... it's blue... 329,' announced Fraser. Whilst he shouted into the microphone, Allie waved the ticket in the air. 'Anyone got blue 329?' he repeated.

Felicity thrust her arm in the air. 'It's me! It's me!' she shouted excitedly.

'That'll will come in handy for the teashop,' chipped in Rona, giving Felicity a nod of approval.

'The next ticket is to win...' Fraser looked over towards Allie who quickly checked the list on the clipboard next to her.

'It's a free newspaper of your choice for a month courtesy of our favourite shopkeeper, Hamish,' shouted out Allie while Hamish stood up and took a bow. He caught Julia's eye as he sat down and looked regretful.

'Winning ticket is pink 173,' Fraser looked over the sea of people who were frantically scanning their tickets.

'It's me, it's me!' bellowed Martha. 'Does it come with free delivery too?' she teased, handing over the ticket to Allie.

'Only because it's you,' shouted out Hamish.

Even though the mood was jovial, all Julia could think about was Flynn. Even though she owned the fact she'd told the villagers that she thought he was untrustworthy, she hadn't called the meeting to hang him out to dry. All she could do was try and put the situation right as soon as she could. For the next five minutes more prizes were drawn, Eleni had won a free walk-an-alpaca day up at Foxglove Farm, Aggie had won one of Eleni's sketches, and Fergus was over the moon to win a free beer every time he came into the pub for the next month.

'The next prize has been donated by Flynn Carter,' announced Fraser. 'This prize is to take a trip on the very first boat that is launched from the Boathouse, which is due to open up in a couple of weeks, followed by an afternoon of water sports.'

Under normal circumstances this prize would have been amazing, however because of the meeting a number of people got up from their chairs and began to filter back towards the bar whilst others just started chatting. Thankfully Flynn wasn't there to witness the undercurrent of unrest. Julia watched Allie swirl her hand inside the bucket.

Eleni leaned in and whispered to Julia, 'You could cut the atmosphere with a knife.'

'Thanks to Hamish,' whispered back Julia.

'It's blue again!' hollered Fraser taking the ticket from Allie. Julia blinked slowly and laid her one blue ticket on her knee.

'It's got to be someone who bought their tickets just after Felicity, the number is 256.'

The room fell deadly silent waiting for the winner to reveal themselves.

Julia swallowed and stared down at the ticket in her hand. She couldn't believe her luck, lying on her knee was a blue ticket, the number 256 staring straight back at her.

Shit.

The adrenalin was pumping through her veins and her hands were beginning to sweat. Her eyes widened – what the hell was she going to do now? The last thing Flynn Carter would want was to take her on a boat trip after what he'd discovered in the last half hour.

'It's you,' hissed Eleni. 'It's you.'

But Julia couldn't answer, she felt paralysed.

'Anyone?' prompted Fraser. 'We are still looking for blue 256.'

Eleni yanked Julia's hand in the air. 'Here!' she shouted towards Fraser. 'It's Julia!'

Julia tried to compose herself quickly and forced a smile, she could feel everyone's eyes on her. Out of all the tickets in that bucket, why did it have to be hers?

Five minutes later the raffle was over, Fraser and Meredith stood proudly next to Allie, who was close to tears again.

'Firstly,' said Fraser, 'on behalf of Allie, Meredith and myself, we would like to thank everyone who has donated a prize and bought a ticket. Tonight, thanks to you guys, Martha and Aggie have counted the money and would you believe we raised just over one thousand pounds? It's outstanding!'

The whole room burst into applause.

'The money will be spent on equipment for the new centre that will be opening up at Clover Cottage in the very near future... watch this space.' Fraser took a breath and turned towards Allie. 'That only leaves me to wish our beautiful, clever daughter a happy six months in the big smoke working on the national paper.' Fraser leant over to the table at the side of him and picked up his glass. 'Here's to Allie.'

'Here's to Allie,' everyone chorused.

'And now I declare the bar back open,' announced Fraser, switching off the microphone and placing it on a nearby table. Allie stood and hugged her parents whilst the majority of drinkers began to queue at the bar. Eleni followed Julia back to their table where Felicity and Isla were already sat back down and watching Julia with amusement.

'Do not say a word,' Julia shook her head. 'Out of all the raffle prizes it had to be me.'

'Do you get a plus one? Maybe you could take Hamish?' joked Felicity.

'I wish I could be a fly on the wall on that date,' teased Isla who was waving over at Allie behind the bar. 'The best thing about one of your mates being the barmaid in your local is you never have to queue for a drink.'

'Mmm, make the most of it, it'll be the last time for a while. And for the record, it's not a date,' added Julia.

'The lady doth protest too much.' Eleni gave Julia a little nudge with her elbow.

Julia knew they were only teasing but began to feel a little restless about the situation. Thankfully, there was a swift change in conversation when Allie appeared at the side of the table with a bottle of wine and glasses. 'I'm not sure what you are going to do for the next six months without your favourite barmaid, and make sure you lot don't disappear without giving me one last hug,' Allie's voice wobbled. 'Right, I need to keep busy,' she said disappearing back towards the bar.

As the girls began chatting about Rory's TV programme, Julia just wanted to go home. The situation had spoilt her evening and she wasn't going to rest until she could.

'I'm sorry ladies, I'm going to get off home. I'm just not in the mood,' said Julia honestly.

'Are you sure? Do you want me to come back with you?' asked Eleni.

'No honestly, you stay and enjoy the rest of the night. I'll see you in the morning.'

'Aww don't go, you can't do anything now about Flynn. Let him calm down. Everything will seem much better in the morning.'

Julia knew that Eleni was only trying to help but all she wanted to do was to curl up in bed and see what tomorrow might bring. 'I know but I'm going to go. I'll say goodbye to Allie on my way out.'

Five minutes later Julia was walking down the High Street heading towards the B&B when she noticed Flynn's car driving towards her. Andrew was sitting next to him in the passenger seat and it looked like they were heading towards Starcross Manor. They were deep in conversation and Julia noticed Andrew looked concerned.

Without warning Flynn stared straight through the window at her. His eyes were cold and hard as he held her gaze. Julia felt uncomfortable and looked away first. By the look on his face he was gunning for her and she knew she was going to have to have a conversation with him tomorrow. With her heart pounding Julia mentally ordered herself to calm down. She hadn't done anything wrong, she just needed to explain everything exactly the way it was – but she had no idea who she was going to face in the morning, the old Flynn or the new Flynn. Only time would tell.

Chapter Nine

J ulia shot up in bed and began to control her breathing. She'd just woken from the most vivid dream, where she had been strolling along a sandy beach somewhere in the Mediterranean, hand-in-hand with Flynn Carter. She'd been wearing a wedding dress and as they'd waded barefoot through the warm seawater Flynn had turned to her and shouted, 'It was you, you turned the village against me!'

Last night's altercation came flooding back for Julia. She gave herself a little shake, the dream had seemed so real, and sitting up in bed she felt not only exhausted but slightly worried about what today would bring. She wasn't a fan of any sort of confrontation.

After taking a minute to rally herself, Julia reached for her phone. Allie had left Heartcross and had posted a selfie just before she climbed on the plane to Glasgow, with the hashtag #seeyousoonHeartcross. She gave the photo a quick like then read the latest news. Woody was stretched out across the bottom of the bed and Julia gave his tummy a quick ruffle before finally slipping out from underneath the duvet.

The B&B was silent as she made her way downstairs, the guests hadn't begun to rise yet, so Julia switched on the radio in the kitchen then flicked on the kettle. She placed two mugs on the table ready for Eleni's arrival.

Woody was off up the garden sniffing frantically after the scent of the foxes and Julia stood in the doorway, staring out across the view. Already she could feel the warmth of the day; according to the news, today was going to be the hottest day on record for years, which meant she and Eleni needed to work hard this morning to get all the bedding changed and bedrooms cleaned before they sweltered in the heat.

With the sound of the crunching gravel outside, Julia smiled; Eleni was right on time. She wheeled her bike up the path and appeared around the corner with a beam on her face and propped her bike up against the wall, before taking her handbag out of the wicker basket attached to the front of the bike. 'Good morning! It's a new day and what a scorcher it's going to be,' chirped Eleni.

'The sooner we get our jobs done, the better. There's fresh tea in the pot too.'

'Perfect,' replied Eleni sidling into the kitchen. 'I can't function until I've had my first cup of the day. How you feeling after last night?' asked Eleni pouring herself a drink.

'Terrible, it must have sounded like *I'd* organised for the contractors to down tools,' she shared. 'And then just sat in front of him revelling in it as Flynn was frantic wondering what the hell was going on.' Julia felt awful and knew that she had to clear the air with Flynn as soon as she could.

After checking on the breakfast things, they spent the next thirty minutes setting up the dining room. Every morning they had the same routine and it worked well. Right on cue the guests began filtering down for breakfast. It was a lovely day to hike the mountain of Heartcross and Julia reminded her guests that it was going to be a hot day and to help themselves to the frozen bottles of water in the cool box she'd left by the front door. The breakfast hall was busy, and Eleni took the orders for the guests' packed lunches before ringing them through to Rona.

'Good morning,' chirped Julia with a smile to Grayson, who'd become a regular at the B&B. Julia knew little about him except that he was away a lot on business and always stayed here. 'How's your breakfast?' she asked as Grayson laid down his knife and fork.

'Don't tell the missus, but Julia you always cook up the best breakfasts,' he answered with a grin. 'Not good for my waistline or my cholesterol levels but always the best breakfasts.'

'I promise I won't tell her,' said Julia brightly.

Once the guests began to disperse Julia and Eleni set to work tidying up. 'Andrew hasn't been down for breakfast yet, should we put a Full Scottish to one side?' suggested Eleni, flinging a tea-towel over her shoulder as she began to gather up the empty plates.

Julia stopped what she was doing for a minute before replying. She hadn't seen Andrew since he and Flynn had driven past her last night. 'I'll take the fresh towels up and check with him.'

'Good plan.'

Julia walked along the corridor, wishing the hikers on their way out a lovely day. A couple of seconds later she arrived outside Andrew's room and rapped softly on the door.

Silence.

Julia knocked again and waited but there was still no answer. She turned the handle and peered around the door. The bed was made perfectly and looked like it hadn't been slept in.

'Hello, it's only me, Julia,' she gave a little shout just in case Andrew was in the bathroom but that too was empty. Quickly she swapped the towels and pulled the curtains back. Andrew's holdall was open on the bed and two chef's double-breasted jackets hung on the rail.

She was just about to leave the room when Julia noticed an open notepad lying on the bedside table. She knew she shouldn't snoop but curiosity got the better of her. Taking a deep breath, she cast her eyes over the words on the page that looked like new menu ideas for the restaurant at Starcross Manor accompanied by a list of suppliers. Feeling a twinge of guilt for snooping Julia laid the notepad back in the same place and picked up a couple of photographs that were lying next to it. The top photograph was of Flynn and Andrew standing on the huge stone steps in the front of

Starcross Manor. Flynn was dressed in a tailored suit whilst Andrew was posing in his chef's attire. The second photo was again of Flynn and Andrew and they were pictured with a distinguished-looking gentleman, dark hair with soft curls, a thin line of stubble on his jawline, also dressed in chef's whites. He looked Italian and vaguely familiar to Julia. They were standing on a sandy bay, with a banquet fit for a king laid out in front of them. Julia narrowed her eyes, she didn't recognise the white building behind with its old-fashioned shutters, purple wisteria and pink roses twisting around the doorway.

'Where are you?' Eleni shouted up the corridor causing Julia to jump. She quickly put the photographs back and hurried out of the room.

'Just coming!' shouted Julia.

Eleni was waiting patiently at the end of the corridor. 'Well?'

'Well what?' replied Julia.

'Does Andrew want any breakfast?'

Julia had completely forgotten the reason why she'd gone to his room in the first place. 'He's not there and it doesn't look like his bed has been slept in. Come on, we need to get those beds made, the bathrooms cleaned and the towels changed. If you do the rooms over the far side I'll take the bedrooms at the top of the stairs.' The day was heating up and Julia already felt hot and sweaty, she pulled at her T-shirt around her neck and took a tentative look in the mirror that hung on the wall in the reception. Her hair looked like she'd put her fingers into an electric socket, it had frizzed into something that resembled a bird's nest. 'I really need to do something with this hair.'

'There's no point worrying about it now,' replied Eleni, picking up the box of cleaning products she'd left on the reception desk. 'Right... Ready... steady GO!'

They were just about to disperse off in different directions when the bell above the entrance tinkled. Julia spun round and froze. Standing in front of her was Flynn and with his lack of smile, she didn't have a good feeling about this.

'Julia, have you got a minute?' Flynn's tone was firm and far from friendly.

'Of course, would you like to come through to the kitchen?' Julia was fully aware there were guests lounging around in the nearby day room and by the look on Flynn's face she assumed this was not a conversation she wanted people over-hearing. 'This way.'

In silence Flynn followed Julia down the hallway and into the kitchen. After closing the door, she turned towards him. 'I was going to come and see you after we'd finished the shift.'

'Julia, I won't beat around the bush, we need a conversation to clear the air.'

Even though Flynn was still being standoffish she was glad he was there.

'I've been nothing but polite and genuine towards you and others since I arrived in Heartcross. So I wondered if you might explain why you're calling meetings and warning the villagers against me.'

Julia felt hot under the collar and knew this was the time to lay all the cards on the table. He was still staring at her, waiting for an explanation, and he didn't once drop his gaze.

Taking a deep breath, Julia spoke. 'When I saw you yesterday, I didn't know anything about why the contractors had cancelled. It was only when I got to the pub that I knew. But did you honestly think that you could turn up in Heartcross and build a hotel that would have an effect on all our businesses and we'd sit back and take it?' Julia was hoping her voice sounded braver than she felt. 'Why all the secrecy, Flynn?'

'Secrecy? What secrecy? I've not hidden the fact from anyone! There's been planning applications stuck to lampposts and in the local newspaper. I've been upfront about everything I've been doing, Julia.' Flynn was direct.

'Except you haven't come directly to any of us because you must have known you wouldn't get the village's blessing. We have long-standing businesses in Heartcross and you just come along with an agenda to make more money. Where do we fit in with all of this?'

Flynn raised an eyebrow, but Julia didn't let him answer.

'A hotel with a swanky spa, swimming pool, gym, restaurants and shops will put this place out of business. Who would want to book a room here when they could have all that less than a mile up the road?'

Julia had to admit Flynn looked a little stunned, his colour paled.

She continued, 'And why do you think Hamish is so

upset? His shop is his life, and now you are opening up another one within your hotel. People will have bought their newspapers before they've even wandered into the village.'

'It's not my intention to put anyone out of business...' interjected Flynn.

'I suppose you are going to tell us all now that a little bit of healthy competition never hurt anyone,' chipped in Julia, hearing her own voice rise a little.

'There will be room in the village for all of us, the hotel will bring in more tourists...'

'And they will be spending all their money within your hotel complex and the Boathouse. It's a win–win for you isn't it, Flynn? But what about everyone else?' Julia finished in a rush.

Flynn looked exasperated, his mouth open. 'Julia, what is going on here? You seem quite hostile towards me all of a sudden, when I've only ever been friendly towards you. All I know is that my contractors cancelled because of you, your actions led to Hamish interfering in my business matters. What am I missing? Why are you telling everyone I'm untrustworthy and trying to tarnish my good reputation?' Flynn was direct, standing his ground. He wanted answers.

'Tarnish your good reputation,' scoffed Julia. 'That's questionable. What was good about your reputation when you offered me thousands less for my grandfather's house due to the economic climate or...?' Julia walked over to the table and grabbed the magazine, she opened it up to the page of the article and slapped it against Flynn's chest. 'Or this, which is all lies.' Her own outburst took Julia by surprise, but these were issues that needed to be addressed. She was so confused by this new Flynn, when she knew, in the past, he had been a very different man.

She felt the tension between them growing as Flynn took the magazine and glanced at the article, with a puzzled look on his face. 'Why are you angry over this?'

Julia shook her head in disbelief, her eyes firmly fixed on Flynn. She pointed at the article. 'Why am I angry over this? Because it's not the truth, is it, Flynn? Was it a ploy to entice people into believing your story to secure bookings for your hotel, increasing your profits?' She bit down on her lip, the knots in her stomach twisting. 'Because I know this isn't what happened. Flynn Carter wasn't jilted, it was you who did the jilting!'

Flynn's jaw fell open. 'Julia, what the hell are you talking about?'

Julia was shaking her head in disbelief, but she felt a sudden stab of unease. Flynn looked dumbstruck by her accusation. 'You know exactly what I'm talking about,' she said, but her words had lost a bit of their strength.

'I really don't.' Flynn was shaking his head. 'I've no idea what you are going on about,' exclaimed Flynn, blowing out at breath.

'Of course you do! Why pretend? You were the one who jilted Anais, leaving her devastated ON HER WEDDING DAY,' Julia's voice rose a notch. 'I'd only nipped out for some pastries and when I returned her beautiful dress was cut to shreds and you'd run off with a woman you were having an affair with, and now you're pretending you know nothing about it.'

Flynn's eyes flickered as he ran his hand through his hair. He exhaled. 'I'm not pretending anything. But your version of events is not the truth. You know what...' Flynn stared into space for a second then placed the magazine back on the table. 'You've painted this picture of me that simply isn't true. Julia, everyone in this village thinks I'm not trustworthy, thanks to you,' he took a breath. 'You've tarnished my reputation and the lies you are spreading about me are damning. I've no intention of causing anyone's business to fold. But now I will do whatever I have to do to get that hotel up and running ready for its opening. No thanks to you... you should have just come and spoken to me first. There was no need for any of this. And as far as Anais is concerned, you are SO far off the mark...'

'I know the truth,' remarked Julia, but she suddenly felt decidedly sick.

'And so do I,' Flynn replied calmly.

'So there's nothing more to say.' Feeling mentally exhausted Julia walked to the door and opened it, gesturing for Flynn to leave.

'Agreed.' He hovered in the doorway and turned back towards Julia. 'You really have got it all wrong,' Flynn said softly.

As the door swung shut behind him Julia took a deep breath. With the emotion pouring through her body, she blinked back frustrated tears. Julia didn't like confrontation of any sort – but how could he stand in front of her and blatantly lie? Unless he had got it wrong?

With a soft rap on the door, Eleni peered around it. 'You okay? Can I come in?'

Julia nodded, 'How much of that conversation did you hear?'

'Most of it,' admitted Eleni, giving Julia a hug. 'You're shaking.'

'I'm so frustrated and fuming… that man… Urghhh. He stands in front of me with his barefaced lies.'

Eleni pulled out a chair. 'Sit down and I'll get you a drink.'

Julia did as she was told, pushing the magazine to the other side of the table.

'Don't take this the wrong way, but Flynn sounded very convincing to me and Jack thinks he's wonderful…' Eleni stared at Julia who looked like she was about to combust. 'It's just… to stand there and lie like that takes some bottle, and why would he need to? It was years ago with Anais and maybe he isn't out to ruin all local businesses?'

'Oh Eleni, I feel like I'm going mad. I just don't know what to think about him any more. You're right, he seemed so convincing that I'd got it wrong about him and Anais, but I was there… In fact, I'm going to FaceTime Anais right now and get to the bottom of this.' Julia reached for her phone, desperate to get answers to the muddled thoughts racing through her head.

'Are you sure about this?' Eleni didn't sound convinced.

'Does she really need to know that Flynn has turned up in Heartcross?'

'Absolutely sure, then at least you can hear it straight from the horse's mouth that I'm not going mad.'

The phone only rang out a couple of times before it connected and Julia was met with Anais's smiley face. She was lounging on a sunbed with a cocktail in hand at the side of the pool.

'Julia! How lovely! How are you? Are you enjoying the sunshine? We are hanging by the pool in this glorious weather.' Anais barely came up for air.

'Anais, hi! It's all good here, just working as usual and maybe grabbing a cocktail very soon too.'

'So to what do I owe this honour, why the video call?' Anais took a sip of her drink.

Julia took a deep breath before speaking. 'I'm not quite sure how to say this, so I'm just going to come out with it. Flynn Carter is here in my village.'

Anais adjusted the sunglasses on top of her head and pulled them down over her eyes, then lowered her voice. 'Flynn Carter is in your village and you thought you'd ring me... why? His name is one I never want to hear again.'

Julia could hear the anguish in Anais's voice. 'I know and I'm sorry, but he's saying things that make no sense to me.' Julia felt awful now that she'd rung Anais, who appeared to look a little unsettled.

'I don't need to hear this, I've moved on. I'm happy. That man... I've got no words for that man after what he did to me,' Anais's voice wobbled. 'You know how untrustworthy, not to mention dangerous, he is, and my advice to you would be to stay the hell away from him. Julia please forgive me, I don't want to talk about this any more.'

'Sorry, sorry, I didn't mean to upset you.' But Anais had already ended the call.

Julia slumped back in the chair, her mood plummeting to an all-time low. 'I've gone and wrecked Anais's day too,' she muttered, letting out a long shuddering sigh. She looked up towards Eleni. 'But Flynn had me doubting myself for a second. He's got a nerve telling me to get my facts straight. I wasn't losing my mind.'

Eleni gave Julia a quick squeeze. 'I didn't think you were losing your mind. Maybe he's changed. People can change you know; maybe he wants to put the past behind him. Everyone deserves a second chance, don't they?' Eleni placed an iced drink of lemonade on the table in front of her then pulled out the chair next to Julia. 'And whether he's telling the truth or not about what happened with Anais is really neither here nor there. What matters is he's opening up a five-star hotel and he has the funds to make it work. And where will that leave you?'

'So what are you saying?' Julia looked up and held Eleni's gaze.

'What I am saying is, we need to come up with a plan B.'

'Which is?'

'I have no idea yet, but let's crack on with the cleaning and have a think.'

Julia nodded.

'And tonight, how about a change of scenery?' Let's go

over to Glensheil, there's a new restaurant opening up near me. We can grab some food away from everything,' suggested Eleni.

'Sounds like the perfect plan to me,' replied Julia, wanting some time out from Heartcross. Following Eleni along the hallway towards the staircase, Julia stopped for a minute and picked up the photograph on the dresser of her and her grandad fishing. She blinked back tears as she remembered how happy they had been then, how worry-free her life once was.

As Eleni carried on chatting as she climbed up the stairs, Julia was oblivious to anything she was saying; all she could think about was Flynn. She felt confused about why he would so strenuously deny that he had jilted Anais, when Julia had been there. And he should have come clean and been open and honest with the community about his plans for Starcross Manor before they discovered them for themselves. All Julia knew was that she'd made an enemy of Flynn and maybe that wasn't the way to go. Once more she thought back to her grandfather. 'Always keep your friends close and your enemies closer.' His words echoed around in her head. Maybe she was going to have to change her approach when it came to Flynn Carter? She just didn't know how she was going to.

Chapter Ten

All afternoon Julia felt dispirited, and the hot weather didn't help. As it was changeover day, new guests could arrive at any time of the day, which meant Julia needed to be present at the B&B all day, which meant she couldn't get away to speak to Flynn even if she wanted to.

Andrew had returned early afternoon and checked out, explaining that his room was now ready up at Starcross Manor. A small part of her was worried that her actions had caused Andrew to leave but thankfully he was his usual friendly self, which was a relief to Julia as she really couldn't face a second confrontation today.

Finally, around four o'clock Julia and Eleni managed to sit down for the first time that day. The pair of them were both exhausted. 'On the plus side, at least we don't have 110 bedrooms to clean and change,' joked Eleni, lightening the mood.

'There is that,' smiled Julia. 'And thank you.'

'What for?'

'For putting up with me today, I know I've been like a bear with a sore head,' admitted Julia, knowing she wasn't in the best of moods.

'It's understandable; you've worked hard to build up a brilliant business. It's your home, your independence, and it's under threat. Anyone would feel the same way.'

Julia tilted her face up to the sun and closed her eyes.

'Jack texted me before. Flynn is still trying to find someone desperately to finish the ballroom on time so that the wedding can go ahead as planned.'

Julia did feel guilty that the innocent couple getting married at the manor had been caught up in the line of fire. 'The community of Heartcross is definitely a force to be reckoned with.'

'I've no intention of ever getting on the wrong side of anyone here,' chuckled Eleni.

They enjoyed another five minutes of glorious sunshine before the final guests arrived, and once they were all checked in Eleni headed home while Julia jumped in the shower. She was looking forward to checking out the new bistro over in Glensheil, and the change of scenery would do her the world of good.

A couple of hours later Julia was standing at the impressive entrance to the bistro. It reminded her of a time she'd visited Paris. Outside was a selection of well-worn tables and chairs, a chalkboard menu and a bustling ambience due to the glorious weather.

Julia spotted Eleni walking up the pavement and gave

her a wave. 'This place looks amazing, good choice,' she said as she perused the menu on the outside board as the waiter approached them.

They opted to sit outside on the street and enjoy the summer evening. Once the waiter took their drinks order, he disappeared back inside.

'This is the life,' exclaimed Julia. 'It's nice to get out somewhere different.'

'It is after that busy day.' Eleni thanked the waiter as he placed a bottle of wine on the table alongside two glasses and handed them a menu each.

'Cheers!' exclaimed Julia as they clinked their glasses together.

'How are you feeling after today?' asked Eleni tentatively.

'Confused. I just don't know what to think,' admitted Julia.

'I agree, it is very strange, but I was talking to Jack whilst I was getting ready… he's going to pick us up by the way and drop you back over the bridge to save you getting a taxi home.'

'He's a keeper,' Julia interrupted.

'And off the record, he's been chatting to Flynn about the hotel situation and can see where he's coming from.'

'In what way?' asked Julia, not quite understanding.

'He thinks that Starcross Manor will bring in more tourists and that can only be a good thing for Heartcross. Everyone has their own budget, think of it like a car…'

'A car? You've lost me.'

'Some people can afford Lamborghinis whilst others can only afford second-hand cars…'

'Great! Now you are telling me Starcross Manor is the Lamborghini and my B&B is the rust bucket that will hardly start in the morning!' Julia chuckled. 'But I know what you are saying.'

'And then there's Foxglove Camping and Isla's campervans. Some people enjoy the great outdoors, they prefer to wake up to the smell of cow dung and cook their breakfast on a BBQ. We are all different.'

When Eleni put it like that maybe she had got it all wrong and Starcross Manor wasn't such a threat to business. But there was still a niggly feeling in the pit of her stomach.

'And I'm intrigued to know what you are going to do with your raffle prize, Jack was telling me that the Boathouse is opening in a couple of weeks' time.'

'I don't even want to think about that at the minute,' Julia said. Spending time alone with Flynn sounded like her worst nightmare.

The waiter came back and took their food orders, and their conversation turned towards Julia's upcoming fortieth birthday. Julia had agreed to leave it in everyone's hands apart from her own, which she was beginning to regret a little now.

'It's all in hand,' grinned Eleni, taking a piece of seeded bread from the wicker basket on the table and dipping it into the oil.

'I dread to think! I spoke to Callie a couple of days ago

and as far as I know she's coming,' said Julia, moving her knife and fork to one side as the waiter placed down a creamy courgette and bacon pasta in front of her, which looked amazing.

'There's just a few little things to tweak but it's going to be fun.'

'I honestly don't mind just going down to the Grouse and Haggis...'

'Nonsense! We can do that anytime of the week,' remarked Eleni, tucking into her plate of lasagne. 'Oh my, this is delicious. Just what I needed.'

'This place is packed to the rafters, it's so popular,' Julia glanced around at the diners and spotted Jack's van travelling up the road towards them. 'Is that Jack?' she asked looking at her watch. 'What time did you ask him to collect us?'

Eleni looked towards the road, her fork poised in mid-air. She narrowed her eyes and focused on the number plate. 'It's definitely Jack,' said Eleni confused, 'but he's way too early.'

A continuous frantic beep of the van horn caught every diner's attention. All heads turned towards Jack's van as it screeched to a halt on the edge of the pavement outside the bistro.

'I've got a bad feeling about this,' exclaimed Eleni, placing her knife and fork down on the table.

They watched Jack jump out of the van. 'Julia, you need to come with me.' He looked stricken.

Julia's heart was suddenly pounding fast. 'What is it?'

'I'm honestly not quite sure. I was driving past the B&B and all your guests are outside on the grass verge, and there's a fire engine parked outside.'

'There's a fire?'

'I couldn't see any flames, I just don't know. Felicity and Rona are there rallying around the guests.'

Eleni flagged the waiter down and paid for their meal before they both climbed into the van.

'Surely it can't be a fire?' She swallowed down a lump in her throat. 'I can't see what would catch on fire.'

Eleni looked across at Julia, all the colour had drained from her cheeks. Julia's head was swirling. What about the guests, were any of them hurt, and where the hell were they going to sleep? She couldn't think straight. They travelled back in silence.

As Jack turned into the road and slowed down, Julia couldn't believe the sight before her. All her guests were sitting on the grass verge clutching their belongings. Jack had been right, there was a fire engine parked at the gates of the B&B, but she couldn't see any flames and couldn't smell burning. Uncertainty gripped her stomach and she clambered out of the van. All she could hear was the continuous alarm ringing out from the B&B. A distressed Julia was mystified as she glanced towards her guests, who all looked wet – in fact they were drenched to the core. What the hell had happened here? She'd only been gone for under an hour.

She ran towards the B&B followed by Jack, whilst Eleni

hurried over towards Felicity and Rona who were currently handing out towels and cups of tea.

As Julia reached the gate the alarm finally stopped ringing.

'Excuse me, Ma'am, you can't go in there. It's not been declared a safe zone yet.'

Julia met the eyes of a burly fireman. 'But I'm the owner,' said Julia, feeling herself crumbling. She just needed to get inside.

'Julia... Julia Coleman?' he asked.

'That's me. Please can someone tell me what is going on?'

'It seems your sprinkler system has been activated... somehow.'

'The sprinkler system?' Julia wasn't expecting that. 'You're joking me, right?'

'I'm afraid not, the fire service are working to shut it down.'

'But that means everywhere will be swimming with water.' An uncontrollable shudder swept Julia's entire body. 'That system activates in every room. Everything will be ruined.' The tears began to freefall down Julia's face as Eleni appeared at her side and slipped a comforting arm around her shoulder.

'I'm so sorry, Julia.'

'What about my guests? Is anyone hurt?' Julia spun round to see the guests looking forlorn with towels draped over their shoulders, feeling completely helpless. 'They are soaked through to the bone,' she noticed.

'Everyone is out safely, maybe a little wet, but all unharmed,' the fireman confirmed.

Julia felt paralysed to the spot. All the guests abandoned on the side of the lane, all their possessions saturated and most probably destroyed by the water. 'Where the hell are they going to sleep tonight?' Julia couldn't think straight, the uncertainty of it all gripping her stomach. 'All the bedding and mattresses will be soaked, the curtains, the sofas.' Julia felt like she couldn't breathe. Her eyes were glued to the B&B.

Eleni put on her best encouraging smile. 'We'll think of something. Won't we Jack?'

Jack raised an eyebrow. 'Of course, we'll come up with a plan.'

'I need to go inside.' Julia's voice was urgent.

'I appreciate that Julia, but I'm just waiting for confirmation that we've managed to disconnect the gas supply, electricity – and thankfully we've just managed to turn the water off at the mains supply.'

Julia was at a loss. 'How has this happened? Why would the sprinkler system be activated if there was no fire? I just don't understand.'

'That's the million-dollar question, but we could hazard a good guess.'

'And that guess is?' Julia was staring at the fireman.

'Usually each individual sprinkler stem head is triggered automatically when the air rising to the ceiling reaches a fire-specific temperature of around 155 degrees. The systems installed these days are more advanced and reliable; the system you have installed in here is unreliable and doesn't even meet the new regulations.'

'But why would it be activated?' asked Julia.

'My guess is today's heat. It's been the hottest day on record for years. In the second storey of the house,' the fireman pointed up above, 'you have skylights, the first sprinkler that was activated was located near that skylight... from what we can tell. Most probably the heat activated a faulty sprinkler...'

'And once one is activated, they are all activated.'

The fireman nodded. 'That's correct. Aside from deliberate sabotage, I would say that would be the cause. But obviously your insurance company will investigate further.'

Julia hadn't heard the rest of the sentence. 'Sabotage?' she said out loud.

'Do you know of anyone who would want to put you out of business?' the fireman was looking directly at her.

In Julia's mind there was only one person who would want to put her out of business... Flynn Carter. Her chest hitched as she snagged a glance towards Eleni.

'I know exactly what you are thinking, but that's just ridiculous. I mean this in the nicest possible way, Julia, but you are small fry compared to Flynn Carter. He wouldn't need to put you out of business this way,' confirmed Eleni in a whisper.

Before Julia could answer a voice bellowed from inside, 'It's all safe now boss.' Another fireman appeared at the entrance to the B&B. 'However, it's swimming in water.'

'Are you ready for this, do you want me to come inside with you?' offered Eleni.

Julia nodded, not trusting herself to speak. Deep breaths she told herself, trying to be braver than she felt. Wiping a tear from her eye she followed the fireman inside. Her anxiety levels were off the scale as she took in the sight of the damage in front of her. Reality struck hard: how was she ever going to get this place back to any sort of normality? Julia felt suddenly helpless.

'I'm afraid it's not a pretty sight inside,' said the fireman, propping open the front door of the B&B. 'Those shoes may not be suitable.'

Julia gulped, she didn't care if her shoes got wrecked, her whole B&B was wrecked. Feeling devastated, she saw that everything she had worked for lay under a tidal wave of water. The desolation was all-consuming, like a scene on TV. The reception was soaked through, the paint on the walls a darker shade than before, where it had soaked up the water. The reception diary sodden, the writing illegible.

Julia paled. With the computer submerged in water, how was she going to notify the up-and-coming guests that they would have to rebook their accommodation? She'd have no record of who'd paid what.

'OMG!' Julia gripped Eleni's arm, panic-stricken. 'Woody, where the hell is Woody?'

'Woody?' repeated the fireman. 'All guests have been evacuated safely.'

'Woody is my dog, he'll be petrified. He's usually under

the kitchen table.' Julia was fraught with emotion as she splashed towards the kitchen.

'He's here, don't worry, I have him.' Woody was clinging like a frightened child to another fireman, his coat drowned, his large dopey eyes were sad and his whole body was shaking from fright.

He really was looking sorry for himself but the second he spotted Julia he thumped his tail slowly.

'He's okay, he was hiding in the pantry, maybe a little shocked but he's not hurt,' said the fireman reassuringly.

Julia took Woody from his arms and was relieved he was safe. She hugged him like her life depended on it, but felt her body quivering with the shock. Everywhere was drenched, the paintings hanging on the walls ruined, the curtains soaked. She stared round at everything in despair, this was going to be a major clean-up operation, each room a mammoth task. She thought about taking a look upstairs but just couldn't face it.

'Julia, we need to think fast,' encouraged Eleni. 'We have paying guests sitting outside needing a bed for the night.'

Julia knew she needed to pull herself together and gave herself a little shake. 'We need to telephone the Grapes Hotel over in Glensheil and see if they have any vacancies.'

'It's unlikely as it's peak season, but I'll try,' replied Eleni, pulling her phone out of her pocket.

'If not, try the George Hotel, even though I'm not sure how the hell I'm going to pay for it all,' added Julia, thinking aloud.

Jack touched Eleni's arm. 'I'll ring one, you ring the

other,' he nodded towards the back door. The pair of them waded through the kitchen and stood out on the patio and began to dial the local hotels.

Julia was surrounded by bedlam. Overcome with emotion she cuddled Woody so tightly and couldn't hold on to the tears any longer. 'What the hell am I am going to do, Woods? This is my life and look at this place.'

Eleni and Jack returned back inside, the look on their faces saying it all. 'I'm so sorry Julia, but there are no vacancies anywhere...'

Julia just couldn't help it, more tears began to stream down her face.

'Please don't cry...' Eleni sloshed her way over to the box of the tissues on the table and reached inside. 'Okay, no tissues, they are all just one lump of sogginess.'

Jack stepped towards her. 'Don't worry, we'll sort this. It's going to be okay,' he said trying to offer a little bit of reassurance.

After placing Woody on the floor Julia flung her arms open. 'How is it going to be okay? My guests are stranded outside on the lane with nowhere to stay and I've no idea where to start with this lot.' Julia felt her chest rising and falling, and all she could do was try and catch her breath. 'I'm sorry Jack, I don't mean to take it out on you. I need to go and talk to the guests, but I have no clue what the hell I'm going to say.'

'Don't shoot me when I say this, but we think you only have one option,' Eleni looked a little uncomfortable.

'I'm willing to listen to any options.'

'Starcross Manor,' Eleni scrunched up her face as soon as the words were out, waiting for Julia's reaction.

'Except that option. Are you kidding me? I don't need Flynn Carter's help – not that he's going to give it to me anyway,' she muttered, wrapping her arms around herself in a soothing manner. Her mind flashing back to the altercation with Flynn earlier today.

'I think he's your only option. There's a number of bedrooms finished, at least they will be able to have a hot shower and a good night's sleep.' Jack's voice was soft.

Of course, Julia needed to get her guests fixed up with a bed for the night as soon as possible, but there was no way on this earth Flynn was going to help her out. And under the current circumstances she didn't feel she could even approach him. Surely there must be another solution.

The fireman appeared in the doorway. 'We're off now, but I'll get a report filed in the next forty-eight hours so you can forward it to your insurance company.'

'Thank you,' replied Julia, still feeling bewildered. She had no idea if the insurance claim would even pay out, knowing the sprinkler system didn't meet any current regulations.

'Oh, and there's a lady called Rona who wants to speak to you. Apparently, the guests are wanting some answers and becoming a little agitated.'

Julia knew that was going to happen, she just wished she had some good news to tell them all. 'I'm on my way,' Julia picked up Woody and began wading back through the water.

Rona was waiting by the gate with a look of concern on her face. 'What has actually happened here?' she asked.

Julia explained about the dated sprinkler system and the extreme heat. Her bottom lip began to quiver, and she felt that her legs were going to buckle underneath her. 'I need to sit down.'

'Sit on the wall,' suggested Eleni, taking Woody from her while Rona wrapped him up in a towel and gave him a quick rub. 'It'll be the shock.'

'This is all my fault.' Julia exhaled. When she'd bought the B&B the survey had flagged up the outdated system, and that whilst it wasn't unsafe, they had recommended that she change it to a more updated version. But the cost had been huge and Julia's main priority had been to get the business up and running. She had been planning to update the system when the building work started on the new extension, but now it was too late.

She pulled herself back to the moment. 'I don't even want to go back in there,' she said, anxiously. 'I don't even know where to start and those poor people. I've wrecked their holidays.'

'It's just an accident, one of those things,' Rona tried to soothe the way, but Julia was feeling distraught.

'Rona, can we move everyone up to the teashop whilst I work out what to do?' asked Julia, thinking aloud.

'Of course, it's already in hand. Drew and Fergus are on their way with the trailer to transport the guests and their luggage, but everyone is wanting to speak to you. They are asking questions that I don't know the answers to.'

'I'm not sure I know the answers either,' admitted Julia, taking a look over at the bedraggled guests who were looking in her direction, but she knew she needed to go and talk to them.

'We are right behind you,' stated Eleni with warmth. 'You aren't on your own.'

A small thread of relief ran through her. 'Thank you, that is a weight off my mind,' she said, ruffling the top of Woody's head who was sitting patiently at her feet.

'In fact, here's Drew and Fergus now,' Jack nodded towards the tractor chugging up the lane pulling the trailer behind. 'And I still think your only option is talk to Flynn.'

Now it was Rona's turn to raise an eyebrow.

'I might not have a choice,' Julia had thought about nothing else in the last five minutes, 'especially if there's no vacancies anywhere in Glensheil.'

'Any vans free up at Foxglove Farm?' prompted Rona.

Julia shook her head. 'No, they are completely full.'

'I think Jack is right, you know,' Eleni touched Julia's arm. 'You may just need to swallow some pride on this occasion. We can't leave them sitting outside for much longer, some of those families have children.'

Julia knew she needed to make a decision, but asking Flynn for help would be so humiliating and she would hazard a guess that he wouldn't be jumping at the chance to help her. But her guests couldn't sleep out on the street, they needed relocating and fast. Taking a deep breath Julia began to walk towards the guests.

After gathering everyone around, Julia took a swift

glance back towards the B&B. It was going to take a lot of hard work to get that place back into any sort of order and she had no idea how long it would take. She was going to lose revenue from the imminent guests arriving in the next couple of weeks and she needed to come up with an alternative plan for their forthcoming holiday bookings, and fast. Julia felt sick to her stomach; maybe Eleni was right, maybe she was going to have to go and speak to Flynn about striking a deal.

As Julia approached, almost immediately, she heard an undercurrent of disgruntled mumblings, but she could absolutely sympathise with them.

'How long are you going to leave us out here?' bellowed one guest.

'Are we setting up camp on the grass verge?' another shouted.

Julia realised that tempers were beginning to fray and she needed to act fast.

'And where the hell are we sleeping tonight?'

Julia raised her arms then lowered them to gain everyone's attention, and thankfully everyone hushed.

'Hi, firstly, thank you all for being patient,' said Julia warmly, trying to calm the situation. 'It certainly hasn't been the easiest of evenings. Secondly, everyone is out and safe. According to the Fire Service, it's more than likely the sprinkler system was set off due to the extreme weather conditions, which was beyond our control, a freak accident.'

'Never mind that, all we want to know is where are we

sleeping tonight?' shouted Mr Cullen who was juggling a small child. 'Some of us are already in need of their bed.'

'Yes, I fully understand that and I'm working hard to try and sort that as soon as possible, but for now we are going to transport you over to Bonnie's teashop.'

'And how long are we going to be there?' Mr Cullen shouted again.

'Please bear with me Mr Cullen, I will endeavour to get this situation sorted as soon as possible, but first let's get you all shifted off the street.'

'And who is going to pay for any new accommodation, I'm assuming that's not coming out of our pocket?' added Mr Cullen once more.

These were all questions that needed answering, but at this very moment Julia didn't have the answers. She felt as stranded as them. For a brief moment Julia closed her eyes and tried to keep her panic at a manageable level. This was hard enough as it was without the constant interruption and negativity.

'I promise you I'm going to do my best to get this sorted as soon as possible, and the sooner we transport you over to the teashop the sooner I can get on with arranging alternative accommodation.' Julia looked over her shoulder and thankfully Fergus and Drew were standing behind her ready to load up the trailer with the guests and their possessions.

'If you would like to head over to the trailer Fergus ad Drew will help you with your belongings.'

'Are you having a laugh, you expect us to travel by that thing?'

Julia knew that Mr Cullen was far from happy, but she really wished he could see the bigger picture. 'Think of it as an adventure Mr Cullen, I'm sure the children will love it.' Julia gestured over towards the hay bales on the back of the trailer.

All of the stranded guests began to walk towards the trailer and handed their bags over to Drew and Fergus, who stacked them up safely. Rona and Felicity quickly began collecting up the empty cups then jumped on the back of the trailer alongside them all.

Drew made sure everyone was sitting comfortably. 'It may be a little bumpy, but I won't go too fast... hold on tight!' He winked at the children before climbing into the cab of the tractor next to Fergus. As soon as the engine started, he beeped his horn and waved his hand out of the window at Julia. She watched the trailer trundle down the road thinking it reminded her of a scene from the war, when all the evacuees were loaded onto carts and shipped away with their possessions. As soon as it disappeared around the corner, she let out a huge sigh – what the hell was she going to do now? Time was ticking.

Chapter Eleven

'**E**verywhere is booked – urghhh, absolutely everywhere.' Looking at her phone in despair Julia felt exasperated. She'd telephoned what seemed like every hotel in Glensheil with no luck whatsoever, not one of them had a spare room.

'Julia, I think you've only got one option.' Eleni gave her a knowing look.

'I agree,' urged Jack. 'Flynn is actually up at Starcross Manor now shooting a video for a wedding advert.'

'Flynn is not going to help me out and I'm not sure I'm willing to give him the satisfaction of turning me down,' replied Julia stubbornly.

'What's the alternative?' urged Eleni. 'Because I can't think of anything.'

Silence.

Julia threw her hands up in the air. 'Okay, okay, it doesn't look like I've got much choice.'

'Flynn is not going to let you down. Do you want me to come with you?' offered Jack.

Julia shook her head. 'No, it's okay, this is something I need to do on my own. Would you both head over to the teashop in case Rona and Felicity need backup? And can you take Woody? I'll be in touch as soon as I can.'

'Of course.' Eleni gave Julia a quick hug. 'It'll be okay, you'll see.'

Unconvinced, Julia rummaged inside her bag for the keys and then got inside the stifling hot car that had been sat in the sun all day. With a sick, sinking feeling in her stomach Julia fired up the engine and immediately switched on the air con, thankful for the cool air blasting out. Nervously she began to drive the short journey towards Starcross Manor.

It only took a matter of minutes before Julia was travelling up the long driveway towards the manor house. She was thankful for the line of green foliage that provided that little bit of shade which shielded her eyes from the blinding sun that bounced off the windscreen. The ducks had the right idea, swimming in the lake and nestling under the cascades of branches at the water's edge to keep cool.

On the drive she'd played out in her mind what she was going to say to Flynn, but now, parking the car, she was struggling to remember the conversation she had rehearsed so many times in her head on the way here. Nervous didn't even cover it as Julia grabbed her bag from the passenger seat and risked a tentative look in the mirror. Her skin was glistening with the heat, the nape of her neck felt damp, and her mouth was dry. She took a swig from a bottle of warm water that had been in the cup holder for goodness-knew-how-long and tried to calm her beating heart.

It was now or never. Plucking up courage, Julia stepped out of the car and looked around. There were approximately a dozen cars parked in the bays, which must be down to the filming that Jack had mentioned. The warm evening air hit her once more as she headed towards the grand entrance of the manor house. She was surprised to see a red carpet trailing the stone steps leading to an open doorway, but again that must have something to do with the wedding video.

Inside the grand foyer there wasn't a soul in sight, and the only sound Julia could hear was her shoes tapping on the slate floor as she began to walk towards the double doors in front of her, which took her down a hallway into another awe-inspiring room – the extravagance of the place took her breath away. She hovered by a table that was littered with books of different colours of materials and quickly flicked through them. Flynn must be choosing his soft furnishings, she thought, walking through to another room that was filled with round tables decorated with pristine white linen cloths, each with a silver candelabra standing proudly in the centre. There was a bar at the back of the room with rows of champagne flutes lined up, and on the stage an array of musical instruments. This place looked like it was about to host the wedding of the century thought

Julia, wandering over to the three gigantic windows that ran from ceiling to floor overlooking the freshly-mown lawns.

Outside there was an intimate gathering on the lawn with everyone dressed up to the nines, the women in long floating dresses holding sun parasols, the men dressed in kilts. Four rows of chairs were laid out on each side of an aisle, with a beautiful wooden archway dressed with gorgeous pink rose foliage. Watching from a distance, Julia heard music through the open window, followed by a man with a camera shouting 'Action' – and that was when she saw him. Flynn was standing at the bottom of the aisle, actually taking part in the video. Dressed in a kilt, accompanied by a dirk and sporran, his three-button waistcoat, white shirt and black bow tie left Julia thinking how handsome he actually looked.

More out of curiosity, Julia was rooted to the spot and continued to watch. Trailed by a camera man and photographer, a beautiful woman floated onto the lawn wearing the most exquisite wedding dress Julia had ever set eyes on and carrying the most simple but stunning bouquet of white roses. Everyone was up on their feet as the actress began to walk down the aisle leaving Julia's view obscured.

Hearing her phone ping, Julia jumped out of her skin. It was a text from Eleni. 'Any luck? Has Flynn agreed? It's 7pm we really need to know what's happening. The guests are beginning to get restless.'

Julia stared at the text and didn't know what to do. She couldn't gatecrash the pretend wedding, and Flynn was surrounded by actors and the rest of the film crew. Hearing a voice shouting 'It's a wrap', she glanced once more towards the lawn to see Flynn shaking everyone's hand. He must have sensed someone was watching him, and he turned and locked eyes with Julia. Her heart thumped as he held her gaze and then began walking towards the manor house. Flynn never took his eyes off her except for a couple of moments when he disappeared through the door. With his footsteps now echoing down the hallway, Julia's heart pounded faster, before the door into the room swung open. The look on Flynn's face made it obvious that he wasn't happy to see her – and who could blame him?

There was no welcoming smile. 'Well, you turn up in the most unexpected places. What are you doing here?' asked Flynn in a stern tone.

Julia felt her cheeks colour fast. She gulped. He continued to stare at her. Feeling uneasy, she knew now that this hadn't been a good idea. The tension between them could be cut with a knife. He stood watching, waiting for Julia to muster up the courage to speak. Knowing this wasn't going to be easy, she swallowed. She had to do something, all her guests were stranded and needed a bed for the night. Taking the plunge, she hoped her voice didn't sound as nervous as she felt. 'There's been an incident at the B&B, the old sprinkler system was activated, the firemen think it's possibly due to the weather conditions… anyway the B&B is submerged in water, everywhere is soaked, and I've got stranded guests with nowhere to sleep. I've telephoned every hotel in

Glensheil and they are all fully booked, so I was wondering...'

Flynn raised a perfectly arched eyebrow.

Julia had started so she may as well finish. 'I was wondering whether there was any possibility you could help me out.' There, she'd said it now, as the words hung in the air, there was no going back. Julia had swallowed her pride and had asked Flynn to help, but judging by the look on his face this wasn't going to be an immediate yes, if even a yes at all.

He gave a short strangled laugh. 'For a second there, I could have sworn you were asking for my help.' He stared straight at her.

'That's exactly what I'm asking for, your help.'

'Are you serious? Have you completely lost your mind and forgotten what you've done to me?'

Julia was just about to answer but Flynn jumped straight back in. 'You've spread rumours about me all over this village and tarnished my reputation, and now you have the gall to stand there and ask for my help.' Flynn's eyes were wide. 'In the last twenty-four hours do you know how many contractors have cancelled on me? And that's all down to you and this community.' Flynn took a breath. 'And do you know what the frustrating thing is about all of this? You are so wrong, about everything.'

Julia knew she was going to get a dressing down and Flynn didn't hold back. 'Starcross Manor wasn't a threat to anyone. All you had to do was come and have a conversation with me. This morning I walked down Love

Heart Lane into the village and not one person passed the time of day with me and now… and now you want to forget all that and ask me to do you a favour.'

Julia felt guilty and embarrassed. She knew she'd made his life difficult, but she'd never wanted people to turn against him. Everything had got out of hand, especially with Hamish taking matters into his own hands.

'I do understand how you are feeling,' she said. 'I really do, and I'm sorry everything has got out of hand. That was never my intention, Flynn.'

Flynn remained silent.

'I've got numerous guests stranded, with children who are soaked through to the bone and really need a bed. And it's more than likely I've put myself out of business before this place ever could.' For a second Julia let her guard down and was close to tears.

'What do you mean by that?' Flynn didn't take his eyes off her.

'I was warned that the sprinkler system was outdated, and I delayed updating it, which means more than likely the insurance company won't pay out. I've got more guests arriving in the next couple of days, and I'm going to lose all my income, and will have to refund all of them.' Julia's voice was getting higher and higher. 'And I've only got myself to blame. Look, this isn't your problem, it's mine. And again, I'm sorry; you're right, I should have come to you first when I discovered this place was going to be a hotel – but I was wary of you, because of the past. And I don't blame you for not helping me, I really don't. I'm sorry to have wasted your time.'

Julia turned and began to walk towards the door, her whole body was shaking, she had no clue where she was going to put her guests, but she needed to go and face the music.

'Julia… wait,' Flynn called out after her.

She stopped dead in her tracks and turned round.

Flynn's face had softened. 'I'm not about throwing families out on the street, especially when there are small children involved. I have rooms ready and made-up that your guests would be welcome to use.'

Had Julia just heard him right? 'This isn't a joke, is it?'

'No, but if I'm helping you, in return you need to help me.'

Julia knew there must be a catch. 'What do you mean?' she queried.

'Tell the village you got me all wrong, and help me to put it right. I need this place finished and up and running. In return I'll help you get the B&B back up and running as quickly as possible.'

'Why would you do that?' Julia felt sceptical, could this really be ruthless Flynn Carter talking, offering to help her out?

'Because I'm not the guy you think I am. We need to agree to disagree and move on, otherwise what are we going to do, spend our whole time fighting?'

His words resonated through Julia. 'We need to agree to disagree and move on.' It was only hours earlier she'd declared war on Flynn Carter, and now she owed him everything.

Julia's thoughts were scrambling all over the place. On one hand the community were going to think she'd completely lost the plot – one minute she was telling everyone how untrustworthy Flynn was, and now she was going to have to admit she'd made a mistake. But this was business, and she needed to separate it from what he'd done to Anais. That wasn't her argument. She needed to concentrate on what was important to her, and that was her B&B.

'Okay, deal,' replied Julia, feeling grateful the guests were going to get a roof over their heads, but also a little uneasy about what the rest of the villagers would think. But she knew she needed to put it right. Tomorrow, Julia would go and find Hamish and talk to him, to try and calm the situation down. It was the least she could do for Flynn after he'd agreed to put up her guests.

'I will put it right Flynn. I will.'

He acknowledged her with a nod.

Hurrying to the door Julia waved her mobile phone in the air. 'I need to get my guests.' She glanced back over her shoulder. 'And thank you.' Julia was genuinely grateful, his generosity had floored her, and she knew he had gone above and beyond when he didn't have to. He was now watching her with amusement as she hovered near the books of sample material by the door.

'Out of curiosity, what are these for?'

'The curtains to frame those windows,' Flynn pointed behind him.

'This is the one you need.' Julia pointed to a regal red colour. 'It will frame those windows perfectly.'

A smile hitched across Flynn's face. 'Go and get your guests.'

Chapter Twelve

The next morning Julia's eyes started to tear up as she fixed her gaze on the flooded debris. Everywhere looked exactly the same, except drenched and forlorn. Lost for words, she bit down on her bottom lip and took in the carnage around her, then blinked back the tears as she noticed the beloved photograph of her and her grandfather, fishing on the river, lying on the floor with a smashed frame, the photograph ruined. Julia picked it up and clutched it to her chest.

'You okay?'

Julia jumped out of her skin, she hadn't heard anyone come in behind her. She turned round to find Flynn, standing behind her.

'Sorry, I didn't mean to make you jump. I'm just checking you're okay. I thought I'd see you at breakfast, but I just missed you. Andrew took care of the guests, I think they all quite liked their breakfast being prepared by a celebrity.' He smiled.

'Thank Andrew for me, I'm sure they loved it. I just wasn't hungry, too much on my mind. I needed to get back here and work out where the hell I'm going to start.'

Flynn held up a bag. 'Breakfast – you may not have been hungry then, but you need to keep your strength up. Looks like there's a lot to do here.'

Julia was pleasantly surprised. 'Breakfast for me?'

'Exactly that. Breakfast for you, sausage and egg muffin with a sachet of brown sauce,'

'Brown sauce, you say. How did you know that was my favourite?' she asked.

'Just a hunch,' he smiled warmly, handing the bag over.

After everything that had happened between them, Julia couldn't believe Flynn had actually brought her breakfast. His kindness touched her.

'What have you there?' Flynn was looking at the photograph that Julia was holding.

'My only photograph of my grandad... destroyed.' Julia always loved the summer holidays hanging out with her grandad, they had so much fun down by the river. Her cousin Callie wasn't one for sitting still for long periods of time on the riverbank, which Julia was secretly chuffed about, because that meant she would get her grandad all to herself.

Flynn took the photograph from her hand. 'Look at you, you must be about...'

'Ten years old. I was cute once, you know.' She attempted a smile.

'And that it seems hasn't changed.' Flynn flashed her a warm smile.

For a second, she studied his face. His hair seemed a little longer and he pushed his floppy fringe to one side. She noticed he had the beginnings of a beard, and his face was tanned from the summer sun.

'That photograph was taken by the newspaper,' she said. 'We'd won a fishing competition. I can remember that day like it was yesterday,' she said, taking the photograph from his hand and laying it flat on the dresser. Feeling a lonely tear slide down her cheek, she wiped it away with the back of her hand. 'Look at me crying. This place has seen enough water in the last twenty-four hours and here's me adding to it.'

'I'm sorry about your grandfather,' Flynn's tone was soft.

'It's only a photograph, I still have the memories.'

'No, I mean I'm really sorry for what I did... your grandfather's house.'

Julia was surprised by his sudden apology and held his gaze. Flynn looked genuinely sorry.

'Back then, all I thought about was making as much money as possible, and I didn't care whose toes I trod on. I saw you, sitting in your car outside the estate agents when you handed the keys over. You were crying, and I saw the hurt in your eyes. I think that moment was a wake-up call for me, and I vowed never to do business like that ever again. I am sorry

Julia. I know that property was worth much more than I paid for it… and that it was your future.' Flynn's voice faltered.

'Thank you, that means a lot,' replied Julia, amazed at the revelation.

'I can't change what happened back then, but let me help you get this B&B back on track. I can sort out all the soft furnishings, curtains etc. My chain of hotels has a dry-cleaning contract and we can turn everything around super-fast.'

'You'd do that for me?'

He touched her elbow, sending shockwaves through her body. 'Yes, I would. We need you to be up and running as soon as possible, and with my contacts we can turn this place around quickly.'

'Why are you being so kind to me after everything?' her voice faltered. Flynn's kind gesture had made her a little weepy.

'Hey, don't get upset. Maybe it's because I admire your fighting spirit, or maybe I admire someone who stands up for what they believe in. That's something about you Julia Coleman – and I think we just got off on the wrong foot.'

His words gave her hope that her B&B would be up and running very soon and she felt grateful for his offer of help, knowing she couldn't turn everything round as quickly without him.

'Thank you, Flynn, your help would be amazing,' she replied enthusiastically, her mood lifting a little. Maybe the clean-up operation wasn't going to be bad as she first thought. Suddenly feeling hungry she peeped inside the breakfast bag. 'I think I've just got my appetite back.'

'Aye aye, what's going on here?' Eleni was standing in the doorway with a quizzical look on her face. 'Are all things amicable?' Eleni flicked a glance between Julia and Flynn. 'Or do I need to call for backup?'

'I don't think there's any need for backup,' joked Julia. 'We are all good, aren't we?' She looked towards Flynn who nodded.

'Thank God for that, as my only option was Woody, and I'm sure he'd only lick you to death.'

Everyone looked down at Woody who suddenly sprang to life with the mention of his name.

'Luckily your cleaning fairies are about to arrive, I've rallied the troops, and here they are now.' Julia couldn't help but feel thankful. Behind Eleni, armed with their mops and buckets, were Isla, Felicity, Meredith and Aggie, traipsing in like they meant business.

'We have mops, buckets, brushes, cleaning products, there's no stopping us now. Oh, and a radio so we can dance along as we go,' said Felicity.

'But there's no electricity,' replied Julia.

'That's why I've got some batteries! Right, what's first? Have we got a plan? It is a bit of a mess isn't it?' Felicity spun around.

Julia really didn't know where to start. 'Maybe work from the top downwards? It might be easier that way.'

'Good point,' chipped in Meredith, looking around

sympathetically then pulling on a pair of Marigolds. 'Let's do this!'

Flynn began making his way to the door. 'I'll let you ladies get on with it, but there will be extra cavalry arriving in approx. thirty minutes.' He tapped his watch.

'Extra cavalry?' queried Julia.

'Jack and the rest of the builders, I've told them to down tools up at Starcross Manor today and come over and help. If you strip all the beds, Jack will bring all the bedding on the truck over to the manor house, we have our own laundrette up there. The boys are going to remove all the mattresses and prop them up outside in the sunshine to dry them out, and any blinds or curtains Jack is going to ferry across to the dry cleaners.'

Julia was overwhelmed, Flynn really was going out of his way to help her and put the past behind them. She noticed the troops eyeing her with curiosity. The last thing they all knew about was the altercation between them in the pub and now here he was, standing on the doorstep helping out just like he was one of them.

'Thank you,' replied Julia, taking a mop and bucket from a very surprised Aggie.

'I'll catch up with you later.' He turned to head outside and then paused in the doorway. 'I'll nip into Bonnie's teashop – well, as long as I don't get blanked,' he rolled his eyes playfully. 'And organise sandwiches to be dropped off for lunch, and when you've finished there will be a drink and a meal waiting for you up at Starcross Manor. But first, I would suggest getting every single window open –

today's sunshine is certainly on your side, unlike yesterday's.'

There was a murmur of appreciation as Flynn stepped outside.

'Spill,' ordered Isla, amazed. 'What the hell is going on here? Why have you suddenly got a new best friend?'

All eyes were Julia. 'Okay…' she took a breath. 'We've decided to put the past behind us and have agreed to move on. I know I said he was untrustworthy, and I was hurt over the way he handled my grandfather's estate but he's since apologised and stepped up to the mark. He's providing the help to get this place up and running again and I can't ignore that kindness.'

Isla gave her a look. 'I really wasn't expecting that. What about the impact of the hotel?'

All eyes were on Julia and she knew they all must think she was barking mad at her U-turn regarding Flynn.

Her view on Starcross Manor had shifted a little bit after thinking about what Eleni had said about people's requirements and budgets. Maybe there was space for all of them? And Julia did have an idea brewing, but not one she wanted to share yet, until she'd fully thought it through.

'Just trust me on this,' urged Julia. 'I've been working on an idea that I think is going to benefit us all. I just need to get it straight in my own mind first.'

'I second Isla, I wasn't expecting that,' admitted Aggie, completely taken by surprise. 'But if you're saying trust you, we can do that. All I'm saying is we need to keep our wits about us too.'

'Agreed,' murmured everyone.

Julia felt guilty for putting her own needs first, but what she had in mind could work to everyone's advantage.

'I'm thinking he's hypnotised you with his good looks,' teased Eleni.

'There is that, I suppose. Anyway, are we ready to begin?' said Julia, rolling her eyes.

With her friends by her side, Julia set to work. They made their way to the top of the house where the sprinkler system was first activated. Julia could kick herself that she'd never replaced the old system but thankfully no one had been hurt, and all the furnishings could be cleaned or replaced. They flung open each window as they went, the blast of fresh air a welcome breeze.

'Okay what's the plan?' asked Felicity, looking around the very first bedroom.

Julia swiped her hand over the excess water sitting on the bedside table. 'How about you and Isla start mopping up the water, and Eleni and I can strip the beds and take the curtains down.'

They all set to work, and within a couple of hours the top floor was complete. Everyone started to move downstairs, except Julia who pushed open the landing window a little wider. She took a moment to admire the blue sky above and found that her thoughts turned suddenly to her mother. Their relationship had been one full of love. Her mum had guided and supported her no matter what, and she'd always been the calming influence in Julia's life, someone she would always turn to first for advice. The one value her mum had always championed had been forgiveness. She had been a strong, fair woman, who had always owned up to her mistakes, apologised when she was in the wrong and always encouraged forgiveness. Julia knew her mum would be proud of her for accepting Flynn's apology, but Julia also knew she'd helped to fuel the fire against Flynn and Starcross Manor, and that she needed to apologise to Flynn too.

Flynn had really come through for her last night and she had to believe and trust everything was going to be okay. Last night the guests had arrived up at Starcross Manor to a buffet of food and hot drinks prepared by Andrew. Not only that, but Flynn had placed laundry bags in each of their rooms and offered to have all their sodden clothes freshly laundered before the guests woke for breakfast. Once more Flynn had gone above and beyond.

Julia was just about to catch up with the others when she threw a bucket of dirty water out of the window.

'Oi! Watch what you're doing!' came a shout from below.

Quickly Julia leaned out of the window and gasped. 'Oh my God, I'm so sorry!'

Jack was standing in the flower bed alongside a couple of builders staring up at the window. Luckily, they'd moved swiftly and managed to dodge the bucket of water that had splashed on the path next to them.

'Better luck next time,' shouted Julia cheekily.

'We are only here to help move some mattresses, not for a shower,' bellowed Jack.

Throughout the clean-up operation her friends kept her spirits up, they laughed, joked and danced along to the radio as they stripped the beds and mopped up the excess water. All mattresses were lifted outside alongside the plush fabric chairs, sofas and anything and everything that could dry out in the sun. The front of the B&B looked like a garage sale with everything sprawled on the front lawn. All the food in the freezers had defrosted and everything had to be chucked away but overall, the damage seemed to be mainly cosmetic – and at least they had the weather on their side.

Flynn was true to his word, and just after 1pm Martha appeared with bags of sandwiches, cakes and drinks. Once again Flynn had taken off the added pressure; no one had to think about preparing food or nipping to pick anything up. He'd thought of everything.

Whilst everyone took a break and refuelled, Julia took a walk to the bottom of the garden and perched on the bench by the side of the stream. This was her first opportunity to dial the insurance company and she immediately felt frustrated by the automated service. Finally, thirty minutes later, she'd managed to log the insurance claim – and although Julia didn't hold out much hope of a pay-out, until she'd completed the forms there was no point second guessing whether they would or not. Julia walked into her tiny brick office that was detached from the main house, and which thankfully had no sprinkler system installed. She looked around the office and sighed, she really did need a clean out in there. Every drawer of the filing cabinet was stuffed to the brim with invoices and bills that went back years and most probably could be destroyed. After the morning she'd had, she had the bug for cleaning up and getting rid; maybe this flood was giving her the motivation she needed.

'You okay?' asked Eleni, popping her head around the office door. 'Here, have one of these.' Eleni handed her a cup of tea. 'Martha brought flasks of the stuff from the teashop. Come and eat your sandwich, everyone is taking a breather and is sitting on the lawn.'

This morning Julia couldn't have asked for more. All of her friends had pulled together in a time of need. Jack and the other builders had made various trips to Starcross Manor ferrying all the bedding, soft furnishings and cushions that could be laundered. Everyone had worked so hard.

'Look at this place, this office is on my to-do list at some point but there's always something better to do.' Julia knew she'd let the office stuff get out of hand.

Suddenly Eleni swiped Julia's arm. 'Is that your laptop?' Julia nodded. 'Yes, why?'

'I was going to ask where it was, but I just assumed it was in the house and water damaged.'

'No, I was working out here last week.'

Julia watched as Eleni hot footed it over to the desk and flung open the lid of the laptop. 'Forty-five percent battery left, which is good as I can't plug it in.' Eleni tapped away. 'Bingo! We have the bookings on this system that are arriving in the next couple of days, it's all linked.'

Julia blew out a breath. 'You are a life-saver.'

'Are you talking about me again?' Flynn appeared from nowhere and was standing in the doorway grinning. Julia noticed the sunlight hitting his slightly tanned face, causing his features to stand out.

'Eleni has just discovered the booking system is linked to my laptop, so at least we can contact the people that are about to arrive. Even though I'll have to deliver the bad news that we'll need to cancel. I don't even want to think about the income I'll lose.' Julia's voice trailed off.

Flynn turned towards Eleni. 'Is it possible to have a word with Julia?'

Eleni looked towards Julia for confirmation, who nodded, and then stepped outside the office. 'Let me help you,' offered Flynn.

'You are already helping me,' replied Julia.

'You don't need to cancel the guests arriving tomorrow. I can put them up at the hotel along with everyone else and there's no charge.'

His words swirled round Julia's head. 'It's a very generous offer but I really couldn't accept that or burden you any more. You are already doing too much.'

'Of course you can. Let me do this.'

Julia was unable to hide her amazement. 'But I don't understand – what's in it for you?'

As soon as the words left her mouth Julia realised that sounded ungrateful. 'I'm so sorry, that came out wrong.'

'Look, I think I owe you... and you're in a pickle. The hotel isn't even open yet and this would be the perfect practice run. Andrew can try out his new menu and I can work on skeleton staff. However, I would need two favours in return.'

Julia raised an eyebrow, she knew there must have been a catch. 'And they are?'

'Firstly, I'll need you on the reception to check your guests in tomorrow. And secondly, you were right about the colour of those curtains. You have a fantastic eye for interior design and detail. I could really use your expertise and magic to make Starcross Manor the best it can be – what do you say?'

Julia was flattered and gave a smile; she knew she was right about the colour of those curtains.

Flynn gave a nod of reassurance. 'Let me help,' he said once again.

Julia never imagined she'd ever be in this situation. And Flynn's offer was amazing and the perfect solution – but then Aggie's earlier words flashed through her mind. *Just make sure you keep your wits about you.* What if her guests began booking their future stays at Starcross Manor instead of her B&B? Was she actually just handing over everything to Flynn on a plate?

'I'm not sure,' she hesitated.

He touched her arm. 'I've no ulterior motive, I just want to help.'

Julia could see in his eyes that his offer was genuine, and she'd be a fool to turn him down. Hadn't Flynn more than proved he had changed? And hadn't they agreed to a fresh start? It was time for her to put her past feelings to one side. 'Thank you, in that case.'

'Perfect,' he answered, as his phone began to ring. 'I'm sorry, I really do need to take this call.' Julia watched Flynn walking towards the stream at the bottom of the garden whilst he took the call.

High-spirited, she walked back to the others, who were all sprawled out on the grass enjoying the afternoon sun. She was going to take Flynn's offer at face value, and knowing that she didn't have to find a way to refund the guests suddenly made her life a little easier.

'You aren't going to believe what's just happened.' Julia sat down next to them on the grass and grabbed a sandwich.

'We are all ears,' exclaimed Eleni. 'I've just been filling in the girls on how spectacular our rooms were last night.'

Julia and Eleni had also stayed at Starcross Manor. Eleni had been comical the second she'd stepped into the grand reception, her head swivelling round taking in her surroundings, reminding Julia of an owl. Once Flynn had showed the guests to their rooms, he'd led Julia and Eleni through a maze of corridors towards the back of the hotel. As they stepped into their rooms it was now Julia's turn to gasp. A huge four-poster bed, a settee, a coffee table, and a view that overlooked the lake made for a magnificent room. Once Flynn had left, Julia peeped inside the bathroom. 'Holy shit,' she exclaimed out loud. There in the middle of the bathroom floor was a sunken bath with tea-lights scattered all around the edge.

Eleni was in the adjoining room. Julia giggled when the door swung open and all she heard was a scream from

Eleni. 'OMG, have you seen the bathroom, it's out of this world.'

Also on the table was a silver cloche full of food for Julia, alongside a bottle of wine with a note, 'Compliments of the Management.' After a bath with bubbles up to her ears, Julia had enjoyed the food accompanied by a glass of wine, then sunk into the king-size bed and fallen fast asleep.

'The rooms were amazing,' confirmed Julia, looking over her shoulder. Flynn was still deep in conversation at the bottom of the garden. 'He's only offered to put up my forthcoming guests free of charge until the B&B is back up and running.'

'Wow! Why?' queried Isla, sitting upright and shielding the sun from her eyes.

'He just wants to help,' replied Julia in a low voice, noticing Flynn had hung up his call and was walking back towards them, looking pleased with himself. Jack appeared from the front of his house and headed over towards Flynn.

'And do you trust him? It all seems a little... actually, I'm not sure what it seems. If it's too good to be true, something isn't quite right,' added Isla who was always the voice of reason.

'It sounds like a perfect plan to me if it takes the pressure off and the guests can still enjoy their break, no brainer in my book,' chipped in Eleni, crossing over her legs and tilting her face up to the sun.

Julia understood exactly what Isla was saying: if something was too good to be true there was usually a catch, but maybe Flynn had seen the error of his ways and it was a genuine offer of help. Only time would tell.

'I think we should trust him.' Julia kept her voice low. 'Is he really going to double-cross me? He already knows how the village might react to that!'

'Mmm, you may have a point. But keep your wits about you.' Isla echoed Aggie's thoughts from earlier.

'Good news,' remarked Flynn, waving his phone at Jack. 'We have the contractors back on side. They'll be delivering the outstanding material first thing tomorrow morning, which means we can get underway with the final construction up at the hotel, and the final touches can be finished down at the Boathouse too.'

'That's a relief,' remarked Jack, giving Eleni a quizzical look, who shrugged.

Julia smiled. She'd spoken to Hamish on the phone earlier this morning and explained that she needed him to speak to his godson and get him to send Flynn the supplies he needed. He'd taken a lot of persuasion, but it looked like he'd come good. Julia was thankful.

Flynn gave Julia a look of appreciation and she gave a discreet nod before standing up and brushing herself down. 'Right, ladies, we need to get back to work.'

'Any jobs going at Starcross Manor?' joked Eleni. 'As my current boss is a slave driver.'

Julia swiped Eleni's arm playfully then pulled her to her feet.

That afternoon there were the fridges and freezers to empty and clean out as well as the guest living room and dining hall, but they were nearly there. Everyone had been worth their weight in gold.

'Julia, I'm going to take the rest of these curtains over to the dry cleaners, but are there any more to be taken down?' queried Jack, giving Eleni a swift kiss to the cheek before she began walking over towards the back door.

Julia shook her head. 'There's no more, it's just what I've piled up on the patio table.'

Together Flynn and Jack heaved several pairs of tweed fabric curtains over their shoulders. Julia was suitably impressed that they made it look so easy. She couldn't help but admire their tanned, bulging biceps, and caught Eleni watching them too.

'Now there's a sight for sore eyes,' murmured Eleni, still hovering outside and Julia didn't disagree.

For the rest of the afternoon they were all hard at work. Bucket after bucket of water had been scooped out. All the books taken off the shelves in the living room were now drying outside, and all the fridges and freezers had been fully cleaned. Julia looked round in amazement: they'd worked so hard it was beginning to look like her old B&B once more.

A few hours later, with her whole body aching, Julia declared they'd finished for the evening. Everyone felt tired, their hands were dry and blistered from the constant scrubbing and cleaning, their hair limp from sweat. Just like at lunchtime, they collapsed on the grass outside, staring up at the blue summer sky. 'Slushy moment alert. I can't thank all of you enough for today, I really can't,' gushed Julia. She would never have managed today without them.

'I'd say it's been a pleasure,' chuckled Felicity, 'but it hasn't.' She held up her hands. 'I've only got one long nail left.'

'You lot have just been the best.'

'What's going to happen to all the mattresses?' asked Meredith. 'Do they need to be taken back indoors?'

Julia sat up and glanced over to the mattresses propped up against the wall, standing to attention like naval officers. 'I think they can stay there tonight, there's no rain forecast and it's another hot day tomorrow.' She lay back down and closed her eyes. She was absolutely shattered. Julia felt like she'd lost all contact with the world today. The day had been manic, but thankfully things were beginning to look a little brighter and hopefully there was light at the end of the tunnel.

'How you feeling?' asked Eleni, lying down next to her. 'Difficult day?'

'Emotionally and mentally drained, to be honest. But we are nearly there. Everything aches, muscles I didn't even know I had. These things come to try us.'

'Don't they just,' murmured Aggie. 'All this humping at my age.'

Everyone burst out laughing.

'But we always to pull together,' added Aggie.

Everyone was quiet and lost in their own world for a moment. Julia contemplated taking a nap in the glorious sunshine, but her stomach growled and all she could think about was a large bowl of pasta, salad, and garlic bread. 'I'm absolutely starving, and I mean starving. Flynn offered us a meal up at Starcross Manor when we'd finished.'

'That he did and look, you've made the headlines,' piped up Isla, opening up the daily newspaper that had been posted through earlier.

'Me, why? What have I done?' Julia sat up and peered over her shoulder at the newspaper.

'Blimey! They don't miss a trick.' The headlines were black and bold. 'Millionaire Property Developer Saves The Day.' There was a photo of Flynn standing outside Starcross Manor with all her guests.

Julia's stomach felt like a tumble dryer going round and around as she began to read the article.

'Flynn Carter, the multi-millionaire superhero, came to Julia Coleman's rescue after a freak accident at the Heartcross B&B left guests stranded.'

'They've quoted some of the guests,' remarked Eleni, reading over her shoulder.

Mr Cullen: 'This place is magnificent, five stars, first class! Mr Carter's hospitality has been beyond generous. No charge for the rooms, full access to all the amenities including the spa and swimming pool. We can't wait to come back.'

Julia sucked in a breath. 'I've got a horrible feeling,' she gave herself a little shake. 'No, I'm over-thinking it...'

'I know exactly what you are thinking,' Aggie interrupted. 'Did Flynn Carter use your unfortunate position to showcase his hotel to guests that frequent Heartcross time and time again? Is this man to be trusted?'

Julia's initial reaction towards Flynn came flooding back – did she need to be wary of him? Was this a ploy by him to pinch her guests? Surely not, he'd gone out of his way over the last twenty-four hours to help her. He'd seemed so genuine about putting the past behind them.

'What do you think Isla?' asked Julia.

'Maybe he is just doing a good deed, but he's standing in front of his new hotel with your guests and they are looking forward to going back there.' She shrugged.

For a second, Julia began to doubt his generosity. Was he just playing her? She started to panic a little.

'Let's stay positive,' declared Eleni. 'Let's not worry about things beyond our control. The hotel will hopefully bring in different types of guests, not everyone can afford hotel prices, and thankfully there are still folk out there who like basic B&B and tents.'

'You're right, I'd prefer to wake up to the sound of the cows mooing and the smell of muck spreading. Hotel rooms aren't for everyone,' declared Isla, shutting the newspaper. 'And after a while you get used to the smell of cow dung.' She sniffed her T-shirt and wrinkled her nose. 'Or maybe not.'

'Are you going to voice your worries?' asked Felicity, folding the paper and tossing it to the side. 'Julia?'

Julia was lost in her own little world for a moment. 'I am, and I've got a plan that I think might benefit the whole community.'

'I love it when a plan comes together,' chipped in Eleni. 'Any hint on what the plan is?'

'Not just yet, but I'm going to talk to Flynn about it first this time. If he is genuine about fitting into Heartcross, I can't see why he would turn down my idea.' Julia was giving nothing away, leaving everyone intrigued. She thought back to the photographs, and the list of suppliers she'd discovered on the notepad in Andrew's room when he'd stayed a few nights ago; that list was the basis of her proposal.

For a moment they all lay back on the grass in silence, until their blissful five minutes were interrupted by the sound of Eleni's phone beeping. She shielded the screen and read the text.

'It's Jack. Dinner is waiting for all of us up at Starcross Manor.'

'I actually can't wait to have a snoop inside,' exclaimed Felicity.

Isla jumped up. 'And I'm starving,' she said brushing herself down.

'I'll have to check that's okay with Fraser, the poor man has been on his own all day running the pub.' Meredith had a look of doubt on her face.

Isla slipped her arm through Meredith's. 'Nonsense, if you go anywhere near the pub, he'll make you feel guilty for having extra time out. We deserve this after today.'

Meredith didn't need any more persuading. 'I'm in. I'm dying to take a look inside too.'

Everyone chattered excitedly as they wandered down

the path towards Starcross Manor, all except Julia who hung back slightly. Once again Flynn had gone out of his way to help them and Julia was so grateful. She thought about the idea whizzing around her head and felt excited. It would make perfect business for Flynn and the community of Heartcross, all she had to do now was arrange a meeting and put her ideas forward, and hope Flynn agreed. She had everything crossed.

Chapter Thirteen

As they arrived at Starcross Manor, Felicity swirled round like a Disney princess, looking up at the impressive ceiling in the reception area. 'Just look at this place.'

'It's quite impressive isn't it?' remarked Julia, noticing Wilbur, Flynn's father, walking towards them. Wilbur had been in the village for a few months, staying with Flynn at his home in Love Heart Lane. He'd become good friends with Rory's parents, Stuart and Alana, and was a likeable chap. Julia had seen him milling around the village but hadn't been introduced to him yet.

'Welcome, welcome, welcome!' bellowed Wilbur, his voice echoing around the grand entrance hall. He was a jolly-looking fellow, with a huge beam on his face, wearing a flamboyant blue velvet suit, sporting a bright-red checked cravat, and leaning on his cane. Even though he had similar mannerisms to Flynn his dress sense was more daring. 'The workers are finally here, are you ready to feast?'

Julia stretched out her hand. 'We most definitely are. I'm Julia,' she said, before introducing everyone else.

'Pleased to meet you all. Now, if you would like to follow me, we've set up the private dining suite for you all.'

They followed Wilbur through the entrance hall into a huge reception room.

'Look at this place,' Meredith was awe-struck, 'that chandelier must cost more than the value of my pub,' she was looking up at the ceiling with her jaw wide open. 'Simply stunning.'

Julia knew all too well how breath-taking this room was, looking out over the gardens of the manor house.

'I wish we'd got changed now,' muttered Eleni, 'this all looks very posh and look at the way we're dressed.'

Julia looked down at her dowdy clothes and couldn't agree more, her bobbled black jogging pants were covered in dust and grime, and her white T-shirt was smeared with dirt. With her hair scraped back into a ponytail and her early-morning makeup long gone, she wished they'd made a little effort to clean themselves up now.

'There you all are,' Flynn was walking towards them and greeted them with a smile.

'Thank you so much for feeding us,' gushed Felicity with excitement. 'It's a wonderful place you have here.'

'It's no trouble, Andrew will be testing out his new menu on you and please do give your honest feedback.'

'Ooo, what are we eating?' asked Isla, rubbing her hands

together. Her stomach rumbled loudly and everyone laughed as she clutched it, mortified.

Flynn clasped his hands together. 'I have it on good authority that for the starter, you'll be sampling crispy duck and watermelon salad. For main you have grilled calf's liver, whipped potatoes, bacon and melted onions, then for pudding...'

'If we have any room,' interrupted Aggie.

'You have lemon meringue with a twist.'

'I can feel my mouth watering already,' exclaimed Felicity.

Julia had to admit she was feeling ravenous too, and couldn't wait to tuck in to the food.

'I'll show them to the dining area, you'll need to get going otherwise you'll be late,' remarked Wilbur looking at Flynn then tapping his watch. 'And where's your tie?'

Flynn was dressed in a classic blue tailored suit accompanied by a white shirt. He pulled a tie from each pocket and looked down at them in his hands. 'I couldn't quite make up my mind.'

Almost immediately, Julia pointed to the navy, white and red-diamond silk tie in his left hand, 'Definitely that one.'

Flynn smiled. 'Good choice,' he answered, handing the other one over to Wilbur.

'Are you off anywhere nice?' asked Julia, intrigued.

'Just a business meeting.'

'Talking of business, I've got an idea to run past you? Something that's going to benefit the whole community. Can we arrange a meeting... to talk about it?'

Flynn narrowed his eyes. 'A business idea? Now I am intrigued. I'll catch you tomorrow and you can tell me all about it.'

'Perfect,' replied Julia, as Wilbur shooed him out the door.

'Ladies, if you would like to go and get yourselves a drink at the bar, compliments of the house, I will be back in five minutes to show you all to your table.' Wilbur waved his cane in the air before he turned and walked off.

As soon as Wilbur turned his back Julia realised they were all staring at her. 'Why are you looking at me like that?' she asked, puzzled.

'That tie is perfect, Flynn,' teased Felicity, mimicking Julia's voice. 'We all saw the way you were looking at him.'

'Don't be ridiculous, the man didn't know which one to wear, I just pointed out the one that went better with his suit.'

'Mmm, that's your story and you're sticking to it,' Eleni marvelled at Julia's embarrassment.

'Let's get that drink,' suggested Julia, trying to brush Eleni's comment under the carpet, knowing full well that Flynn wore the suit well and it complemented his physique perfectly.

They all began to walk towards the bar when they heard a commotion over by the huge glass windows. All of Julia's B&B guests were huddled together in a group and pointing at something in the gardens. 'What's going on over there?'

asked Felicity, standing on her tiptoes, trying to snag a look over the bobbing heads.

They curiously ambled across the room to take a look. 'Wow! Look at that,' exclaimed Julia.

All of them witnessed a red-and-yellow helicopter hovering over the centre of the lawn. Julia noticed the pilot wearing dark glasses, arched over the controls, and as the blades slowed, he landed the helicopter.

'OMG!' exclaimed Isla, pointing at Flynn who was hunched over, holding the lapels of his jacket as he was seen hurrying across the lawn.

'How the other half live, eh? That's some hell of a business meeting,' added Eleni, staring out across the lawn.

They watched Flynn climb inside the helicopter and the door closed behind him. Once more the blades began to spin and the helicopter lifted effortlessly off the ground, and within seconds took to the sky. The room was a buzz of excitement, the children's eyes glued to the machine in the sky until it had completely disappeared behind the clouds.

After returning to the bar they ordered their drinks, and within minutes Wilbur reappeared. 'Follow me ladies, let me take you through to the private dining area.'

Julia raised an eyebrow at Eleni; she could get used to this. As they followed Wilbur Julia heard her phone ping and after delving into her bag, saw it was Flynn's name flashing up on the screen.

She read, 'Good choice of tie.'

'What are you grinning at?' Eleni narrowed her eyes at Julia.

'Nothing, absolutely nothing,' she smiled.

'Seb will be your waiter for the evening,' announced Wilbur, gesturing towards the man at the far end of the room leaning against an oak easel. At the mention of his name Seb looked up and fiddled with his cufflinks as he began to walk towards them. 'Good evening ladies,' he said politely. Julia noticed his accent wasn't Scottish, maybe Southern.

'VIP area,' whispered Isla to them all. 'Just look at this place.'

'Please do relax and enjoy your food. I'll leave you in Seb's capable hands,' announced Wilbur, lightly placing his hand on Seb's back before exiting the room via a different door at the far end of the room.

'If you would like to follow me,' Seb gestured to the tables in front of the windows, but this time the view overlooked the lake.

They all sailed forward, feasting their eyes on the exquisite dining area laid out before them. The interior was warm. Huge paintings of landscapes hung on the walls in burnt-gold frames and Julia was mesmerised by the vast slate floor.

'OMG, is that an original by Wallsey?' questioned Eleni, stopping dead in her tracks and gazing at the piece of artwork hanging on the wall. Eleni knew her artwork like the back of her hand.

'Yes,' replied Seb, briefly casting a glance towards the painting. 'He's a friend of Flynn's and I think he's showcasing some of his new works of art here at the hotel in October.'

Julia could tell by the look on Eleni's face she was suitably impressed. 'That must have cost a fortune,' she mumbled under her breath giving Julia a look of amazement. 'And I have to come to that exhibition, Wallsey is a hero of mine.'

'Probably mate's rates,' whispered Felicity. 'And you could eat your food off that floor,' she said pointing at the marble floor.

'Luckily, we have tables for that,' replied Seb, amused, as he pulled out a chair for each one of them.

'And this is why this magnificent manor house is called Starcross Manor,' Seb swooped his hand up towards the ceiling, everyone gazed upwards and gasped. There was no denying Starcross Manor was going to be a year-round showstopper. The retractable roof was drawn back and the warm summer evening flooded into the airy dining room.

'And in winter, stars will twinkle through that glass roof, candles will flicker on the tables and log fires will burn away...'

'It's just wow!' exclaimed Eleni. 'I've never seen anything like it.'

The elegance, panache and charm blew them all away, Julia knew this was place was instantly going to be a hit with anyone that passed through the doors, Flynn's flair for grand designs was off the scale.

'And this door leads through to a secret garden where you can feast or drink champagne beneath the swaying lanterns.' Seb swung open the doors and revealed the beautiful hideaway. 'But today, as you may already know, your meal will be prepared by the world-famous Andrew Glossop... and here he is now.' Seb waved his hand towards the kitchen door that immediately swung wide open. Felicity gave a strangled squeal as Andrew walked into the dining area dressed in his chef's outfit.

'He's a lot younger than I pictured,' whispered Meredith. With his hands clasped together he sauntered towards them wearing his pristine white chef's jacket, black and white houndstooth pattern trousers with his toque blanche resting on his head.

Julia noticed everyone had suddenly fallen silent, they all seemed star-struck.

'Good evening ladies, I'm Andrew, and it's my honour to cook for you all this evening.'

Andrew walked around the table and shook everyone's hand. 'Lovely to see you again, Julia and Eleni. Has Flynn told you what's on the menu tonight?'

They both nodded.

'Excellent! And apparently if there are any bad reviews tonight my trial period is over,' he joked. 'And please do take one of these,' he handed out a complimentary voucher to everyone. 'A free ticket to come and join me in one of my cooking masterclasses.'

There was a ripple of approval around the table. 'This is amazing, thank you, please do tell us more,' Meredith wanted more information, this was right up her street.

'It involves spending the day with me while I inspire

you to explore your passion for cooking. Come and live out a dream, from artisan bread-making to fresh pasta, learn about quality ingredients with an informative tasting experience. Let's excite the palate! I can guarantee it's all good fun. Or there's the luxury chocolate-making workshop, complete with prosecco, gin and martinis, or general cake-baking... Think about it! Food for thought, no pun intended,' he said, returning to his kitchen.

Julia couldn't help but think there was passion and honesty about this man, his voice quickened with excitement when he spoke about food. He was definitely going to be a huge hit here at Starcross Manor.

'A luxury chocolate-making workshop, could you imagine?' remarked Aggie, clearly impressed. 'Even though I don't think I've got the patience to make the chocolate, I just want to eat it, and I do eat way too much of it, but when you get to my time of life... a bar of chocolate and a glass of wine is my treat, empty calories in abundance!'

'Only one glass? More like a bottle of wine,' teased Meredith giving a little chuckle.

'Maybe we could do something like that for my birthday?' suggested Julia, thinking it sounded like fun.

'Your birthday is already planned!' admitted Isla. 'Well, nearly, all we...'

Eleni put up her hand like an over-zealous traffic warden. 'Stop right there! Do not give anything away.'

'At least give me a clue, how will I know what to wear?' asked Julia, taking a sip of her wine.

The girls looked at each other around the table. 'Okay,

she does have a point,' admitted Felicity. 'We can't have her turning up in heels.'

'Mmm, you will need normal clothes and sturdy flat shoes or trainers,' confirmed Eleni. 'But that's the only information we are giving you.'

'Oh, and be ready for ten o'clock,' added Isla.

'Ten o'clock?'

'Yes, but ten o'clock at night,' said everyone in unison.

'It's going to be fun,' Felicity gave a huge grin as Seb started walking towards them balancing their starters. 'And here's the food.'

'Wow! Wow! Wow! This looks amazing,' chipped in Isla, swerving the conversation in a different direction as Seb placed the starter down in front of her.

Julia's phone pinged again. 'I need your help,' came Flynn's text. 'If you're free tomorrow let me know!'

Julia was intrigued, what did Flynn want her help with? She closed her eyes for a second trying to conjure up his presence, the smile he gave her when she picked out his tie and his lovely, manly smell. How things were changing in such a short space of time. Her heart gave a little leap as her eyes skimmed the text again. When she saw him tomorrow she was going to use the time to convince Flynn of the idea she had, so all the community could work together to boost everyone's revenue. Remembering her grandfather's old words of wisdom: out of everything negative always comes a positive. Julia had everything crossed.

Chapter Fourteen

The next morning Julia woke up early and watched the beautiful sunrise from the bedroom window of Starcross Manor. She was thankful it was going to be another hot, sunny day, which was a godsend. The contract cleaners were arriving today to give the mattresses a clean and hopefully they would be back on the beds by the end of play today. The worry over all the curtains and bedding being washed or dry-cleaned had been completely taken out of her hands thanks to Flynn, and everything was due back by tomorrow.

Even with a busy morning ahead, it was still too early to head over to the B&B. The electrician and gasman were due there sometime after 10am, and hopefully they would give the place the all-clear so the B&B could get back on track. After pulling a brush through her hair and dabbing concealer on a spot on her chin that had sprouted from nowhere overnight, Julia powered up her laptop and thought back to last night. It had been a wonderful evening, the food was divine and the wine flowed freely. They'd all sat out in the secret garden until just after midnight, except Meredith who needed to get back to help Fraser at the pub.

As soon as she'd typed in her password, Julia flicked onto the B&B's Facebook page and was amazed by the number of new notifications, and began to click on them. To her dismay, there had been a number of reviews left by the guests in the last twenty-four hours, and even though they weren't exactly putting the B&B in a bad light, they were singing the praises of Starcross Manor:

Mr Cullen... B&B four stars. 'My family and I have stayed in the B&B on numerous occasions. The atmosphere is friendly, the place clean and easily accessible to all amenities, however a new hotel is opening up in the village which includes a pool, spa and gym, and restaurants at affordable rates, do give Starcross Manor a go!'

Mrs Williams... B&B three and a half stars. 'We have stayed at this fabulous B&B for a number of years. Unfortunately, due to a flood we were transferred to a brand-new hotel less than a mile away and what an absolute treat. Starcross Manor was amazing, the kids loved the pool, I loved the spa while my husband disappeared to the gym. The grounds are beautiful and the mouth-watering food is not to be missed by celebrity chef Andrew Glossop.'

Will Blake... B&B four stars...

Julia couldn't read any more. It wasn't as though any of the reviews were putting the B&B in a bad light – and they were absolutely right about how fabulous Starcross Manor was. But she needed to talk to Flynn before all of her regular guests began to jump ship. But what if Flynn didn't go for her idea? She gave herself a little shake, she was worrying for no reason. Of course he was going to go for her idea, as she was certain he didn't want to be on the wrong side of the villagers. She knew the proposal she was about to put to him meant exciting times for the community of Heartcross. Feeling much more positive, she determined to talk to Flynn as soon as she set eyes on him.

With time still to kill, Julia shut down the lid of her laptop and packed her swimwear inside her rucksack with the latest book she was reading, and decided to explore the pool area. After closing the bedroom door behind her, Julia wandered down the vast corridors towards the spa area. This would be the perfect place for some quiet contemplation before heading over to the B&B. Julia had read the welcome pack in the room and knew the contents of the brochure back to front, from the beanbags, twinkly lights and floating canopies of the snooze room, to the light and airy atrium lounge, she was looking forward to finding her own little haven for the next hour.

Stepping inside the starlit cave Julia grabbed a towel from behind the reception desk. Everywhere looked so peaceful, there was no doubt this place was going to be an instant hit. After slipping into her swimming costume and pulling a fluffy white robe around her body, Julia dipped her toe in the salt-water vitality pool. There were jet massage pools, luxury whirlpools – this hotel had everything. For a second she felt all her stresses melt away, and sat on the steps in the warm waters of the hydrotherapy pool, the gentle currents and body massage jets making her skin tingle. She opened her book and began to read until she heard footsteps padding down the corridor and the creak of a door. The noise made Julia jump and she was startled to meet Flynn's gaze.

His chest was bare, his hair slicked back, and his lounge pants looked super sexy clinging to his toned waistline. Julia's stomach churned nervously. For a second she was distracted by the aroma of his aftershave, her whole body tingling in his presence. She averted her gaze and gave herself a little shake to pull herself together. This was the perfect timing to talk to him about how she thought the community could all work together, and she couldn't afford to be distracted by Flynn's hot body.

'Good morning, what a lovely surprise, you are up with the larks,' he said, walking over towards her with a beam on his face. 'I wasn't expecting to see anyone here.'

Julia closed her book and put it on the side. She noticed he was carrying a package which he placed on the bottom of the sun lounger before sitting next to it.

'Me neither,' she replied warmly.

'I always start my day with a quick swim. The joys of owning a hotel.'

'How was your business meeting?' asked Julia, remembering back to last night when she'd watched Flynn climb aboard the helicopter.

'Very successful, it must have been down to the tie,' he

said with a playful glint in his eye. 'And how was your food?'

She tipped her head to one side and felt a flush of warmth surge through her body. 'Definitely must have been down to the tie – and last night's food was amazing. Absolutely exquisite. Andrew is going to be a huge hit, especially with his masterclasses too.'

'He is, isn't he? And now we have the contractors back on board, thank you so much.'

'I couldn't have a cancelled wedding on my conscience.' As soon as the words left her mouth, she wanted the ground to swallow her up. She hadn't been thinking about Anais's wedding, but it may have sounded like a little dig.

Thankfully, Flynn didn't seem to notice and stood up. 'Have you got a minute? Your eye for detail is better than mine. Come and tell me what you think.' Flynn stood up and Julia pulled the robe around her and slipped her feet back into her shoes. She followed him through a door and immediately Julia was taken aback by her surroundings. This room was a lounge area with brown leather wingback chairs dotted around coffee tables, the walls dressed in gold and beige with another impressive chandelier. Flynn led Julia over to a table laid out with limited-edition luxury candles.

'What have we here?' she asked immediately picking up a candle and taking in the aroma. 'That is heaven, I'd say a flirtatious fragrance...'

Flynn was looking at her with amusement. Julia inhaled the scent again. 'Peony... I can definitely smell Peony.'

Flynn took the card next to the candle. 'It is indeed, Peony and Blush Suede.' He was clearly impressed. 'Here, what about this one?' Flynn passed her another candle.

Once again Julia inhaled. 'That's Honeysuckle. My absolute favourite.' She read the card next to the candle. 'Yes, it's Honeysuckle! I'm good at this. What are all these for?'

'This is something I need help with, I may be able to build hotels and design the most luxurious of rooms with breath-taking chandeliers, but all this is beyond me. As soon as I smell one candle, they all seem to merge into one.'

Julia worked her way through the samples on the table, smelling each one before choosing. 'Honeysuckle, it's got to be Honeysuckle. That is just heaven. What are they for?'

'To put in the wedding guests' rooms as a little extra. I've been left in the lurch. My usual wedding planner has relocated to London, leaving all these finer details to me and I've no idea what's needed.'

Julia brought her hands up to her heart and acted all dreamy. 'I love a good wedding. If I was getting married, scents and the little extras would really help to make it a special day. I'd have welcome drinks on arrival, little sweets such as macaroons, chocolate in your room accompanied by a bottle of wine or champagne. There have to be flowers in your room... pale pink, subtle and stunning. A butler service is a must, giving you tips and advice on the area, etc. etc. I can just picture it now.'

'It sounds like you have your wedding all planned out. Is there a lucky man in your life?' His hazel eyes captivated hers. For a split second he glanced down at her lips but then looked away.

'Not yet,' she replied, feeling the spark of electricity between them.

Julia didn't think this was the best time to share that she'd had the whole of her wedding mapped out since she was a little girl. She'd even got scrapbooks full of wedding dress designs and flower bouquets.

'Here take one of these,' Flynn handed her a candle, their fingers brushing against each other. Julia met his gaze again.

'Are you sure?'

He nodded and she gratefully took it. 'I don't suppose you want a job on the side as a wedding planner for the hotel?'

Julia laughed and shook her head. 'No thank you, but stick with Honeysuckle and pale stunning colours and you can't go far wrong.' Holding her candle Julia felt flattered that Flynn had asked for her opinion. 'And along that back wall, in that dead space, a gorgeous indoor water fountain would enhance this room beautifully.'

Flynn stared at the vacant wall and for a moment looked like he was deep in thought. 'I always thought that space needed something. That is something I'm going to think about.' He placed his hand in the small of her back as they walked back into the spa area. 'What was it you needed to talk to me about today?

'Have you time?' asked Julia, dangling her legs back in the pool.

'Shoot,' said Flynn, glancing up at the clock. 'I've plenty of time.'

Julia took a deep breath. 'I admit it was probably me who set the rumour mill into overdrive about you, and I do regret that. After the flood at the B&B, you really stepped up to the mark and I know that's made people see you in a very different light. And this place is just stunning, Flynn. There's going to be a lot of traffic passing through this hotel, which means a lot of business for you, but we – the community – need to be a part of that.'

'Go on. I'm listening.'

'Your suppliers…'

'I use the same company for all my hotels. It's easier that way, I can keep track of everything in one place,' butted in Flynn.

Julia felt a stab of dismay and bit down on her lip. 'But would you be open to changing that for Starcross Manor?'

'And the reason being?'

'To help our community. Work with us, source your meat and dairy from the local suppliers like Foxglove Farm. You can't get better quality, it's within a stone's throw from Starcross and everything will be super fresh… milk, cheese, eggs, beef, chicken, venison… the list is endless.' Julia could feel her voice rising with excitement. 'Then there's the local ales from the pub, vegetables and herbs from Hamish's allotments. There could even be a local information pack in each room including local events that are available – like the walk-an-alpaca day,' added Julia with enthusiasm, thinking Isla would be inundated.

Flynn remained silent, and while she had his full attention Julia wasn't going to stop. 'Then there's Bonnie's teashop – their afternoon cream teas are nearly world-famous, why not let them branch out and provide their cream teas here in your restaurant? No one can bake a scone like Rona. There's chocolate chip, raspberry, maple syrup, apple, cranberry, cheese, pumpkin, almond, hazelnut...' Julia was getting breathless.

Flynn burst out laughing. 'Okay, okay I get the picture. I definitely know where I'm going for my scones.'

'Then there's me,' suddenly her voice was serious again. This was about her now, and saving her business; she just hoped Flynn would be on board. 'My B&B is my life and I love everything about it. Before I learnt about Starcross, I was just about to extend, but now I'm unsure whether it's worth the financial commitment. This morning numerous reviews were left on my Facebook, not so much saying anything bad about the B&B, but singing the praises of this place and it got me thinking. Can we work together? I don't want my business folding,' Julia's voice faltered, emotion spiked through her as her eyes brimmed with tears.

'Hey, don't get upset,' Flynn was up on his feet, and crouched down next to Julia at the water's edge. 'Tell me what you are thinking.'

She swallowed hard, trying to get a grip on her emotions; this was her future and she didn't want to lose the B&B. 'I was wondering if, for any guests that book the B&B, we could perhaps come up with some sort of agreement that my guests can use the facilities here at Starcross Manor at some sort of discounted rate? I think that will give them the best of both worlds. The B&B is within their budget, and they still have the option to go swimming or use the spa and the gym if they wish to do so.' There: she'd said it now, it was out in the open. Julia had her fingers crossed behind her back but from Flynn's expression she couldn't gauge what he was thinking. With a pounding heart she tilted her head to one side, waiting for Flynn to answer.

There was an excruciatingly long pause before a smile began to hitch on his face. 'I think it sounds like the perfect solution all round. I think it's a brilliant idea that all the produce is sourced locally. Andrew will absolutely love that, and you are right: everything will be beyond fresh, and it'll boost the community's businesses.'

'Really?' Julia felt relieved.

'Really,' answered Flynn. 'Marvellous suggestion. I don't even know why I didn't think about it.'

Julia was fit to burst. This was brilliant; she knew her guests would love the opportunity to take a swim or have a spa at discounted rates, and with this added extra bonus, surely that would mean the extension at the B&B was a definite must. The only thing she wished was that she had spoken to Flynn sooner rather than declaring war on him. It was funny how life seemed full of worries one minute, then – whoosh – it could all be fixed by just having that one conversation.

'I can't thank you enough, everyone will be over the

moon.' Julia couldn't wait to share the news with everyone, this would give them all a boost.

'Can we keep this to ourselves just for the minute? I'll organise a meeting here at Starcross and invite the village to attend. Let me break the news to them.'

'Good plan,' replied Julia. Pressing her lips tightly together to keep from smiling, she leaned back on her hands and splashed her legs in the water like an excited child, causing Flynn to laugh and shield himself from the water.

'Watch out,' he laughed warmly.

'Sorry, sorry!' Then she splashed her legs one last time before throwing her head back again. It suddenly felt like a huge weight had lifted off Julia's shoulders.

'I was never out to sabotage your B&B, you know,' said Flynn seriously. 'With the tourist industry in Heartcross rocketing, people want choices, and they will continue to book the B&B. Everyone likes different things, everyone has a different budget.' He paused. Now it was Julia's turn to listen. 'And thank you, Julia.'

'What are you thanking me for?'

'For working with me and not throwing me back out to the lions. Those villagers can be pretty lethal if you get on the wrong side of them.' A smile touched Flynn's lips.

'You better believe it. Heartcross is a passionate community and one I'm proud to be a part of. We look after each other.' Julia spun her legs out of the water and stood up. 'I better be going, I need to get up to the B&B.'

'Before you go...' Flynn took the parcel he'd placed on the sunbed next to him. 'This is for you.'

Julia was surprised. 'For me?'

'Yes, for you. Here,' Flynn handed it over.

It was average size, not particularly heavy and wrapped up in old-fashioned brown paper, with a label on the front which read 'To Julia' scrawled in old-fashioned ink. Completely taken by surprise, she stared at the package in her hands.

'Go on open it,' he encouraged, giving Julia a warm smile.

She carefully unwrapped it. The insides were hidden beneath delicate lilac tissue paper. Her heart skipped a beat; there was another label inside which read *Just for you x*.

With her hands slightly shaking, she trembled with anticipation – she had no clue what she was about to discover. Then, amazed, she stared at the contents, and tried to slow her breathing. 'Surely not,' she whispered to herself. Staring back at her was a newly-framed photo of her and her grandad fishing, the exact same photo that had been ruined by the flood. Flynn must have contacted the newspaper to track down this photograph, and then gone out of his way to have it framed. Julia's eyes brimmed with happy tears. Flynn's kindness was overwhelming, and without thinking she stood on her tiptoes and pressed a kiss to his cheek.

'This is just… just… I'm actually lost for words. Thank you.' This was the best present she'd received in a long, long time, and she had Flynn Carter to thank for it.

Chapter Fifteen

'Pinch, punch, first of the month.'

Julia was walking down the grand staircase towards the reception of the hotel and was chuckling at Eleni's text. She usually included a long list of everyone she wanted to pinch or punch, but today she seemed to have made peace with the world.

The phone pinged again, a second text from Eleni, 'I'll meet you at the B&B in an hour. There's some last-minute birthday plans I need to take care of.'

Julia's birthday was this weekend. It had soon crept up on her, and with the flood at the B&B she'd totally put it out of her mind. Later that evening she had a FaceTime call with Callie and couldn't wait to see her – she knew as soon as they started chatting about the birthday plans excitement would begin to kick in.

Standing on the grand stone steps at the entrance of Starcross Manor, Julia paused for a moment and inhaled the fresh morning air as she took in the view. Beyond the lake she noticed the deer roaming free, grazing on the lush grass at the edge of the woods, and it was a real picture-perfect moment. She glanced at her watch. She still had time to kill, so decided to take the scenic route back to the B&B. Julia headed around the lake towards the woods, a place she would often walk Woody.

Clambering over the rickety old stile, Julia took the bridle path that ran from the woods to the edge of Primrose Park. Again, the view was spectacular. A cow mooed from a nearby field, making her jump. There were sheep dotted up on the mountain top, and goats at the bottom of the valley. She ducked under a low-hanging branch then stopped to admire a deer that loped back into the woodland. It was such a beautiful place, and she felt lucky to live somewhere as magical as Heartcross. This was home, and she could never envisage living anywhere else – and thankfully now, with the deal she'd struck up with Flynn, for the community and herself, everyone would be a winner.

Up ahead, she heard the clomping of hooves and a familiar woof. She was amazed to see Woody running towards her, his ears flapping and his tongue hanging out. By the time they'd finished drinking their cocktails last night it had been late, and so Woody had stayed at Foxglove Farm for the night.

'Well, hello there!' Woody padded excitedly from one paw to the other, wagging his tail madly. Julia bent down and hugged him tightly. 'It's only been a night, but I've missed you!' she exclaimed as he licked her face.

Isla pulled on the reins, and Honk the pony halted. 'Good morning!' sang Isla. 'Fancy seeing you here.'

Julia stood up and rubbed the pony's nose, and Honk nudged her back. 'I thought I'd blow away the cobwebs on the way to the B&B. How's this one been?' She looked down at Woody, who was still jumping up to her knees as Julia ruffled the top of his head once more.

'He's been as good as gold, better behaved than Drew,' she chuckled. Isla looked down fondly at Woody. 'We've been down the valley and thought we'd make our way back through Primrose Park, it's stunning this time of year.'

'It sure is,' replied Julia.

'And the cockerel had us up at the early hours, so I thought whilst the kids were sleeping, we'd get out for a walk and a ride. Not to mention Drew has been driving me insane.'

'Why, what's he been up to?'

'Boys and their toys. I think he loves his new sausage machine more than me,' Isla rolled her eyes then laughed. 'Honestly, he's like a kid in a sweet shop. He thinks he's going to take over the world with all his new sausage recipes, not to mention bacon and black pudding. He's even designing his own packaging for his brand of Foxglove Farm delights.'

'To be fair, he does make the best sausages around,' admitted Julia, her mouth watering at the very thought of a sausage sandwich smothered in brown sauce. The B&B had only ever sourced their meat and dairy products from the farm, and they were always a hit with guests.

CHRISTIE BARLOW

'He did say when your electricity is back on, call up at the farm and take whatever you need to stock your fridge and freezer.'

'That will be amazing, thank you.' Julia had a feeling Drew's farm products might become world-famous sooner than he thought, if Flynn was going to strike a deal to supply Starcross Manor. Who knew where that might lead to?

'And what have you there?' asked Isla, looking at the parcel in Julia's hand.

'A present from Flynn. The photograph of my grandfather that was ruined in the flood...' Julia turned the photograph towards Isla.

'Now, that is a thoughtful present.'

'Isn't it just,' replied Julia, feeling a flutter of warmth. 'And we've had a long chat about business. Everything is going to be okay. I'm going to give Jack the go-ahead to begin my extension as soon as possible.'

'Julia, that's brilliant news.'

'Isn't it just.'

'So, what's changed?'

Julia tapped the side of her nose. 'All will be revealed very soon, but let's just say I've surprised myself with my business negotiation skills.' Julia was upbeat, the village would welcome the news that Starcross Manor was going to support all the local businesses in any way it could. Hopefully even Hamish would be won over.

Isla pulled on the reins and turned Honk around. Julia walked at the side of them both whilst Woody ran in front,

226

sniffing under the hedgerows as they began walking towards Primrose Park. 'You certainly have changed your tune,' Isla narrowed her eyes at Julia.

'I think I overreacted when I first set eyes on him again. Sometimes you have to forgive and forget, and move on.'

'You do. I forget I'm meant to be a grown-up at times.'

'I thought it was about time I became a proper grown-up, especially with my fortieth just around the corner... and why is it I still feel twenty-one?'

'I don't feel like I'm twenty-one,' admitted Isla. 'I'm feeling knackered running round after two small children, a husband who is as bad as the kids. And my grandmother. In fact Martha has more energy than all of us put together. I need some of whatever she's on.'

Laughing and chatting away, Julia crossed on the wooden bridge that arched over the stream, whilst Honk splashed his hooves through the water, followed by Woody.

'Molly's over there.' Julia pointed before pushing open the heavy wooden farmer's gate leading into Primrose Park.

Molly was the local vet from Glensheil, and she often worked closely with the vet's practice in the village. Whilst Rory was off living his African dream, Molly had stepped in to help Stuart at the practice and cover some of Rory's shifts.

'One, two, three, four... five dogs,' counted Isla. 'She's got her hands full there.'

'Morning,' shouted Julia across the park, and Molly lifted her head.

'I'd wave but I have my hands full,' she shouted back.

Honk plodded over slowly – unlike Woody who had taken off at high speed and was now amongst all the other dogs, barking excitedly and weaving in and out of Molly's legs.

'Wow! Where have all these dogs come from?' remarked Julia, thinking that was way too many to handle.

'It's my turn today, let's call it a trial.' Molly raised her eyebrows.

'A trial?' questioned Isla.

'Dog-walking, it's becoming very lucrative. We thought we'd give it a trial period over at the surgery, as an extra string to our bow, and – no word of a lie – within less than a week we are fully booked. We've advertised for staff, but I'm that busy I've not even had chance to look at the applicants yet.'

'That's a very good business,' said Julia, knowing a friend of hers back in her old town was doing exactly the same thing and making a hefty profit. 'Are you walking back?' Julia nodded towards Molly's van parked at the edge of the park.

'Yes,' she answered and handed a couple of leads to Julia as they walked. 'I heard there'd been a flood at the B&B.'

Julia explained about the dated sprinkler system, and that all the guests had had to be evacuated to Starcross Manor.

'Starcross Manor,' repeated Molly amazed. 'I thought Flynn Carter was the sworn enemy?'

Julia blushed. 'Well, I might have been a bit harsh about

him. He's really helped me out and it gave us both a chance to clear the air. All I can say is, watch this space.'

'I wasn't expecting that. I also noticed the Boathouse will be opening soon; with that and Starcross Manor, this Flynn Carter seems to be taking over the world.'

'He does, but this time it's going to have great benefit to our little community… sometimes we just need to give people a chance. But I can't say any more.' Julia zipped her lips with her fingers.

'Isn't she annoying when she knows something we don't?' Isla joked, leaning forward and patting Honk on his neck.

'I suppose that's a bit like us knowing all about your birthday celebrations when you haven't got a clue? I can't wait,' remarked Molly, teasing Julia.

'Shush! Don't say any more, Julia has no idea what we have in store for her yet.' Isla tipped Molly a wink.

Molly mirrored Julia's action and zipped her lips with her fingers. 'Two can play that game,' she chuckled, loading all the dogs into the van. 'I'll catch you both later, morning surgery looms.'

They watched Molly drive off in the van and Julia opened the gate wide whilst Honk plodded slowly towards the lane. 'Once I've cleaned the vans up at the farm I'll come over to the B&B and help you with whatever needs doing.'

'Thanks Isla,' replied Julia, extremely grateful for the extra pair of hands. 'I'll see you later.'

They headed off in separate directions and Julia walked along the High Street with Woody close to her heels. The village was already alive with people. She said good morning to the multitude of street artists selling their paintings in the quaint courtyard at the side of the post office. Already, giggling children enjoying their school holidays were racing down the road clutching their fishing nets, most probably off to try and catch the fish from the brooks at the foot of the mountain. The sun was already beating down and it was going to be another glorious day in the village of Heartcross.

With a spring in her step Julia strolled up Love Heart Lane towards Bonnie's Teashop and admired the triangular bunting draped across the stone wall at the front. Already there were customers sat under the yellow-and-white awning enjoying breakfast. She felt good about her chat with Flynn and couldn't wait to share the news with the villagers. Just as Julia was about to walk inside the teashop her phone pinged with a message from Flynn. 'I've arranged a meeting up at Starcross Manor on Sunday evening at 7pm, do help spread the word.'

'Good morning!' chirped Rona smiling from behind the counter the second she spotted Julia. 'A Full Scottish to eat in or take out?' she asked bending down and slipping Woody a dog biscuit from the jar.

'No offence, but I'm not sure I'm fancying a Full Scottish,' replied Julia with her eye firmly on the array of beautiful pastries and cakes arranged in the numerous glass-domed stands on top of the counter. She immediately fancied a cinnamon swirl the second she laid eyes on them and pointed. 'One of those to take out, please. They look delicious.'

'Baked by my own fair hands this morning,' said Rona, triumphantly slipping one inside a white paper bag.

'And how are you this morning?' Felicity looked over her shoulder at Julia as she pulled open the oven to check on the tray of sausage rolls.

'All is good in the land of Julia Coleman, and it will be even better when my gas and electricity is switched back on.' Julia gave a smile. 'And I have news, there's a meeting up at Starcross Manor on Sunday at 7pm. I've been in negotiations and there's good news for all the villagers.'

Immediately, Rona stopped what she was doing and wiped her hands on the tea towel. 'Good news? What good news? I've already decided Flynn is going to have a fight on his hands if he thinks he's poaching my afternoon tea clients.' Rona gave Julia a look that meant *no one messes with me*. She reached down behind the counter and pulled out a sign. 'Starting from today it will be two-for-one on all afternoon teas. Let's see what he's going to do about that!' She waved the handmade sign in the air. 'This place is prime location at the foot of the mountain, those hungry ramblers want sausage rolls, packed lunches, a Full Scottish to start their day, an afternoon tea to finish. However, if my trade is affected...' Rona gave Julia a wicked smile and wagged her finger. 'I'll play dirty if I have to!'

'Rona, it's good news especially for the teashop, trust me.' Julia lowered her voice. 'Your afternoon teas are going to be the ONLY ones in Heartcross.'

Rona raised an eyebrow. 'Really? I'm intrigued. We always knew we could count on you,' Rona patted Julia's hand over the counter.

Julia had to do everything in her power not to spill the beans, but she'd promised Flynn. She felt like a fairy godmother turning everyone's anxiety and worries into something positive. Rona's trade for afternoon teas was about to double and the only worry she'd have was having to bake twice as many scones. 'But I have to say, I would never want to get on the wrong side of you, Rona Simons.'

Rona winked and slid a flask of tea over the counter. 'Take this and go and get that B&B reopened.'

'I will,' replied Julia, rummaging for some loose change in her pocket, but Rona put her hand up. 'On the house and no arguments.'

'Thank you,' replied Julia gratefully, grabbing the flask and the bag.

With Woody walking at the side of her, they took off back towards the B&B. She was hoping it was good news today and the power to the house would be up and running again by lunchtime. All she needed now was a date to start her extension – this was the first step to her own little business empire expanding and she was excited. That feeling of failure that she'd had when she discovered Starcross Manor was going to be a hotel had completely evaporated. Working with Flynn instead of fighting against him had given Julia food for thought, and she had all sorts of ideas swimming around in her head.

Chapter Sixteen

It had been a busy day; the eerie silence of the B&B at the start of the day had been so different by the time Julia had finished and Isla had finished. True to her word, Isla had turned up at the B&B with her sleeves rolled up and ready to help, and after Flynn had dropped off all the soft furnishings, they'd worked non-stop, making beds, hanging curtains and pushing the cushions back into the covers. Within a few hours everywhere seemed almost back to normal.

The gas and electricity had been declared safe, the Aga was back up and running, the boiler was relit and the hum from the fridge was a welcome sound. Julia smiled at Woody who was stretched out on the sofa in the kitchen like nothing had ever happened.

'Hello!' Eleni shouted up the hallway.

'In here,' bellowed Julia, flicking on the kettle.

Eleni walked into the kitchen holding up a pint of milk. 'Thought you might need supplies.'

'You are a life-saver!' exclaimed Julia, taking out three mugs from the cupboards and throwing a teabag in each one.

'How's it going?' Eleni looked around, suitably impressed.

Julia did a triumphant punch to the air. 'We've smashed it, worked our socks off,' she high fived Isla who grinned.

'It's times like this when I am thankful it's mainly wooden and tiled floors. Could you imagine if it had been carpet?' remarked Julia, pouring the boiling water into each mug. 'That would have needed to be ripped up. All the curtains are hung, the clean bedding is back on the beds, and this place is absolutely spotless. It feels like we've done a proper spring clean.'

'You are like wonder women!' exclaimed Eleni. 'Everywhere does look like it's back to normal. What's the plan? When can you reopen again?'

'Hopefully as soon as possible! How's it gone up at Starcross Manor? Were the new guests okay with the change?' checked Julia.

'Everyone is happy,' reassured Eleni. 'Oh, and I've got one more surprise for you.' Eleni's eyes danced with excitement as she waved her hands at them. 'Come on, come!'

Julia and Isla followed Eleni down the hallway towards the reception. Julia's face lit up – there standing on the desk was a computer. 'Oh my gosh. Where has this come from?' she asked, wiggling the mouse and tapping on the keyboard.

'Don't get too excited, it's second-hand, but Jack mentioned that Flynn had just bought a new computer for the office and this one was going begging. It would have only got thrown in the skip. So I asked Flynn and he said take it... so I did! Here it is!'

'Wow! Incredibly generous.' Julia couldn't believe it, this was going to help out enormously.

'What else is he throwing in that skip?' joked Isla. 'I think we need to take a look.'

'I can ask Jack?'

'I was joking,' said Isla. 'Let's get that cup of tea, I'm parched.'

As Eleni continued to fire-up the computer Isla followed Julia back into the kitchen. 'He's really going out of his way to look after you,' noticed Isla. 'First accommodating all the guests, then the dry cleaning. Jack and the lads helping with all the mattresses, now computers...' She tilted her head at Julia. 'Is there something you aren't telling me? I can see a sparkle in your eye.'

'We've come to an understanding to put the past behind us, and that's what we're doing.'

'And I suppose the fact he is drop-dead gorgeous is something you haven't noticed?'

Julia could feel Isla's eyes upon her, her amused face watching her every move.

Trying to keep the smile off her face was a challenge for Julia in itself. Of course she'd noticed his handsome rugged looks, it was difficult not to.

Julia managed a sarcastic smile. 'Actually, I haven't noticed at all.'

'Really,' probed Isla, still teasing.

'The computer is up and running,' announced Eleni, waltzing into the kitchen, 'what have I missed?'

Isla and Julia exchanged a glance.

'Nothing whatsoever, only Julia not noticing how handsome Flynn actually is.'

'Ha! I knew it!' replied Eleni, with a grin.

'We shall leave this conversation right here,' ordered Julia flashing a huge smile, whilst shaking her head in jest.

'The lady doth protest too much.' Isla put her fingers up to her eyes then pointed them in Julia's direction. 'I'm watching you.'

'Ha ha, watch all you like,' laughed Julia.

———————

Julia arrived back home just after 4pm, after restocking her fridge and freezer with produce from Foxglove Farm. Feeling a bubble of happiness rise in her stomach, she climbed the stairs back to her own private quarters with Woody by her side. As much as the hotel was an extravagant treat, there was no place like home and Julia couldn't wait to soak in the bath with bubbles up to her neck and a glass of wine in hand, before tucking into the sausage casserole that was bubbling away in the bottom oven of the Aga.

After balancing her wine glass on the edge of the bath, Julia turned on the tap and took a moment to watch the warm water swirl around the tub. She added a splash of luxurious bubble bath that Callie had sent her last Christmas and lit the tea-light candles on the windowsill. This was just what she needed. As she lowered her aching muscles into water, the bubbles rose to just under her chin. With her shoulders relaxed under the warm water she closed her eyes for the next ten minutes.

Julia thought about the water damage to the B&B, and on the whole knew it could have been a lot worse. She would never have got it up and running again so fast if it hadn't been for all her friends and Flynn helping out the way they had, and she knew she was so lucky to have that support.

Taking a sip of her wine, she glanced at the screen on her phone. It was an hour until she'd arranged to FaceTime Callie and discuss her imminent arrival for the upcoming birthday celebrations. Julia had everything crossed that Callie could stay for a few days, it would be fantastic to have a proper catch-up.

Julia couldn't quite believe that she was nearly forty – where had the time gone? A few days ago, celebrating had been the last thing on her mind, but now she began to feel excited. Feeling the water beginning to cool Julia finished her wine, climbed out of the bath and slipped straight into a comfy pair of lounge pants and a T-shirt. Once she'd ventured downstairs, she devoured the casserole in a matter of minutes and checked the time. There were a few minutes to spare until her FaceTime call with Callie as she settled on the sofa.

The phone rang out for a few times before the call connected. Julia beamed at Callie. 'Well hello there! You look... actually you look kind of harassed,' remarked Julia, narrowing her eyes at her cousin's image on the screen. 'Where are you? I thought you'd be settled down with a large glass so we can make plans for the weekend.' Julia could barely hear Callie, the background noise was loud and muffled.

'So sorry, I totally forgot we'd arranged to FaceTime. It's really not a good time,' Callie was shouting and barely looking at her phone.

'Are you okay? Have you really forgotten me?' Julia pulled a sad face, this wasn't like Callie at all. They always chatted for hours on their FaceTime calls.

'I know, it's just it's full-on at the minute and I'm on my way out.'

Once again, Julia struggled to hear her, but then could have sworn she heard someone telling Callie to hurry up. 'Where exactly are you? It sounds like you're at the airport or a train station, who are you with?' Julia moved closer to the screen to try and see where Callie was but her phone kept slipping down and now it seemed like she was running.

'I'm just…' Callie seemed breathless.

'Put the phone down,' ordered a voice as someone pulled on Callie's arm – a voice that Julia thought she recognised.

'Is that Allie? Are you with Allie?'

'I'm sorry, I can't talk right now. I'll call you next week,' confirmed Callie, her voice petering out with all the background noise.

'You better not call me next week, it's my birthday this weekend, and you better be here,' Julia was beginning to feel panicky. What the hell was Callie playing at?

'I'm so sorry, I won't be able to make your birthday, but I'll make it up to you… promise,' came the muffled reply.

'What do you mean, it's my big birthday, you have to be here.'

Click. The phone cut off.

With her heart in her mouth Julia stared at the blank screen and felt deflated. What was so important that Callie would miss her big birthday, and where the hell was she running to? It didn't make any sense. They'd spoken a few weeks ago and Callie had been looking forward to coming to Heartcross. What could have changed so quickly? Julia was close to tears, and took a sip of her wine. The whole conversation felt bizarre.

'It looks like it's just you and me then, Woody,' she said to the dog who'd curled up next to her on the sofa. She ruffled his tummy and he rolled onto his back without a care in the world. Julia was still staring at her phone feeling disappointed. She had no idea what the girls were planning but it wouldn't be the same without Callie there. She'd been looking forward to catching up with her and finding out all the gossip and now she didn't even know the next time she'd see her.

Picking up her iPad she flicked onto social media and punched in Callie's name. She scrolled through her latest posts on Facebook, but her last post was a couple of days ago and there was nothing about what she was up to right at this very minute. She gulped the wine from the glass and immediately filled it up again.

Next, she thought about Anais. She wondered if she owed her old friend an apology for ringing her regarding Flynn, and searched for her profile, but was surprised to see her name no longer came up. *How strange*, thought Julia, scrolling through her friends list, but she'd completely disappeared. What the hell was going on? Why would Anais delete her account? Mystified, she placed her iPad down on the coffee table and sighed. Tonight was not going to plan at all.

The sudden pinging of her phone caused her to jump. Julia was hoping it was Callie, but was surprised to see Flynn's name appear on the screen. She swiped the message and smiled. He was searching for advice again. She studied the photo he'd sent through and replied, 'Less pattern, more colour and texture, preferably bright colours, maybe pink!'

His reply was almost instant. 'I'm not sure about pink!'

'Trust me!' she replied, knowing that colour would look fabulous for that particular room at Starcross.

As she leant back on the cushion, she couldn't help but

notice how quiet the house was – it was completely silent except for Woody, who was softly snoring. The whole ambience of the place felt a little different without the hustle and bustle of her guests. 'You've got the right idea Woods,' she said stroking his fur. 'Maybe it's time for an early night.' Julia leant her head back on the settee and put her feet up on the coffee table. Woody opened an eye and snuggled in closer. 'It's a good job I have you,' she said fondly, knowing that he always provided that comfort and was always by her side.

She picked up her phone and pinged a text over to Eleni, 'I'm beyond gutted, Callie can't make my birthday.'

Almost immediately she received a text back, 'Oh no, don't be sad, we will have the best time I promise! See you in the morning x'

That was easier said than done. Julia had a hollow feeling in her chest and felt completely empty. It just wouldn't be the same without Callie – what was so important that she couldn't make her birthday?

Her phone pinged again, this time it was a message from Jack. She swiped and read, 'Good news! We've been working overtime at Starcross Manor and are slightly ahead of schedule. I've re-juggled some jobs which means we can begin work on your place in less than two weeks!'

Julia blew out a breath, her day was full of highs and lows, and this was definitely a high. This was brilliant news, and with the deal struck with Flynn, she could offer her guests the whole range of amenities up at Starcross Manor.

'I suppose we can't have everything, Woods,' Julia

murmured, still thinking about Callie as she wrapped herself up in the grey woollen throw on the arm of the settee and munched her way through a family-size chocolate bar that she'd treated herself to earlier from Hamish's store.

Chapter Seventeen

The next few days flew by, and the B&B was thankfully full of guests and running smoothly again. Julia had been up with the larks and had spent the last hour walking Woody through the woodlands, and was now back with her first cup of tea of the morning.

The back door swung open and in walked Eleni, armed with a handful of colourful wrapped presents and a bottle of prosecco, which she placed down on the table before throwing her arms around Julia and giving her a hug. 'Happy birthday, boss!' she sang.

'Thanks, so much! Even though I don't feel any different to yesterday. And all this?' Julia nodded to the presents on the table. 'That's way too many presents.'

'These are what you call relevant presents, things you will need for tonight.' Eleni looked like the cat that got the cream as she reached for two champagne flutes from the cupboard before popping the cork.

'Relevant?' queried Julia, picking up one and giving it a quick feel. She couldn't guess what was inside. 'And isn't it too early to be drinking?'

'Nonsense, it's your fortieth. I thought we should start as we mean to go on.'

Julia smiled at Eleni's enthusiasm. Since Eleni had heard that Callie couldn't make her birthday, she'd made it her mission to keep Julia's spirits high. She watched as Eleni poured two glasses of fizz and clinked her glass against Julia's.

'Now open your presents before we get those breakfasts underway.' Eleni ushered Julia to the table and pulled out a chair.

'I feel like a child,' said Julia excitedly, picking up the first present. 'It's quite light,' she ripped open the package to discover a flashlight. She looked at Eleni confused. 'Okay, that's a little different. And that is for?'

'My lips are sealed! Wait and see,' came the reply.

A little puzzled, Julia put it to one side and tore open the next present, which contained a pen and notebook, and a two-way radio.

'Okay, now I'm even more confused. The last time I saw one of these... Callie and I used to run around the woods playing hide and seek, and used these to give each other clues.'

'I can confirm we will not be playing hide and seek... well, actually that might not be strictly true.' Eleni gave a small chuckle. 'Come on, open the next one.'

Julia continued to tear open the presents, which revealed

numerous gadgets and gizmos. She had no clue what they were for. Mystified, she stared at the presents. 'Whatever happened to chocolates and champagne? Not that I'm meaning to sound ungrateful.'

'I've brought chocolates; in fact, homemade chocolates from the teashop,' Felicity was smiling in the doorway. 'Happy birthday! Mum and I just thought we'd send these over ahead of tonight.' Felicity took a swift glance over the table and grinned. 'Fully prepared, I see.'

'Fully prepared for what?' Julia narrowed her eyes hoping to squeeze any little bit of information out of Felicity, but she wasn't for sharing.

'My lips are sealed! Enjoy your day!' Felicity waved her hand above her head. 'Catch you later, alligators!' And with that she disappeared as quickly as she'd arrived.

Taking a sip of her fizz, Julia saw her phone screen was full of notifications, people wishing her happy birthday by text or on Facebook. She was just about to put her phone down when it began to vibrate in her hand.

'It's Callie,' she said excitedly, quickly swiping the screen – but as soon as the call connected there were three pips and the screen went blank.

Immediately Julia tried to call her back, but the call wouldn't connect. She tried again, but still nothing.

'Don't worry, she'll ring you back,' reassured Eleni.

'I'm beginning to feel like she's not even bothered.' With that empty feeling in her stomach again, Julia sighed and laid her phone down on the table. 'Or avoiding me for some reason.'

'Maybe she's got stuff going on in her life we don't know about.'

'I'm Callie's family, I would know, surely.'

The phone vibrated again, and Julia pressed her lips together in a secret smile. She was chuffed to see a text from Flynn, wishing her a happy birthday.

'Is that Callie again?' asked Eleni.

Julia shook her head and noticed the kisses at the end of the text.

'Don't dwell on Callie, she will have a perfectly good explanation, I'm sure. This is your special day and the sooner we get on with the chores, the quicker we can properly start celebrating.' Eleni threw her an apron.

'Bring it on,' replied Julia.

The day flew by and before Julia knew it, it was ten o'clock at night. After consuming a couple of glasses of champagne, Julia was standing outside the B&B quizzing Eleni about the night ahead.

'And why are we waiting here?' Julia tried one last time to squeeze any little bit of information out of Eleni, who'd not once slipped up about tonight's plans, even though she'd witnessed Eleni whispering on the phone on numerous occasions – she still hadn't been able to work out exactly where they were going this evening.

Eleni tapped her watch. 'And here they are now. Right on time.'

Julia followed Eleni's gaze to see a white minibus driving up the lane towards the B&B.

'A minibus? Why do we need a minibus?' queried Julia, as it pulled up next to her on the kerb and the door was flung open.

'After you,' Eleni gestured with a grin.

Julia stepped on board to wild applause and curtseyed in front of all her friends.

'Surely someone can tell me where we are going?' Julia looked hopefully towards Aggie, Rona and Martha who were looking mischievous on the back seat of the bus.

'All I know is the last time I was up this late, I was giving birth,' Rona gave a chuckle, and everyone laughed.

'I'm assuming we aren't going clubbing as everyone is dressed in combat pants and hoodies?' Julia looked towards Polly hoping for some sort of clue.

'I'm not sure, the only memo I received was, bring a backpack and a torch, but Alfie made me a pile of sandwiches in case we got stranded.'

'Stranded? Why would we be stranded?' Julia looked alarmed.

'Alfie was a boy scout, always be prepared.'

Isla was wielding a microphone, and blew into it as Julia and Eleni took the only two spare seats at the front of the bus. 'Right, we should only be in this for ten minutes max, so let's have a sing-song, any suggestions?'

'I Will Survive!' shouted out Julia.

For the whole journey Julia had her eyes peeled towards the window. The bus headed down the gravel road at the bottom of Love Heart Lane and headed over the bridge towards Glensheil, but Julia noticed they weren't heading into town. They took the winding, bumpy road at the edge of the river, and then the bus began to weave its way slowly up the side of the hilly, rocky terrain.

'Why are we heading to old man Marley's?' Julia's eyes were wide as she stared at Eleni, who was grinning in Isla's direction. 'Are we actually heading to Heartcross Castle?' quizzed Julia, holding on to the side of the seat as they bounced their way along the rocky road.

'Maybe,' replied Eleni.

'Why? Is old man Marley still alive? Please tell me I'm not having birthday tea with him?' Julia felt alarmed. As far as she knew, Heartcross Castle had not been open to the public for years. Old man Marley was a recluse, no one had seen him for years, and as far as everyone knew he rattled around in the place all by himself.

'It's too late for tea, maybe supper,' chuckled Felicity. 'And this place has been open to the public for a couple of months.'

'Girls, my heart is hammering so fast,' Julia looked up at the giant stone gatehouse in front of her.

'Don't worry, I'll look after you,' offered Molly, showing solidarity but looking as pale as Julia felt right now.

The minibus parked up and the driver turned towards Isla. 'I'll wait no more than an hour.'

Isla saluted. 'Understood.' She took the microphone, looking like a professional tour guide. 'Okay so we have arrived, and what an impressive place this is!'

Alarmed, Julia was still looking up at the castle. She wasn't one for even watching a scary movie, and that castle looked very much haunted to her.

'Heartcross Castle was built around 1660 according to the history books, situated on the bend of the River Heart – and can you see those holes on the battlements? They are called murder holes, that's where boiling tar and human waste were poured to kill invaders... pretty gruesome, eh?'

Julia interrupted, 'Forgive me, but am I able just to remind everyone this is my fortieth birthday, a time for celebrations, a time to drink wine and maybe enjoy each other's company, and we are talking murder holes... just saying.'

'This is going to be a birthday to remember! I promise,' grinned Isla.

'You aren't wrong,' replied Julia looking at Eleni in dismay as the penny dropped. Julia's face paled. 'We are going ghost-hunting? Aren't we?'

Isla squeezed her arm. 'Yay, she's got it! This is going to be so much fun!'

'You never know who you might meet,' said Eleni, zipping up her hoody.

'Mainly dead people,' answered Julia still feeling a little bewildered. 'And which part of it is going to be fun?' Julia was still staring up at the murder holes.

'Mark my words, this is going to be the best birthday ever. Here, take a swig.' Eleni pulled out a hip flask and handed it to Julia, who immediately took a swig of the single malt.

'Here we go!' Eleni tucked the hip flask away and linked her arm through Julia's.

Waiting outside the bus stood a lady Julia didn't recognise. She was all trussed up in a bomber jacket, with a beanie hat pulled firmly down on her head, clutching a clipboard.

'Gather round, gather round. I'm Dawn, your ghost-hunting guide, and I believe we have a birthday amongst us tonight.'

Everyone pointed towards Julia.

'Happy birthday! And a very special welcome to you. Hopefully tonight we are going to make contact with the laughing trickster, the sleeping maiden, and the jolly warden. They do like a good birthday.'

There was an undercurrent of excited chatter from her friends. Julia looked around and brushed against Eleni's arm, who jumped out of her skin and screamed. Then Julia screamed.

'It's only me, you idiot,' exclaimed Julia blowing out a breath. 'There's no need to scream.'

Eleni brought her hand up to her chest. 'Don't do that again, you frightened the life out of me.'

'Give me the hip flask, I need another swig,' demanded Julia, in an attempt to calm herself down.

Dawn continued, 'Heartcross Castle dominates the skyline of Heartcross. With 150 steps, it was built to have a panoramic view of the surrounding land. Doesn't it look magnificent? For one night only we have use of the gatehouse here at Heartcross Castle. We will not be venturing into the main castle as Mr Marley is still in residence, however I can guarantee this will be the best experience ever.'

Julia took an extra swig from the flask and handed it back to Eleni. 'It's definitely a birthday to remember.'

'I told you so. This is going to be amazing,' she whispered in Julia's ear. 'I promise.'

Dawn clapped to get everyone's attention. 'Before we step inside, I'm going to talk a little about our spirit friends, please use your notebooks to write anything down... what you sense, hear and smell. Use your temperature gauges, and keep your wits about you.'

Julia couldn't help but notice that every single one of her friends were hanging on Dawn's every word and had whipped out their notebooks from their rucksacks.

'Okay, we are looking out for sulphuric scent...'

Martha whispered to Rona, 'That could be Aggie's perfume.' And Rona gave a little chuckle.

'Listen out for growling, powerful energy, and knocks that come in threes.' Dawn glanced around at everyone standing in front of her.

Felicity tapped three times on Isla's shoulder who spun round and swiped Felicity. 'Stop doing that!'

'But first we say a little prayer for protection and guidance.' Dawn handed out a laminate card to everyone.

'Read with me...'

To the earth and those who lie beneath

To the paths we are about to walk and to those who trod them before us
To the homes we will enter and to whom they once housed
To this city and its echoes
Know we come in blessing and we wish you only peace

Julia was saying her own prayer – she hoped to see her next birthday.

Once everyone had said their prayer Dawn took back the cards and continued. 'If you encounter a real ghost, don't be scared, simply send out positive thoughts. Don't charge into each room, remember this is their house and you are simply the guests. Common courtesy is the key. Please do not start running around taking pictures left, right and centre. The spirits were once people too, always investigate calmly.'

'There's nothing calm about the way my heart is beating at the minute,' Julia muttered under her breath.

'The only spirit I want to talk to is gin,' chipped in Aggie.

'Let the spirits know you mean no harm, ask their permission to take photographs. Invite them to be in your photo. If they respond, talk to them, manners go a long way. And don't forget, when you leave, thank them for having you and ask them not to follow.'

'Ask them not to *follow*?' repeated Julia looking alarmed.

'Will the ghosts want to talk to us?' asked Felicity, hanging on Dawn's every word.

'If it feels like they want to talk to you, tell them you are open to a conversation, but if you feel an overwhelming urge to leave, take that as a serious warning that you have invaded their space and say another prayer out loud. Always leave the location as you found it.'

'Are we allowed to touch things?' asked Meredith, joining in the questions.

'You can touch walls and tombstones, but don't move any stones or alter the location in any way. Messing about with the scene can get you into trouble with the spirit world.'

'I need another swig.' Julia tugged at Eleni's arm. Never before had she been in need of a drink so much to steady her nerves. She couldn't actually believe people did this for fun.

'Okay, are we ready?' asked Dawn, hurling her backpack onto her shoulders. 'Stay safe.'

Julia was far from ready, but Dawn was already powering her legs towards the door of the gatehouse. Everyone linked arms and followed in silence. Julia wasn't even sure if she actually believed in ghosts, but that belief was about to be questioned.

Dawn swung open the creaky door to the gatehouse and stepped inside. Julia gripped Eleni's arm tighter. 'Look up at the castle,' whispered Julia, her heart was thumping so fast she thought it was about to burst out of her chest at any given moment. There was only one light on in the castle and Julia saw a figure standing in the window.

'That's old man Marley, he's watching us. Maybe he's an

actual ghost. No one has seen him for years,' replied Eleni, treading carefully down the stone steps that led to a very dark room. It took a while for Julia's eyes to adjust, and everyone gathered around Dawn's torchlight.

'Do not leave me,' ordered Julia, not letting go of Eleni.

'Okay, let's have hush for a moment... Hello,' Dawn called out, her voice echoing all around, 'we mean no harm and have come to talk to you.'

Julia's eyes had adjusted to the darkness and she noticed Dawn was holding a gadget like she'd received for her birthday: an EMF gauge. 'We know you are here,' continued Dawn.

Everyone was rooted to the spot. The only thing Julia could hear was the sound of dripping water.

Rona was holding a temperature gauge. 'The temperature has plummeted, that's a good sign isn't it?' she whispered in the darkness. 'Possibly a ghost.'

Julia couldn't see how that was a good sign. All that meant was it was more than likely there were ghosts floating about – although Julia had no real idea what a ghost actually looked like.

'Do you want to talk to us?' encouraged Dawn softly. 'We would like to talk to you.'

Julia could hear a gentle knocking sound. She could feel her body shaking, she was actually frightened. With her feet rooted to the spot, she bit down hard on her lip. Eleni was scribbling down on her notepad. Meredith had whipped out her phone. 'Is it okay to take photos?' she asked getting into the spirit of things.

The knocking sound became louder. Julia wanted to scream. She wanted to run for the hills, literally.

'That means you can take photos,' confirmed Dawn. 'The spirits are saying yes.'

'OMG, there is someone here. What's that smell?' Julia's mouth had gone dry, her whole body covered in goose bumps and she shivered.

Meredith took numerous photos with her phone. 'Look,' she exclaimed lighting up the screen, 'there's a dark shadow over there.' Felicity took exactly the same photo in the same place, and now the shadow was gone.

'Can you feel that presence, can you sense someone?' Dawn walked through to the next dungeon. 'If you want to split up, you can use your two-way radios.'

Julia didn't want to split up from anyone, she wanted them all to stay together.

'Look at that shadow over there... by the split in the wall,' pointed out Molly, slowly walking in the darkness towards the window.

Once more they heard a knocking sound. 'That noise is coming from the next room, let's go.' Isla had no fear whatsoever. Julia had watched *Most Haunted* on TV numerous times and had laughed at how scared everyone appeared, but she wasn't laughing now. This kind of thing was more up Callie's street, she was the braver of the two. Julia didn't want to search for ghosts, she wanted to be safely tucked up in bed.

'My gauge is flickering off the scale,' whispered Dawn.

'We definitely have the spirits with us. I'll try and talk to them.'

Everyone fell silent.

'Hello,' said Dawn. 'Is there anyone there? We've come to talk to you.'

Deadly silence. Julia was gripping Eleni so hard she was more than likely to draw blood at any second.

'We come in peace, and if you would like to talk to us please let us know you are there.' Dawn was speaking softly, her phone lighting up the gauge, which was going mental.

'Please knock three times,' she encouraged.

Julia held her breath.

Knock… knock… knock.

Julia squealed, 'I don't like this, I need to get out of here.' She tugged at Eleni. 'Get me out of here.'

The tapping continued.

'Don't be scared, they aren't going to hurt you. These are good spirits, friendly spirits, and no doubt are in need of some company.'

Julia's eyes were wide; she felt herself shaking, then all of a sudden a white shadow floated past the open door in front of them.

'Whooooo,' came a voice.

Then another figure dressed in what looked like a white sheet floated past. 'Whoooo!'

'Talk to us,' said Felicity. 'Have you got anything to say to us?'

The two figures hovered in the doorway. 'Actually yes,'

came a voice followed by a giggle. A voice that Julia instantly recognised. 'Happy birthday to you!'

Callie whipped off the white sheet and was beaming at Julia in the light of everyone's phones and torches. 'You didn't think I'd miss your birthday, did you?'

Julia exhaled, her whole body trembling – she didn't know whether to laugh or cry.

'OMG! I could actually murder you!'

'And then you would actually be searching for a ghost,' giggled Callie, throwing her arms wide open.

'Feel my heart, it's going to pound out of my chest.' Julia's hands were still clutched to her chest as she stepped forward and hugged Callie, but not before shaking her shoulders in frustration. 'Now the next question is, who's under that sheet?' queried Julia, letting go of Callie. She stretched out her arm and pulled up the sheet. A grinning Allie was standing in front of them. 'Happy birthday! I've never had so much fun in my life!'

Everyone squealed and stepped forward to hug Allie. 'Welcome home!' Meredith squeezed her daughter. 'I thought you couldn't get time off?'

'I wouldn't have missed this for the world! That was so much fun.'

Everyone seemed to forget they were standing in the middle of a dark, damp tower looking for ghosts. The mood had turned from dark and sinister to jovial in a matter of seconds.

'I'm glad you lot have had fun. I actually thought I'd have a heart attack!' Julia was still shaking her head in disbelief that Callie and Allie were standing in front of her, but was relieved there weren't actually any real ghosts.

Julia turned towards Dawn. 'Are you not a real ghost hunter?'

Dawn shook her head and laughed. 'No, I'm not a ghost hunter, far from it. I'm Allie's partner on the newspaper. I heard there was a special birthday going on, and blagged an invite. I hope you don't mind?' Dawn stretched out her hand. 'Happy birthday! And I'm sorry, they talked me into this, you looked absolutely petrified.'

'I *was* absolutely petrified, and I have to say – not meaning to sound ungrateful – disappointed you all brought me ghost-hunting. I was thinking of sacking you all as friends if we ever got out of here alive!'

Isla snaked an arm around Julia's shoulders. 'Now it's time for your proper birthday to begin!'

'You mean there's more? I'm not sure I can take any more.'

'There is, the minibus is taking us back over to Starcross Manor. We've another surprise.'

'Now that sounds more up my street! Let's get out of this place!' Clutching Callie's arm, Julia dragged her outside into the fresh air. 'Can we finally go and drink champagne?!'

'Absolutely we can,' declared Callie, giving Julia another hug before climbing back onto the bus. 'Let the party begin!'

Chapter Eighteen

W ith everyone in good spirits, the minibus pulled up outside Starcross Manor and the driver jumped out and opened up the boot. Everyone began collecting their overnight bags.

'Here's yours,' exclaimed Eleni. 'Honestly, trying to sneak this out of the door and gather your things together was a task in itself – and don't worry about Woody, Drew's been to collect him, he's spending the night at Foxglove Farm again.'

'You lot have thought of everything, haven't you?' Julia was impressed. She couldn't wait to see what was in store for her now. As the minibus drove off Julia noticed Flynn standing at the top of the stone steps outside the entrance to Starcross Manor. She gawped at him, his suit was exquisitely cut, sharp-looking and well-fitted. Julia thought he wouldn't look out of place in a movie, maybe with an Aston Martin by his side.

He began to walk down the steps towards Julia then stretched out his hands and took hold of hers. Their eyes locked before Flynn kissed her on both cheeks. 'Happy birthday,' he whispered.

Her heart was thumping so hard she let out a calming breath and smiled up at him. 'Thank you,' she replied.

Smiling, Flynn held up a bunch of keys. 'Here you go, enjoy your evening,' he said touching Julia's arm. 'Happy birthday again.' He kissed her cheek softly and turned and walked back up the steps leaving Julia weak at the knees as she watched him disappear back inside the manor house.

'What are these keys for?' she asked, turning back towards the others.

Eleni took them from her. 'Come on, we aren't staying in the hotel.'

Julia looked at her quizzically. 'Where are we staying then?' she asked, looking down at all the overnight bags.

Eleni grinned, then raised her hand. 'Follow me.'

Carrying their bags everyone followed Eleni, who strolled through the illuminated gardens of Starcross Manor. Julia had no idea where they were going as they took the gravel path which led to the woodland then stepped into a clearing. Bringing her hand to her mouth Julia gasped. She stared at the circle of log cabins, all swathed in twinkling fairy lights hanging from their crooked roofs. Outside log cabin number 4 was a cluster of gold, silver, and white balloons dancing in the light breeze with 'Happy Birthday' bunting trailing the small picket fence. It was picture-perfect. 'This is amazing! Absolutely amazing.' Julia gave a little squeal and squeezed Callie's arm. 'It looks like something out of a fairy tale.'

'You haven't seen anything yet,' grinned Eleni.

'How did you know all this was here?' Julia asked Eleni, still taking in her surroundings.

'Jack mentioned it was your birthday to Flynn and he offered all this for the evening. Andrew has made up a late-night buffet and there's as much champagne as we can drink, and tomorrow we can nurse our hangovers and have a lovely lie-in.'

'I just can't believe this. This is just how I imagined my birthday to be,' exclaimed Julia, thankful that her birthday celebrations were back on track. 'I can't wait to see inside.'

'After you,' Eleni swept her arm open wide whilst Julia opened the door to the first cabin.

Julia stood in the middle room and gave an incredulous stare. 'Pink,' she muttered under her breath. Everywhere was dressed in pink, from the soft furnishings to an enormous bouquet of pink peonies dressed in a huge pink ribbon on the coffee table. Julia leant forward and inhaled their scent. She was shaking with excitement as she opened the tiny white envelope attached to the cellophane.

'Happy birthday! Enjoy your night, Lots of love Flynn x.'

Julia felt her heart give a little flutter. Next to the beautiful flowers were numerous wrapped gifts.

'These are you proper presents,' Eleni squeezed her arm.

'I can't believe you've done all this for me.' Feeling on top of the world, Julia looked around the room. The one-storey cabin was cosy, there was a wood-burning stove in the living space, giving it a welcoming feel, and the huge windows at the far end of the room took full advantage of the magnificent views. There was a flat-screen TV, a top-of-the-range kitchen and a wine rack full of champagne.

'Take a look outside,' urged Eleni.

At the back of the log cabin there was a wooden terrace area, once again decorated with balloons. Just to the right of the terrace was a private hot tub, and a profusion of red roses sprawling over the high hedgerows on either side of the hot tub, giving privacy but not concealing the stunning view of the countryside.

'I can't wait to sit in the hot tub with a glass of champagne alongside you lot. You really have excelled yourselves. I'm feeling so loved it's unbelievable.'

'Us oldies are going to set up camp in the far log cabin for the evening,' announced Aggie, looking towards Meredith, Rona and Martha.

'There's nowt old about me,' argued Martha. 'I'm more vintage,' she teased.

'Polly, Allie, Dawn and Molly are next door, leaving me, Flick, Eleni, Callie and birthday girl in this one,' confirmed Isla looking at the sheet they'd already drawn up. 'Is everyone okay with that?'

They all nodded.

'Great, go and put your bags in your rooms and we'll meet back here... we have champagne to drink!' continued Isla.

Everyone dispersed off in different directions leaving

Julia doing an impression of a starfish as she sank into the plush sofa. 'I can't believe all my friends and you...' she wagged her finger at Callie, 'are all here. I was so upset with you.'

'I do feel a tiny bit guilty about that,' Callie grinned, pinching her thumb and forefinger together.

Within minutes, everyone gathered back in the kitchen of Julia's cabin. They wandered outside onto the decking and admired the glorious buffet prepared by Andrew laid out on the trestle tables, and in the middle of all the food stood the most magnificent birthday cake Julia had ever seen. 'I'm just speechless, everything looks amazing.'

Rona smiled. 'Obviously, the cake is made by your favourite bakers at your favourite teashop.'

'And there's even a miniature Woody on there!' exclaimed Julia. 'You lot have certainly redeemed yourselves after that ghost-hunting malarkey.'

'I think we need a toast to the birthday girl,' Eleni gathered everyone around and lined up the champagne flutes on the table. She handed the bottle of champagne to Callie who immediately popped the cork. Everyone chimed in at the same time, 'Happy birthday Julia!' as Callie filled up all the flutes. 'We need a second bottle,' she laughed. When all the glasses were full everyone clinked them together. 'Hip-hip hooray!' everyone chorused.

'I now declare the buffet open.' Julia swiped her arm towards the mountain of food.

Julia looked round all of her friends. This was just perfect; everyone was having a great time. They sat around the wooden tables whilst they ate and drank, all except Callie who was bending down and flicking a switch on the decking next to the hot tub. There was a loud gurgling sound and bubbles began to rise to the surface.

After the buffet was demolished everyone disappeared back to their cabins to change into their swimwear. Eleni was putting together a birthday playlist in the living room whilst Julia was the first to slip into the hot tub. 'This is the life,' she murmured letting the warm bubbles soothe her body. Being surrounded by the rural beauty, tranquillity, and her friends, she felt relaxed and happy. Stretching out her arms around the edge of the tub, Julia looked up at the night sky, the stars taking her breath away.

'Penny for them,' asked Callie with a smile, twisting her ponytail into a bun and slipping into the warm water next to Julia. She cupped the bubbles with her hands then stared up at the stars. 'Look at that view.'

'I can't believe you are here. I didn't think you could get away. You had me fooled.'

Callie was silent for a second and looked over towards the door to see if anyone was coming.

'What is it? I know that look. What's wrong?' Julia sat up straight in the water.

'Heartcross is a beautiful place – do you think it has room for one more Coleman?'

'Heartcross is indeed a beautiful place. Another Coleman?'

'Dan and me have gone our separate ways,' admitted Callie, taking a sip of her drink.

'What? And you didn't think to *tell* me? Why? When?' The questions spilled out – Julia had to admit she was shocked by the news.

'I made the decision the night the B&B was flooded, and moved out the following morning. I didn't want to burden you. You had other stuff to deal with.'

'That might be so, but you are never a burden... ever. What happened?'

Callie sighed. 'As time went on, I needed more from our relationship. Dan just had no ambition, no drive. There was a chance to expand his dad's business, but he wasn't interested. All he wanted to do was ride the waves, and I began to feel suffocated, isolated, and bored if I'm truly honest. I'd been doing the same thing day-in and day-out for years.'

Julia was gobsmacked, this was not what she'd expected. She thought Callie and Dan were the perfect couple. She even thought any day now they would announce their wedding plans – not that they had gone their separate ways.

'But don't think I'm sad,' continued Callie. 'I'm not at all. I'd made the decision a while back, and it was more about the timing.'

'It's not just a relationship, it's your job as well. You will have lost everything. What's the plan now?' asked Julia, concerned.

'Well actually, I've got an interview on Tuesday,' revealed Callie, with a beam on her face.

'That's brilliant – an interview, what for?' quizzed Julia.

'Restaurant Manager, at a place called Starcross Manor – ever heard of it?'

Julia's mouth fell open. 'You're kidding me?'

Callie laughed and shook her head.

'Does this mean you are coming to live in Heartcross?' Julia had her fingers crossed in front of her and squeezed her eyes shut. 'This is the best birthday present ever.'

'If you know of anyone with a room to rent...' Callie tipped Julia a wink.

'And that means you will be working for the famous Andrew Glossop.'

'I know, can you imagine? All my friends will be well jealous.'

'And funnily enough, you might actually know the owner of Starcross Manor. Did you recognise the guy on the steps when we arrived?'

'No? Who is he?'

'Remember Anais Brown and that wedding that went pear-shaped? The one I was bridesmaid for?'

'Ha, I do! That wedding was the talk of the town, and not for the right reasons.'

'Well, the guy who dumped her at the altar... Flynn Carter... owns all this.' Julia swept her hand in the air. 'And what do you mean, not for the right reasons?'

'Flynn Carter owns this place, Starcross Manor?' Callie was amazed. 'Wasn't he the one who flattened Grandad's house?'

'The very one.'

'Wow! That's a turn-up for the books. Did he recognise you?' asked Callie, topping up the champagne.

'Not at first, but I soon reminded him. You won't *believe* what I found when I arrived.' Julia took a breath and told Callie all about the untruthful magazine article. 'Flynn declared to the world that *he* was the one who'd been dumped!'

'But he *was* the one who was dumped,' shared Callie, nodding at her cousin. 'Everything in that article was the truth.'

'Don't be ridiculous. Why would you say that? I was *there* that day. When I came back from the shops, Anais was distraught, her wedding dress cut to shreds, and Flynn had left her for someone else... on their wedding day! And when I FaceTimed her the other day after Flynn denied that he'd jilted her, she basically told me to stay away from him as he wasn't to be trusted. And now she's disappeared off Facebook, which is all very sudden and bizarre.'

Callie shook her head. 'Okay, the way he went about Grandad's house was wrong – but you managed to make your start in life, and I received some money too...'

'And he has apologised for that,' interrupted Julia. 'And he's helped out so much to get the B&B back up and running after the flood, including putting my guests up in his hotel rooms. I couldn't have done it without him.'

'But going back to the wedding for a moment – Anais Brown wasn't the victim that day. She'd been having an affair with Brendan Stack, a petty criminal. Flynn's career was taking off, he was on his way to making his first million, and Anais couldn't believe her luck when he walked into her estate agents that day. And here's the reason I know... remember Louise, my good friend? She worked in that estate agents too.'

'And is that how you know all this?'

Callie nodded. 'Louise's parents were Anais's godparents, and best friends with Anais's parents. She'd spun them a line that she'd been jilted to save face, but the truth was, Flynn had discovered her little game. She and Brendan were planning on ripping off his fortune, but Flynn knew something wasn't right, so a couple of days before the wedding he produced a pre-nup for Anais to sign, which of course scuppered her plans. She wasn't going to be able to divorce him in a couple of years, taking half of everything.'

Julia let out a low whistle. 'Are you absolutely sure about this?' she asked, thinking that, with the performance Anais had put on that day, she deserved an Oscar.

'Absolutely sure. Everyone thought Flynn was to blame, his only downfall was falling in love with Anais – but luckily for him, he never married her.'

'It's like something out of a movie,' Julia was genuinely amazed. 'I'm absolutely gobsmacked. How can anyone be that devious?'

'Anais was.'

'How did it all come out?'

'The truth always comes out. Apparently, Anais called her parents, putting on an act just like she did with you, but forgot to end the call. They heard her talking to Brendan and heard everything... disowned her.'

Julia was still shaking her head in disbelief. 'She actually cut up the wedding dress, tried to slur his name, and it was all her.'

'It was all her. Apparently there were angry family members hounding him at the time and so Flynn took himself away from social media, and he never told his side of the story. He just tried to move on and wanted the whole sorry affair to go away.'

'And why did you never tell me any of this?' Julia's jaw was still somewhere near the bottom of the hot tub. She couldn't get her head around the lies Anais had told. The shame of it all – and poor Flynn. Julia knew she'd been wary of Flynn, but she'd told everyone in the village that he was untrustworthy, and he had gone out of his way to help her. 'I feel dreadful.'

'He's probably a nice, genuine bloke,' replied Callie.

Julia was feeling guilty and ashamed that she had treated Flynn so badly. She cringed thinking about the confrontation in the kitchen at the B&B after she'd stumbled across the magazine article at the dentist.

'There's no point feeling dreadful.' Callie was the voice of reason. 'If you didn't know, you didn't know, and all you did was act on what you saw that day.'

Callie was right, but that still didn't help the churned-up feeling in Julia's stomach. She knew she really needed to apologise to Flynn – again!

'Do you think that's why Anais has taken herself off Facebook after I contacted her to tell her Flynn had turned up?' Julia couldn't believe she'd been taken in by Anais, who had deliberately gone out of her way to ruin Flynn's reputation just in case the truth had been discovered. Now knowing the truth, Julia was impressed with how Flynn had conducted himself with such dignity, unlike Anais who had manipulated the whole situation.

'Oh yes, without a doubt, Brendan went down for armed robbery, and I know she got married again. Anais wouldn't want her past coming back to haunt her. Her parents still don't speak to her.'

'I'm not surprised!' Julia couldn't get it out of her mind, it was just awful what she'd done to Flynn, but Callie was right: the truth always comes out.

'Forget all that now.' Callie looked up at the stars. 'That view is amazing!' She clinked her glass against Julia's. 'Happy birthday, and I'm sorry about the ghost-hunting, we didn't mean to frighten you.'

'You're not sorry at all!'

'You're right, I'm not,' Callie laughed.

Julia lowered her shoulders into the water and took a sip of her champagne. 'This is the life. I think I'm going to quite like being forty!'

'But the question still remains: if I'm successful in my job interview here, would you have room for me?' Callie tipped her head to the side and placed her glass on the edge of the tub before putting her hands together in a prayer.

'As much as it's sad you've split up with Dan, his loss is my absolute gain. I've always room for you.'

'Thank you, thank you. Fingers crossed I get the job,

because even though I've only been here a few hours, Heartcross seems a very special place.'

'It is,' agreed Julia.

Just at that second music started playing out from the speakers at the side of the hot tub. Julia looked up to see all her friends spilling through the patio doors. Everyone was dressed in their swimsuits holding their glasses of champagne. 'Let the party begin,' jollied Eleni, dropping her towel and slipping into the hot tub next to Julia and Callie. She looked between the pair of them. 'What have I missed? Any gossip?'

'You aren't going to believe what I'm going to tell you!' Julia told Eleni as she topped up her champagne glass.

'I'm intrigued,' admitted Eleni. 'Very intrigued.'

Chapter Nineteen

Julia was curled up on the settee with Woody by her side, and Callie was sprawled out in the armchair with her legs dangling over the edge. They'd been up until 4am, chatting and laughing in the hot tub, followed by a mini disco on the decking. They'd all fallen into bed and each cabin was woken up just after ten o'clock with a light rap on the door. With a slight hangover, Julia managed to manoeuvre herself out of bed to discover a waiter wearing a huge smile standing next to a trolley containing numerous stainless steel cloches and pots of tea and coffee, and singing 'Breakfast!' at the top of his voice. Each log cabin received the same treatment and when the waiter wheeled the trolley onto the decking, they were amazed to see a Full Scottish breakfast being served for each and every one of them, courtesy of Flynn.

'How was your birthday?' Callie asked, smothering her breakfast in brown sauce.

'The best, one I'll remember for a long time,' Julia said with such warmth. This was what living your best life was all about: good company, the best food, and the perfect location.

'I'd say he was a keeper,' whispered Callie in Julia's ear.

'Who?'

'Flynn. He's got a soft spot for you. Look at all this, not to mention last night's feast, endless bottles of champagne – and those gorgeous peonies.'

When Julia's head had hit the pillow last night, she had to admit the last thing on her mind before she fell asleep had been Flynn. Jack had been right: he was a good, genuine man. Yes, when he'd first started out in business, he'd been young and thirsty to make money, but he'd proved he'd changed his ways, certainly in the last few days.

The fluttering in her stomach had changed from an anxious one to a warm one every time she saw him. He wasn't the man Anais had made him out to be – far from it – and her opinion of him had started to change even before Callie had told her the truth. Last night had been perfect enough, and she really wasn't expecting breakfast. Her thoughts of Flynn were interrupted as a knock sounded on the log cabin's door.

'I'll go,' said Eleni, bounding towards the door before anyone else could offer.

'It's Flynn,' shouted Eleni, walking back through the log cabin followed by a cheery Flynn holding another silver cloche.

'How's the birthday girl?' His eyes twinkled as he looked towards Julia.

'Maybe a little bit of a sore head,' she grinned.

He held out a small gift bag in front of her. 'I have one more present.'

'Really, for me?'

'Yes, for you!' Flynn handed over the bag.

Sheer pleasure mixed with apprehension ran through Julia as she looked inside.

'Ta-dah!' Julia threw her head back, and laughed, and waved a packet of paracetamol in her hand. 'You really have thought of everything, this is the best present.'

'Now they have been safely delivered, I need to go and get ready for the meeting tonight. I hope to see you all there – and don't worry about tidying up this place, I've got the cleaners lined up for when you leave.'

'Thanks Flynn, all this has been amazing.' Julia meant every word.

'It's my pleasure.'

As he walked back through the log cabin followed by Julia, he looked over his shoulder. 'Pink,' he said, 'good choice.'

'I told you pink would be the best. The furnishings in here are amazing.'

As Flynn stepped outside, he turned towards her. 'I hope the hangover isn't too bad.'

'Not too bad,' she replied, not wanting to admit her head was pounding and sleeping for the rest of the day seemed like the perfect plan. 'Flynn, I meant it when I said thank you for all this, and the flowers, they were stunning. It was a fantastic evening.' Without thinking about it, Julia leant forward and placed a soft kiss on his cheek.

'What was that for?' he asked softly, his lips dangerously close to hers.

'For making my birthday the best,' her voice wavered, exhilarated by the electricity between them.

'I'll see you later,' he murmured, still holding her gaze.

'You will.'

Leaning against the door frame Julia wrapped her arms around her body and watched Flynn disappear up the path towards the woodlands. Never for a second did she ever think she would be thanking Flynn Carter for the best birthday. It's funny how you never know what is round the corner, and Julia was first to admit she'd massively misjudged Flynn when she'd first bumped back into him after all that time – but now Julia was looking forward to bumping into him a little more. Her heart gave a little leap at the very thought.

Chapter Twenty

I t was a quarter to seven and Julia and Callie moseyed through the grand entrance of Starcross Manor. Callie marvelled at the beauty of the place. Last night when they'd arrived it had been dark, but now in the early evening light she stood and took in the beauty of it all. 'Okay, I can see why you might have been worried about the future of the B&B, this place is magnificent!'

'And tonight, everyone will find out about our arrangement and what Flynn has planned for them. I can't wait to see everyone's faces.' Julia pushed open the door and Callie stepped inside and whistled.

'I feel like I'm trespassing inside a royal palace or somewhere. Look at this place. So this is what a five-star hotel looks like.'

Julia noticed a sign with an arrow in front of the grand reception desk. 'The meeting is through there,' she pointed to the double doors to the right of the reception. As they walked through the foyer and followed the arrows Julia heard the sound of water. She smiled as she noticed the floor-standing fountain in exactly the place she had suggested. The water was cascading into a small pool at the foot of the fountain. It was stunning, the sound of water soothing, and the perfect centrepiece for the room.

The signs led them to a room Julia hadn't been in before. It was a typical conference room with rows and rows of chairs facing a small stage and a lonely microphone on a stand right in the middle of it. Along the back wall was a long table full of cups and saucers next to aluminium urns with a wide selection of teas, coffees, and plates of biscuits. The windows were again floor to ceiling with magnificent regal-like drapes framing the windows.

Eleni had saved them a couple of seats a few rows from the front. Everyone from the village was there waiting in anticipation to find out what Flynn had to say. Julia felt a little guilty knowing exactly what was going on, especially when she noticed a red-faced Hamish armed with a notepad and pen – even though she'd managed to talk him into doing the right thing regarding the contractors, he obviously wasn't going to let anyone walk all over him. As soon as Flynn stepped into the room the babble of voices died down and everyone quickly became seated.

Julia's eyes were fixed on Flynn as he walked onto the stage and stood poised in front of the microphone. Looking like he'd just walked off a catwalk, he oozed class wearing a modern, classic pin-dot weave wool blazer slipped over a two-tone striped crew neckline tee – a relaxed take on business wear, but sophisticated and sexy.

'He does scrub up well, doesn't he?' whispered Callie in Julia's ear, and she wasn't going to disagree. 'I'll enjoy working for him when I do get the job.'

Julia nudged Callie's arm. 'You are full of yourself.'

'You better pray I do get that job, because then I won't be under your feet.'

'Can't wait,' Julia rolled her eyes playfully. It was great to have Callie back and of course Julia had everything crossed that Callie did get the job if it meant she was sticking around for a while.

'Thank you all for coming,' Flynn looked around the room and acknowledged everyone with a nod of the head. 'I bet you are all wondering why I've invited you here this evening, so I'll cut to the chase and won't leave you all hanging on. I'm here to put your minds at rest,' he took a breath and looked directly at Julia who felt herself blush. 'Starcross Manor is not here to jeopardise anyone's business; in fact, quite the opposite. I want to work with you all to make our businesses the best they can be. I want to support the community the best I can. Last week, I had a meeting with Julia Coleman and Julia kindly pointed out to me the uncertainty that surrounded the opening of Starcross Manor. It is my belief we can work together, and I would really like to become a part of this fantastic community in Heartcross. I do believe there is enough room and business in this village for all of us.' Flynn took a breath and looked down at the piece of paper in his hand.

Julia took a swift glance around the room and all eyes were on Flynn, he was holding their attention.

'Firstly, I have one of the best chefs – world-famous Andrew Glossop – cooking up a storm in my kitchen here at Starcross Manor. We believe in only the best fresh local ingredients and produce, so I'm proposing, if it's okay with you...' Flynn looked over towards Drew and Isla. 'That you can supply all of the meats, eggs, milk, cheese and potatoes on a daily basis to this hotel.'

By the look on Drew's face it was more than alright. 'That will be very lucrative,' muttered Isla, looking impressed.

'And I believe you make the best sausages.'

'You better believe it,' replied Drew, looking very proud.

'Hamish,' Flynn scanned the room. 'I believe you grow the best fruit, veg and herbs from the allotments, so we would like to work with yourself to supply seasonal fruits and veg.'

Immediately, Hamish's face softened, and he nodded his appreciation.

'Also, the shop here at Starcross Manor will work with you and will get all our supplies of newspapers and fizzy drinks from you, so that the village shop will continue to grow and flourish.'

Everyone burst into a round of applause. It reminded Julia of a political speech. Flynn was just about to be elected by the whole of the community. He carried on with such charisma, he had the village hooked on his every word. 'I believe only the best cream teas will ever come from

Bonnie's teashop, so I would like to propose we double your afternoon orders and you supply Starcross Manor.'

Felicity looked towards her mum and they both turned back towards Flynn. 'I'm proposing we extend Bonnie's teashop into the café here at Starcross. Any cakes and scones will be made by yourselves and sold here.'

Rona was beaming and nudged Felicity. 'Perfect.'

Felicity bit down on her lip and nodded at her mum, knowing the potential to supply the hotel could be a huge boost to their income.

'Each bedroom here at Starcross will hold an information pack, which will include any local business in this community – walk-with-alpaca days, roast dinners at the Grouse and Haggis...' Flynn searched the crowd for Fraser and Meredith. 'And I'd like to talk to you about supplying the local ales to our restaurants, too.'

Fraser gave Flynn a look of gratitude.

'As you know, this hotel offers numerous facilities, including the spa, swimming pool, gym, golf course... that really sounds like I'm boasting now,' he rolled his eyes then focused back on track. 'I want you as residents of Heartcross and your families to make use of these facilities. These will not just be for the guests, but for all of you, at heavily discounted prices, and that goes for all the guests at the B&B, and all the guests staying at Foxglove Farm, too.'

There was a ripple of approval all around the room.

'There will special discounts for villagers at the restaurants, for beauty treatments and the spa, and this will also include all water sports at the Boathouse when it opens. My dad Wilbur is currently passing out a printed sheet with all the details.'

Flynn carried on talking about all the benefits of the hotel and the events he had planned throughout the year too.

'He can't take his eyes off you,' Callie whispered. 'Do you notice he keeps looking over in your direction?'

Julia had noticed, and each time she found her body erupting in goose bumps.

'Please, please do come and have a chat with me about anything that is worrying you, and you have my word we will work together as a community to find a solution. Finally, I'd just like to give a special mention to Julia Coleman.'

All heads turned towards Julia who felt an instant blush to her cheeks.

'Julia kindly pointed out to me all the fabulous things your businesses have to offer and how we can all work together. So a huge thanks should go to her too.' Flynn held out his arms and began clapping, the whole room followed suit.

There was a buzz in the air, everyone was happy. Julia knew offering the use of the facilities at Starcross Manor was going to boost her bookings and profits. This was a win–win situation for her, but Flynn had really excelled himself and had been brilliant standing up there. He'd gone out of his way to put everyone at ease and had won the hearts of the villagers. Julia had no doubt he was going to fit in very well with village life.

'And on a final note,' Flynn raised his voice to gain everyone's attention, 'the Boathouse will be open for business next weekend and in two weeks' time I will be holding a garden party here at Starcross Manor to celebrate the official opening and would be honoured if you could all join me.'

'I wouldn't miss it for the world, boss,' Callie gave a little salute and Julia couldn't help but smile at her cousin's confidence about landing the job when she hadn't even gone for the interview yet.

Flynn stepped away from the microphone, and Julia watched as he began to shake hands with the villagers. She watched as he stood talking to Drew and Isla, and smiled to herself. Drew really could launch his sausages worldwide if he started supplying all of Flynn's hotels. She knew too that she had a lot to thank Flynn for. Her B&B could have been make-or-break but Flynn had decided to work with the community to help make everyone's business the best they possibly could be.

Everyone was on a high, the room was charged with excitement and possibilities, everyone looked relieved. 'That's a turn-up for the books isn't it,' Isla joined Julia. 'Drew is beyond excited, and offering our guests all the facilities here... you did well negotiating those deals.'

'It's going to be fantastic for everyone,' replied Julia casting a glance over in Flynn's direction. Finally, the crowd around him had been begun to ebb away.

'Will you excuse me for a minute, I just want to say thanks to Flynn myself.' Julia made her way over towards him. She also owed him an apology. The revelation regarding Anais was at the forefront of her mind and she couldn't believe she'd fallen for her lies. 'Flynn,' Julia tapped him on his shoulder. 'On behalf of us all I want to say thank you,' she said as he spun round.

'You are very welcome. I hope everyone's minds are at rest.' Flynn touched her elbow sending a spark of electricity through her body.

'Flynn, I need to speak to you. I know, I got you all wrong…' Julia looked over her shoulder, this wasn't the time to get into a conversation about Anais but she wanted to make it clear that she needed to apologise. 'I need to apologise.'

But Julia didn't have time to say any more, Flynn's phone was ringing. 'Are you in a rush to get home?' he asked, looking at the number on his phone. 'I really need to take this.'

'No, no rush.'

'Andrew is through there,' Flynn nodded towards the door. 'I'll be with you in five minutes max.'

Julia walked towards the door and on the other side she was amazed to discover a balcony that resembled something from a French château. There was a wrought-iron bistro table and chairs with a bottle of Chablis chilling in the middle of the table. Andrew was sipping a glass of wine and looking out over the stunning view, a view that looked across at the lawns.

'Hi,' said Julia causing Andrew to look up.

Andrew smiled. 'How are you? Is the village on side?

Flynn negotiates million-pound deals but I've never seen him so nervous as tonight.'

'May I?' Julia touched the chair.

'Of course, join me.' Andrew gestured for Julia to take a seat.

'Nervous? Was he really nervous?' Julia couldn't imagine Flynn ever being nervous.

'Petrified. Those villagers have some clout. Never in all his time have a group of villagers been able to shut down his contractors within twenty-four hours. It's one hell of a powerful community.'

Julia grinned. 'It is that. Thankfully, they all now think he's wonderful.'

'That's good, otherwise I would be out of a job. Glass of wine?' Andrew nodded towards the bottle chilling in the middle of the table.

'Perfect,' replied Julia, looking out at the view.

As Andrew began to pour the wine, Flynn appeared at the side of the table.

'I'm glad that's over! How do you think it went?' He looked towards Julia.

'You had them eating out of your hand,' she replied with a smile.

'Honestly, when I walked into the room, the look I got from Hamish...'

'But you charmed him. And his vegetables have won prizes.'

'Really?' Flynn raised an eyebrow.

'Oh yes, he wins the best marrow every year at the

Heartcross Summer Fair,' she grinned. 'Because no one else grows marrows.'

'Very funny,' replied Flynn.

'I'm going to leave you pair to it, I have a buffet to plan,' Andrew stood up. 'Have a lovely rest of the evening,' he said before walking off.

'How's the hangover?' asked Flynn, pulling out a chair and sitting down.

'Better. Thanks again for everything you did for me last night. It was a brilliant birthday.' Julia took a breath. 'But actually, I need to apologise to you.'

'Apologise? You didn't get reckless in the log cabins, did you?'

'Ha, no,' Julia flicked her hair over her shoulder and nervously looked into his eyes.

'You've gone all serious on me,' he noticed. 'What's the matter?'

'Flynn, I'm so sorry. When I told everyone you were untrustworthy, I was wrong and mistaken. Can you forgive me?' blurted Julia, feeling awful about her actions.

'I wasn't happy, believe me, but I thought we'd put all that behind us?'

'I know and we have, but I know I was wrong. I've been a total idiot.' Julia explained how Callie had turned up and revealed the truth about Anais.

Once Julia had finished talking, Flynn poured himself a glass of wine.

'I have to admit that morning in your kitchen, I was

fuming,' declared Flynn. 'It was like my past had come back to haunt me, and I had no way of proving any of it. I was dumbfounded when you told me that she actually cut up the wedding dress.' Flynn blew out a breath and raked his hand through his hair. 'She really was something wasn't she?'

'She really was, I feel like I never knew her at all,' admitted Julia, disappointed in herself for not taking a person as she found them and judging them on someone else's opinion.

'I let someone into my life that I thought I'd fallen in love with and they tried to take advantage of me, and I've been very wary of people ever since, if I'm truly honest. I disappeared off social media due to the online abuse from her so-called friends and family. I couldn't believe what I was reading,' he took a breath, the hurt on his face was clearly visible. 'The things they called me, accused me of having an affair, I was bewildered by it all. I didn't even know where any of that information had come from, but I soon realised it must have been the lies spun by Anais to save face after I'd discovered their plan to try and rip me off. It was one of the worst times of my life.'

Julia remained silent and listened as Flynn continued, 'There had been no grand gesture on my part to get down on one knee, Anais actually asked me to marry her. I said it was all too soon. We moved in together first, and she convinced me that it was never too soon if you felt the person you had met was the right one. I felt humiliated I'd fallen for the whole scheme. I wanted the ground to swallow me up. All I could do was take myself away and heal in my own time.'

'I'm so sorry Flynn, I really am.'

'It's not your fault. Now you can understand what a brilliant con-artist she is, she had you fooled too.'

Julia nodded, Flynn was right. The performance she'd put on the morning of the wedding was outstanding and believable.

'I honestly never thought I'd ever hear that woman's name again, or ever wanted to.'

Julia nodded. 'How did you discover her plan?'

Flynn sat back in his chair and rolled his eyes. 'Just by luck if I'm truly honest. I had no clue what she was up to. I believed everything she said to me. I hadn't been sleeping well and I wasn't sure whether it was down to the pressures of work etc. So I set up an app to record my sleeping activity and placed the iPad next to my bed. I'd gone downstairs to make a drink, answered a few important emails and then went to sleep. The next morning Anais had left for work and I noticed the app had recorded activity before I'd climbed into bed. I clicked on it to discover her conversation with the fraudster she was having an affair with, and that's when I decided to draw up a pre-nup which I knew she wouldn't sign. She kept thinking I would change my mind, but I still hadn't changed my mind on the wedding day, and that's why she did what she did. What I wasn't counting on was the fact she tried to slur my name and reputation. I was the victim, not her. However, what's the saying? What doesn't kill you makes you stronger.'

Julia exhaled. 'I'm so sorry. I wish…'

'Julia, I would rather put everything behind us. All this is in the past and that's where I would like it to stay.'

'Can we start again… again?' suggested Julia.

'That sounds like the best plan to me,' replied Flynn. He turned to look at the view. 'I'd never get bored of looking at that view. It's magnificent.'

'I know what you mean.'

'Would you possibly be free tomorrow afternoon?' Flynn's voice sounded a little nervous.

'Yes, I could possibly be,' replied Julia, intrigued. 'Why, what are you thinking?'

Flynn swallowed. 'Would you like to come out on a date with me?' he asked hopefully.

'A date…' Julia bit down on her lip.

'Don't feel you have to,' Flynn cut in quickly as Julia hesitated to answer.

'I'd love to,' she replied, nervously fiddling with her watch strap.

'One o'clock tomorrow, meet me at the Boathouse.'

'It's a date!' she replied, giving him a darting glance before her mouth broke out into a silly grin.

Chapter Twenty-One

'Apparently Jack said Flynn's hoping to expand into hiring out mountain bikes, he's surprised with all the mountainous terrain that no one has jumped at that idea sooner, and it would fit in perfectly at the Boathouse... are you listening to me?' Eleni shouted across the landing to Julia. 'And then there's plans for the steam-powered cruise, it's going to launch from the Boathouse, takes you down the river and sails around Heartcross Castle.'

Still there was no answer from Julia. Eleni put down her duster and poked her head around Julia's door. 'Am I talking to myself? Woah! What's going on here and where's Callie?'

Julia was sitting on her bed amongst a pile of clothes looking hot and frustrated. 'My clothes seem to be getting smaller every time I try them on, and Callie has gone exploring with Woody, she's checking out Heartcross.'

Eleni chuckled. 'With the calories we burn on a daily

basis you'd honestly think we would be stick-thin. That's a hell of a lot of clothes that don't fit you.'

'You are stick-thin! And I can't find anything suitable to wear, well not suitable for a date with Flynn. Look at all these, so dowdy.'

'There's got to be something,' reassured Eleni, picking up a couple of items then raising her eyebrows. 'And presumably you are going to do something with your hair?' Julia's hair was scraped back in its usual ponytail.

Julia brought her hand up to her hair. 'What's wrong with my hair?' she asked, sounding a little hurt and taking a quick glance in the mirror.

'When was the last time you ever had your hair styled, or even had the split ends cut off?' Eleni flicked the bottom of her hair. 'Those split ends have splits on splits.'

Julia couldn't actually remember the last time she went to the hairdressers. She found it a chore heading over to Glensheil just for a haircut and always found other stuff she could be doing. Julia was one for simplicity, she didn't have time to style her hair each morning; all she ever did was wash it, then for practicality tie it up in a ponytail.

'I *do* dye my hair,' Julia replied in her defence, 'those grey hairs keep creeping back in every six weeks, but I suppose that's about as far as it goes.'

'You can't go off for a hot date with straggly ends and your hair scraped back in a ponytail. At least make some effort.' Eleni began to mess with Julia's hair. 'I think you should have it cut just above your shoulders, give it some life. I'll get the kitchen scissors.' Eleni sniggered.

'Do *not* cut my hair,' Julia ordered, but couldn't help but smile at Eleni's suggestion.

Julia risked a second look in the mirror and gave a theatrical sigh. 'You are right, I need to do something with it,' she flicked it outwards. 'And I do need to be taking better care of myself, but there's no chance I'm going to get this cut by 1pm this afternoon.'

Eleni bit down on her lip then pointed at Julia. 'Maybe, just maybe… get yourself downstairs. I'll be with you in five.'

Julia had no clue what was going on in Eleni's mind as she bounded towards the door and back across the landing.

A couple of minutes later Julia was nervously sitting in the kitchen. Eleni returned dragging Petra behind her, who was a regular at the B&B and had only arrived this morning. Petra was a sales director who frequented Glensheil at least six times a year, but who preferred the quiet side of the bridge and adored Julia's B&B.

'Petra used to be a hairdresser,' announced Eleni triumphantly.

'Really?' quizzed Julia, wondering how Eleni would even know this.

'I did indeed, and am still handy with my scissors,' replied Petra, reaching inside her bag. She pulled out a red velvet wrap tied up with a ribbon. Inside was a brush, a comb and the shiniest pair of scissors Julia had ever set eyes on.

'And you still take your scissors everywhere you go?' asked Julia, amazed.

'Not usually, but the girls in the office wanted their hair cut this week.'

'This is meant to be. But you need to go and wash your hair – hurry, we haven't got much time,' Eleni ordered, looking rather pleased with herself.

Ten minutes later and feeling a little nervous, Julia sat down on the chair and Petra whipped an old towel around her shoulders. She brushed through Julia's hair then clearly announced she had never seen split ends like it, leaving Julia mortified.

'I think we need quite a few inches off this to spring it back into life so it starts looking healthy again,' announced Petra, taking control of the situation.

'Really that much?' Julia wasn't liking the sound of that, and was beginning to feel nervous.

'Yes really, it needs a really good cut,' confirmed Petra.

'Above the shoulders… look, this would suit you.' Eleni, who had been Googling the latest trends, swung her phone towards Julia.

'I think you are forgetting, I do not look like that model and I'm about twenty years older,' argued Julia.

'I disagree, I think with your heart-shaped face that look will really suit you.' Petra was now standing in front of Julia pulling down her wet hair around her face to level it out.

Eleni excitedly clapped her hands together. 'Go on, you will look amazing.'

'Okay, okay but not too short,' Julia finally agreed, and Eleni let out a squeal.

Petra got to work, and masses of Julia's hair fell to the

floor. Julia couldn't look and kept her eyes closed. For the first time in a long time her hair was now resting just above her shoulders.

Fifteen minutes later Petra switched off the hairdryer and walked in front of Julia blasting hairspray all over her. 'Stop!' said Julia, choking on the spray.

'All done!' Petra stood back and admired her work. 'You look FAB-U-LOUS!' she strung out the word. 'What do you think?' she turned towards Eleni.

However, Julia was panic-stricken at all the hair strewn all over the floor. 'Please tell me I *do* have hair left and *don't* look ridiculous.'

Eleni was beaming. 'Honestly, you look amazing!'

Just at that second the back door swung open and in walked Callie. 'Oh my God, what have they done to you?' On her face was a look of horror then she burst out laughing. 'Only joking! You look so different... stunning in fact. It really suits you.'

Petra held the mirror in front of Julia. 'Take a look yourself, what do you think?'

It took a second for Julia to even recognise herself, when she saw the face of a pretty girl staring back at her. 'It looks so different,' she said amazed, finally tearing her eyes away from the reflection. 'It just doesn't look like me. I absolutely love it.' Julia couldn't stop swishing her hair from side to side.

'It's taken years off you!' added Eleni. 'It really does suit you.'

'Thank you so much Petra, what do I owe you?' gushed

Julia, standing up and brushing the loose hair from her body. She walked over to her bag and pulled out her purse.

Petra put up her hand. 'You owe me nothing, it was my pleasure.'

'Are you sure?' asked Julia, looking in the mirror once more, still mesmerised by her appearance.

'I'm more than happy to help. Enjoy your date.'

'Thank you, thank you so much.'

Eleni began to sweep up the hair from the floor. 'I can't get over it, you look like a different person.'

Julia felt different, in fact she felt like a million dollars. She was surprised how different a haircut could make her look and feel.

'Now for your make-up and clothes,' suggested Eleni, putting the broom back in the cupboard.

'As long as you don't make me look like a clown.'

Eleni was undeterred. 'Now there's an idea, what do you reckon Callie?' Eleni giggled. She reached inside her bag and brought out her make-up bag then tipped the contents onto the table. 'Okay we need subtle, we need natural.'

'And it's hot out there again today. I'll go and have a look through your clothes, between us all we'll get you sorted,' Callie disappeared out of the kitchen and headed for Julia's bedroom.

Eleni ordered her to sit on the chair in the middle of the kitchen. Julia couldn't help but smile at the concentration on her face. 'You look so serious.'

'This is serious. How you feeling about your date?' probed Eleni.

'Nervous... excited, I just hope I don't make an idiot of myself somehow.' Julia was looking forward to the afternoon. The weather was glorious and the only details she knew were to meet Flynn at the Boathouse at 1pm and that he was bringing lunch.

'Now keep as still as possible, otherwise you will end up looking like a clown,' Eleni teased as she switched on the radio and set to work.

Fifteen minutes later, Eleni stood back and studied Julia's face like she was a professional make-up artist. 'Mmm, I just need to blend the eye shadow.' Eleni narrowed her eyes. 'There, I think you are all done.' Eleni handed Julia the mirror and waited for the verdict.

For the second time today, Julia stared at her reflection and did a double take. She tilted her head from side to side. 'Is that really me?' she asked open-mouthed. 'I look...'

'You look smoking!' interrupted Eleni, really pleased with her efforts, 'even if I do say so myself.'

In a matter of an hour Julia was transformed and amazed by the results. 'You have actually made me look quite decent.'

'Did you doubt me?' asked Eleni putting her hands on her hips.

'Maybe, just a little,' replied Julia, with a grin. 'All I need now is some clothes.'

Julia and Eleni walked back upstairs and into her bedroom to witness Callie stumbling across a clothes mountain. 'Do you never clear out your wardrobe? And what the hell is this?' Callie held up some sort of baggy brown tweed dress. 'This needs to go, no arguments.'

Julia wasn't about to argue. She couldn't ever remember sorting out her clothes, they'd just hung there, year after year. Half the stuff she couldn't even remember buying in the first place.

Callie took control and threw it on top of a pile of clothes already on the floor. 'That pile there is for the charity. And what is this?' Callie looked amazed at the garment she was now holding up in her hands.

Immediately Julia took the oversized pantaloons from Callie's hand and threw them down in the growing charity pile on the floor. 'They were all the rage once you know!'

'Put these on with that T-shirt... simple but stunning,' ordered Callie, handing Julia a pair of skinny jeans with a simple pale blue T-shirt.

Julia held up the jeans, they looked like they'd shrunk and she couldn't remember the last time she'd tried to squeeze into them. Whipping off her jogging bottoms she sat on the edge of the bed and pulled the jeans onto her ankles. 'I'm not sure I'm going to get these on!' She stood up and attempted to pull them over her thighs. Julia forced some jollity into her voice, 'I'm going to die if I wear these, I can't even fasten them.'

Much to Callie's and Eleni's amusement Julia lay on the floor and wriggled and writhed, pulling and tugging until the jeans were around her waist. The tightness of the denim felt like it was about to cut off her circulation.

'OMG! Pull them off me, I can't breathe, I'm overheating.'

Laughing, Eleni and Callie took a leg each and pulled with all their might, toppling over onto the pile of clothes on the floor.

'Okay, no jeans, maybe just a simple pair of shorts, that T-shirt and a pair of Birkenstocks.' Callie threw her a pair of denim shorts. 'Let's keep it simple and classy.'

With ten minutes to go, Julia set off from the B&B with a handful of cheers from Callie and Eleni as she strolled down the path. This had been the first date she'd been on in a while, and she felt nervous.

With her new hair swishing from side to side Julia clutched the duffle bag over her shoulder stuffed with a swimsuit and a towel, and waltzed down towards the river oozing confidence. She felt like a new woman. Why hadn't she had her hair styled sooner? Her face was beaming, her heartbeat racing and she tried to imagine the day ahead. For the first time in a long time she felt good about herself and pressed her lips tightly together to suppress her smile. It was only a five-minute walk to the Boathouse and as she ambled along the path at the edge of the river she stopped in her tracks and lifted up her sunglasses to stare. The river looked like a mini St Tropez, with boats of all shapes and sizes bobbing on the water. Julia noticed the Boathouse had been painted and stacked up outside were paddleboards and canoes, and floating on the water outside the Boathouse was the most magnificent yacht Julia had ever set eyes on – and there was Flynn waving straight at her from the deck.

'Wow!' Julia muttered under her breath. 'That doesn't look like a cheap specimen.'

'It's not!'

Julia spun round to see Jack standing behind her.

'Where did you come from?' she held her hand to her chest. 'You made me jump.'

'Sorry! I've just dropped off the lunch for Flynn – and you're right, that yacht isn't cheap, it's worth over a quarter of a million,' continued Jack. 'It's an absolute beauty.'

'That's bigger than some of the houses in the village, including my B&B,' exclaimed Julia, her eyes still firmly fixed on the boat.

'That boat is everything a boater wants – beauty, function and performance. The cockpit is smartly executed, a double adjustable helm, a portside lounge, state-of-the-art audio and flat-screen TVs, it's the finest of the finest on the water.' Jack was in awe, he sounded like a salesman as he reeled off all the features. 'And you get to be the first one that sails in her today.'

Julia was completely taken by surprise, she wasn't expecting anything of this magnitude; she was expecting more of a tiny speedboat, this was something the rich and famous owned – but then again, thinking about it, Flynn was a successful property developer. 'All I know is that boat is worth more than the value of my B&B, and the extension I'm building.'

Jack laughed. 'You mean the extension that *I'm* building. Now go and enjoy yourself.'

Julia carried on walking along the path and noticed

Flynn had left the boat and was now walking towards her. He looked casual but handsome dressed in a white T-shirt and a pair of navy smart shorts, Julia couldn't take her eyes off him.

Flynn's smile was wide. 'Your hair,' he noticed straight away, 'you've done something different with your hair. It really suits you. You look amazing,' he said, holding out his hand to help Julia over the rocky ground, the touch of his skin sending shockwaves through her body. Her heart gave a little leap when he stepped forward and pressed a kiss to her cheek.

'Thank you,' she replied, catching a whiff of his inherently spicy masculine fragrance. For a brief moment she closed her eyes and inhaled, there was something about a man's scent that caused her to feel a warm fuzzy feeling inside.

'Are you ready to set sail?'

'We are actually going to sail? I thought we were going to have lunch on the boat?'

'Absolutely, we are going to set sail. I'm taking you to a very special place for lunch.'

Inside Julia began to panic a little. She'd only ever been on a boat once in her life and it hadn't gone well. As a child her parents had taken them on a family holiday to France, which was an extravagant treat back then. Julia remembered that ferry crossing like it was only yesterday and could still remember the swirling motion sickness she'd endured. She'd spent the whole crossing bent down with her head in a paper bag as the travel sickness took over her life for a few hours. Even when she finally stepped off the boat she could still feel herself rocking. Julia prayed to God that she didn't go throwing up in front of Flynn Carter – the sheer embarrassment.

Flynn was still holding Julia's hand as they walked along the wooden jetty. He finally let go when they got to the end and he pointed towards the tied bottle of champagne that was hanging down on the side of the boat.

Julia looked puzzled.

'I know I'm not in the navy, but this is the first official outing of this boat and I do love this tradition.'

'I'd be too worried about chipping the paintwork and not to mention the waste of champagne.'

Flynn grinned. 'Go on, grab the bottle.'

Julia brought her hand up to her chest. 'Me? You want me to smash it.'

'Why not? I can't think of a better person. Go on,' he encouraged. Flynn stood on the edge of the jetty and leaned forward to grab the rope.

For a split second Julia hesitated, then grasped hold of the bottle from Flynn. 'This is an absolute first for me, I've never launched a boat before,' she revealed, feeling a sudden sense of importance. 'And what's the boat called?' asked Julia, her eyes scanning the side of the boat.

'*Starcross*,' replied Flynn.

Julia took a deep breath, she hadn't got a clue what to say but then remembered a line she'd once seen in a movie. 'I name this ship *Starcross*, and may she bring fair winds and good fortune to all who sail on her.' Julia swung the bottle and brought her hands up to her head. To her amazement the bottle didn't smash, it bounced.

Flynn stifled a laugh.

'Oh my gosh, the bloody thing is plastic,' remarked Julia, hooting with laughter and playfully swiping Flynn's arm. 'And here was me panicking that I wouldn't have enough wellie to smash the thing.'

'Sorry, I couldn't resist. Did you honestly think I would chip my paintwork?' he gave her a cheeky wink. 'Let's get you on board and you can have a glass of the real stuff.' Flynn took her hand in his and helped her onto the deck of the boat. 'Are you ready to set sail?' he asked.

'Aye aye Captain,' she saluted. 'I'm more than ready.'

Chapter Twenty-Two

The *Starcross* was not just an ordinary run-of-the-mill kind of boat, it was more like a mini mansion on water, with all its mod cons and leather upholstery. In her head Julia pretended she was a Bond girl about to accompany her 007 on a secret mission. It oozed expense and class. She'd never seen anything like it. There was a separate deck up above on the roof, and another at the back of the boat. There was a champagne bar, a TV larger than the local cinema screen, and oversized white leather seats. So this was what it was like to be a millionaire, with expensive toys and champagne on tap.

'This is amazing; you really have done so well for yourself,' exclaimed Julia, admiring her surroundings.

'Thank you... shall we?' Flynn gestured towards the front of the boat. 'Let's get her started and on our way, then we can pour you a drink.'

Julia followed Flynn over to a wooden crate which he opened and pulled out a life jacket.

'Don't worry, it's just a precaution. You are precious cargo, and I don't want anything happening to you.'

This declaration from Flynn was met with a flip from Julia's stomach that had nothing to do with the fact they were on a boat. He'd just said she was precious cargo, and Julia quite liked that.

'Here let me help you on with it,' offered Flynn, holding out the jacket as Julia slipped her arms into it. She turned to face him and felt her heart pound as Flynn leaned in extra close and with a short sharp tug zipped up the life jacket.

'How does that feel?'

'Snug,' she replied. 'Very snug.'

'Good,' he said, not making eye contact. 'That's exactly how it needs to feel.' Next, he grabbed the buckles and pulled the first one in tight. Julia inhaled.

'Just breathe normally,' he said, moving on to the second buckle.

Julia observed the concentration on his face. She noticed he was biting down on his lip, which she found quite sexy. Trying to avert her gaze was unsuccessful, she couldn't take her eyes off him. This wasn't helped in the slightest by the scent of his aftershave again, which was beginning to stir up feelings inside her. Flynn pulled in the last buckle causing Julia to gasp, bringing her back down to earth.

'Sorry, is that too tight?'

'It just took my breath away for a second,' she admitted.

She couldn't help but notice both the amusement and

challenge in his eyes, which bore into hers and Julia dropped her gaze to his lips. She couldn't help it.

'Shall we get this show on the road, or this boat on the river?' He took her hand and led her to the two black leather-bound seats surrounded by numerous dials and levers on an oak wooden dashboard, which reminded her of a cockpit on a plane. 'How do you know what you are doing?' she asked, sliding into one of the seats. 'It all looks so complicated.'

'It's simple really, all you do is put the key in the ignition.'

'Really?'

'Yes really!'

Julia was mesmerised, it didn't look as simple as that to her. She watched Flynn take out the key and insert it into the ignition; it really was just like starting a car. 'Are you ready?'

Julia felt a tiny surge of excitement and trepidation. 'I think so!'

As they left the tiny bay and picked up speed, the boat bumped along the river. Julia's hair began to waft in the breeze. The boat was beginning to slap the waves hard now with each fall, and Flynn checked whether she was feeling sick, but Julia was far from feeling sick, she was enjoying every minute of it. There were no other boats on the river and their only witnesses were the gulls that were circulating above in the clear blue sky.

'You may need sun cream on,' suggested Flynn, 'because of the breeze you think it's not that hot, but believe me, an hour later you'll look like a lobster and won't be able to move your neck and shoulders. I get caught out all of the time.'

Luckily, Julia had already coated her neck and arms with sun cream before she left. The boat was now incredibly fast-moving. Each time it hit a wave Julia let out a peal of laughter, the rush reminding her of when she was a little girl on a fairground ride.

'As soon as we turn that next corner' – Flynn nodded, and Julia followed his eyes – 'it will become a lot calmer. Don't forget to keep hydrated, the sun is very hot today.' Flynn pressed a button in front of him and at the side of Julia's seat a lid popped up, causing her to jump.

'Water,' he said.

'Wow! I feel like I'm in a movie,' she said, taking the bottle of water.

Flynn smiled at her. 'Now sit back and enjoy the view.'

That's exactly what Julia had been doing, she'd kept snagging a glance at Flynn's tanned forearms steering the boat, but after giving herself a secret smile she sipped her drink and focused on the water around them ahead. Everywhere was so peaceful, Julia had never ventured up this stretch of river. They cruised past a number of glorious bays that Julia didn't recognise or even know existed. There were children splashing at the water's edge and dog-walkers ambling along some of the coastal paths. They sailed past harbours and attractive villages with colourful houses, followed by greater expanses of sand and taller cliffs, with impressive views, the coastline becoming more indented with coves and estuaries.

'I feel like I've been transported back to my childhood,' admitted Julia, her eyes wide, taking in the view.

'What do you mean?' Flynn asked, slowing down the boat.

'Look at all those secret coves, I feel like I'm in a *Famous Five* novel.'

'They are impressive, aren't they?'

'I'm not sure we are even in Scotland; this scenery is so spectacular I feel like actually I should be in Switzerland or somewhere.'

'It's pretty special, isn't it?' Flynn gave her a sideward glance and held her gaze.

The way he stared, the warmness of his words, made Julia's whole body tingle. 'Okay,' he said, slowing the boat right down. 'We are nearly there.'

Taking Julia by surprise, Flynn steered the boat slowly through numerous weeping willows that hung over the water's edge and manoeuvred it carefully around a cluster of rocks. This looked like a private driveway on water. The *Starcross* trod calm water whilst Julia took in the view. The white rugged cliffs overhung, protecting a tiny secluded beach of sparkling beige sand. Julia breathed, 'Beautiful.'

Carefully, Flynn guided the boat to the tiny jetty and directly in front of them stood a house that wouldn't have looked out of place on the French Riviera. Julia recognised the place from the photo that she'd seen in Andrew's room at the B&B. Flynn, Andrew and another man had been posing outside.

'This place is gorgeous,' Julia said, awestruck. She couldn't take her eyes off the beauty all around her.

'It sure is, isn't it?' replied Flynn.

Julia watched as he securely tied up the *Starcross* then he made his way back over towards her.

'You can take the life jacket off now, if you want?' he suggested, taking the key out of the ignition.

She exhaled. 'Yes I want!' immediately unclipping the buckles and packing it away in the box.

'Have you brought a swimsuit with you?' he asked, reaching for a couple of towels that were folded neatly on a shelf.

'I have,' she held up her duffle bag.

'There's a bedroom and bathroom through there. If you want to get changed.'

Julia was curious to see what the bedroom on this magnificent boat was like, and she pushed open the door and stepped into a room that felt more spacious than her actual bedroom at home. The décor reminded her of a hotel room. There was a double bed with white linen, built-in wardrobes, a TV attached to the wall, a chest of drawers, a sofa and coffee-maker on top of the dressing table. At the far end of the room was another door leading to an en suite bathroom. Risking a tentative look in the mirror she was horrified: the tip of her nose was already bright red and there wasn't a scrap of makeup left in sight. Flynn had been right about the sun cream. With the coastal breeze she hadn't felt herself burning at all. Quickly she reached in her bag and tried to calm down the redness by dabbing a little foundation on the edge of her nose, but it really didn't make that much difference.

Returning to the bedroom Julia kicked off her Birkenstocks and got changed into her swimsuit, pulling her shorts back on over the top. When she stepped back onto the deck Flynn was waiting on the jetty. He'd changed into a pair of swimming shorts too.

'Where are we?' asked Julia, focusing on the view in front of her and taking in the beauty all around. There wasn't another soul in sight and it really felt like she was stranded on a desert island. 'Whoa! Look at that!'

Flynn smiled as Julia watched the water cascading down the mountainside which ran into the bay.

'It's utterly breath-taking,' she murmured. 'It's like a secret hide-away.' Julia stepped down from the jetty. Her feet found the sandy sea bottom as she paddled at the edge of the shallow water. 'I feel like I should be on holiday.'

Flynn joined her, the water gently lapping around their ankles. 'Welcome to The Lakehouse,' he said proudly. 'This is my next project.'

Julia's eyes grew wide. 'And The Lakehouse is...'

'A soon-to-be restaurant with its own private bay. The only way in and out is by Carter's water taxis. This is going to be the place everyone is talking about. Reservations will be booked months in advance and you are the first person I've ever brought here – well except for Andrew and my brand-new Italian chef Gianni.' Flynn snaked his arms around Julia's waist and they both took in the white building standing in front of them, with its old-fashioned shutters, purple wisteria and pink roses tumbling all around the doorway. Up on the roof Julia noticed the balcony with table and chairs overlooking the secluded water.

'It is absolutely beautiful,' she said, still taking it all in.

'Do you want to see inside?'

'Of course!'

Hand-in-hand they walked across the sand towards The Lakehouse. Julia wondered how Flynn had even discovered this place of outstanding beauty in the middle of nowhere. She imagined sitting on the roof terrace sharing a candle-lit dinner, weddings taking place on the jetty with the waterfall trickling down the mountain. It had such a romantic feel about the place. 'This place is certainly something special, Flynn.'

'I think so,' replied Flynn opening the door to the restaurant. 'After you.'

The inside of the building was just as breath-taking as the outside, with its shimmering central dining bar and signature large windows overlooking the bay. Its oak panelling and striking art hanging on the walls gave it a warm and luxurious feel. There were approximately fifteen tables, spaced to allow a sense of privacy, and in the corner of the dining area stood an ebony baby grand piano. Julia knew this place was going to be an instant hit.

'It's all been set up for the publicity photos,' said Flynn, walking to the centre of the room.

'The whole place is amazing. Even though I'm not sure I'll ever be able to afford to eat here, it looks way out of my league.'

'That's simple, you can always be my guest.'

A tiny thrill ran through Julia's body at that suggestion. 'Well in that case you may find it hard to get rid of me,' she joked but wanting to see Flynn's reaction.

'Sounds perfect to me,' his eyes skimmed her briefly before walking over to the piano. Julia followed him. He was flirting with her, and she liked it. There was a gentlemanly confidence about Flynn as he sat down at the piano and lifted up the lid.

'Do you play?' asked Julia, leaning against the piano.

'Funnily enough I do.' He looked up towards Julia with a magnitude of warmth and smiled, then began to glide his fingers gently over the keys with ease. Julia was captivated, she closed her eyes and listened, allowing herself to be lost in the music. When he stopped playing, she opened her eyes to find Flynn watching her. The intensity of his gaze caused her to tingle, she could feel the raw chemistry between them, her heart beating wildly.

'Did you like?'

'You, Flynn Carter… are a man of many talents. I really wasn't expecting that.'

He closed the lid and pushed the stool back under the piano. 'Come and take a look at this.'

Taking her by the hand, Flynn led Julia up the stairs at the side of the bar. The short spiral staircase took them out onto the roof terrace, which benefited from its south-facing exposure as well as the panoramic sea views and mountain terrain in the background.

'Can you imagine sitting here and watching the beautiful sunsets?'

Julia blew out a breath. 'Actually, I can. Look at that...' Julia held her arm out. 'Goose pimples. This place has actually taken my breath away.'

'It's magical isn't it? Romantic.'

'It's that alright. It's like something you'd find in a magazine and only dream of visiting.'

'This is where I need your help.'

'My help?' she asked amazed.

'I need this area to stand out. I need to make this space as outstanding as that view, and with your flair for interior design... I'm thinking you could guide me on the right track. I want this place to be special. Can you help me?'

Julia had 101 ideas running around her head. 'Oh Flynn, I'd love to. What's the timescale?'

'As soon as possible,' he said with a grin.

'No pressure then.'

'Once the water taxis are up and running and the staff are in place, I'm ready to open,' he said turning back towards Julia.

'Is this the time to tell you my cousin Callie has an interview with you for Starcross Manor?'

'I'll let you into a little secret. I've already recruited for the manor. The job application is actually for this place.'

'Ooo, fingers crossed,' replied Julia, thinking Callie would love to work here.

'Hungry? Let's go and get a glass of champagne and a bite to eat. I'm actually starving after missing breakfast.'

They walked back down the stairs and into the main restaurant before stepping out onto the sand. Julia kicked off her shoes and carried them as they walked back towards the boat, the fine grains of sand underfoot giving warmth from the sun beating down.

'You wait there,' ordered Flynn, touching her arm affectionately, causing her to feel the flush of warmth in her body again. That feeling wasn't one she'd felt for a long time, and being in Flynn's company felt so easy and natural.

Julia watched him walk back towards the boat, then glanced back towards The Lakehouse. She had a million and one ideas already running around her head to transform that beautiful roof terrace.

Sitting down on the sand, she brought her knees up to her chest and tilted her face up to the sun. Flynn arrived back playfully kicking the water towards her whilst holding up a picnic basket. 'Lunch.' He placed it on the sand and rolled out a red tartan blanket.

Julia went to peep inside the lid. Jokingly, Flynn gently snapped the lid down causing Julia to jump and their fingers to brush against each other. Once again Julia felt that spark ignite.

'We have champagne and...' Flynn reached into his back pocket, 'sun cream, your face is looking a little burnt.'

Julia gratefully took the tube. 'It feels a little burnt, in fact more than a little burnt. And what have we got in here?' she asked, lifting up the lid and watching Flynn's every move in case he swiped the lid again. 'Wow! You have come prepared,' said Julia, suitably impressed. The picnic basket was packed to the brim with delicious-looking food. 'You have gone all out.'

'Always prepared… well, Andrew is,' he grinned. 'We have chorizo Scotch quail's eggs; smoked salmon; ham, pea and mint pastries; super salad wraps; egg and cress club sandwich; strawberry and cream cheesecake; rainbow fruit skewers…'

'Woah! Stop there!' exclaimed Julia, feeling overwhelmed. 'How many people are you feeding?'

'You can never have too much food,' Flynn patted his stomach.

Julia patted hers. 'Oh yes you can! It's true what they say: as you get older, it's harder to lose the pounds, and I think what's the point in starving yourself? But then when you look like this…' She stared down at her stomach.

'You look alright to me,' Flynn flicked his eyes up and down and gave her a cheeky smile. 'But if you aren't going to eat, that means more for me.'

'I'm going to eat, don't you be eating mine!'

'Champagne first,' said Flynn, passing her a glass before popping the cork from the bottle, which flew through the air and landed in the water causing Julia to jump.

'I have to say this is a first for me: a champagne picnic in a secluded bay.'

'And dare I ask, are you having a good time?' Flynn had his fingers crossed held in the air and squeezed his eyes shut.

Julia laughed. 'I'm having the best time,' she replied and genuinely was. She couldn't remember the last time she'd felt this happy and relaxed.

'Me too,' replied Flynn, resting his hand on her knee as he began to lay the food out onto the blanket. Once he finished, he lifted his glass. 'Here's to new beginnings, love, laughter and lots more.'

Julia chinked her glass against his. 'New beginnings.'

They sipped their champagne and stared out across the water in silence. In the distance there were two sailing ships and the only thing Julia could hear was the lapping of the water against the sand. Everywhere was calm and tranquil. 'I feel like I'm twenty-one again. This place reminds me of a girly holiday back in the day. We could be in Corfu with this sunshine and those views,' said Julia reminiscing.

'I know what you mean. Right at this moment I feel like I haven't got a care in the world, except you and me sat here, enjoying all this.'

Feeling relaxed Julia passed Flynn a plate, and for the next ten minutes they tucked into the food with murmurs of appreciation. Everything tasted so good. When Flynn had finished eating, he lay down on the sand and rested his head on his hand. As he stretched, his T-shirt rose up, revealing a flash of his toned, tanned stomach. 'This is the life,' he murmured, catching the rays on his face.

She risked a glance. 'So why haven't you got anyone special in your life? Anyone would jump at this kind of lifestyle.'

He opened one eye and looked in Julia's direction. 'And don't we know it.'

Julia chuckled. 'Yes, sorry, I didn't mean...'

'I know,' he interrupted, turning his face back towards the sun. 'But I could say the same about you.'

'I suppose that special someone just hasn't crossed my path yet.' Julia dug her feet into the sand and glanced back towards The Lakehouse. 'So tell me, how did you discover this little piece of paradise?'

Flynn sat up. 'This was actually my grandparents' place. I spent many a summer here as a boy. It was my favourite place in the whole world.'

'Wow! I wasn't expecting that.' Julia hadn't realised Flynn's family was originally from around these parts.

'Back in the day, this was a famous restaurant, quite an exclusive place, and many rich and famous people frequented here. But when my grandmother passed away my grandfather's heart was broken, and he couldn't face keeping the place going without her. It was never sold and has been standing empty for a long while. My dad was thinking of turning it into a house, but once I'd won Starcross Manor in the auction and secured the purchase of the Boathouse, I thought it would be the perfect time to re-open this place.'

Flynn began to peel the T-shirt from his broad shoulders and folded it up at the side of him. 'And do you see that rock up there?' Flynn pointed. 'As a kid that was my favourite place to dive from.'

As Julia looked up Flynn was already on his feet and

striding over to the rocks. She watched him confidently climb up the jagged rockface in what seemed like a couple of seconds.

Surely, he really wasn't going to dive from that cliff? Julia's heart began to gallop. She stared out at the glittering water. There might be huge rocks under the surface, it looked too dangerous to her. She suddenly felt queasy watching him. He waved over to her before focusing back on the water.

'What are you doing?' she shouted, up on her feet. 'It's too risky.' But Flynn didn't hear her, he'd already launched himself off the cliff. Her heart was in her mouth, she screwed up her eyes and watched him glide through the air.

SPLASH, the water rippled all around him as he plunged from the rock into the bubbly cobalt-blue water. Time slowed and finally he surfaced. Julia exhaled, *Thank God*. Just watching Flynn took her breath away and she couldn't take her eyes off him. With his hair slicked against his head, he swam effortlessly until he was safely back in shallow water. He stood high in the water, bare chested. His shoulders were broad and there wasn't an ounce of excess flesh – he was clearly a man who worked out. The way he lifted his arms was almost sensuous. Finally, he swam closer to her then stood up. His skin glistened as he raked his hand through his wet hair. Julia had to pinch herself; this man was so gorgeous. She felt drunk-happy, and it wasn't from the champagne. This was the most relaxing day she'd enjoyed in a long time.

Flynn's eyes smiled. 'Come on in, it's beautiful in here,' he pleaded.

'Don't ever do that to me again,' she said. 'You nearly gave me a heart attack.'

He grinned. 'Don't worry, I know these waters like the back of my hand… come on in,' he repeated, ducking his shoulders under the water. 'It's not that cold once you're in.' Flynn bobbed his head under the surface and then emerged from the water. 'See?'

'I'm coming!' she shouted, peeling off her shorts. The sun was glorious on her skin as she walked towards the edge of the water.

Flynn had swum out a little further as Julia was navigating the rocky ground underneath her feet. Carefully putting one foot in front of the other, her concentration was broken as she heard buzzing and frantically swished her hair. Her heart began to beat in big apprehensive thumps as she let out a squeal and swiped away the dragonfly that was trying to land on her shoulder, only to stumble on a rock. Julia stretched out her arms to try and steady herself, but it was too late – she shrieked and lost her balance and was sat on the seabed with the water lapping all around her shoulders.

'You okay?' Flynn shouted out, striding through the water like some sort of superhero towards her.

Julia managed a little wave, reassuring him she was okay, but before she knew it, his two big strapping arms were yanking her to her feet. He grinned. 'What are you doing down there?' he said, gently pushing the damp tresses from her face.

'That blooming dragonfly toppled me off balance,' she said, shaking her head laughing. 'Well, at least I'm in now, and look at my hair,' she cast her eyes upwards and brushed her wet fringe to one side.

'You look beautiful to me,' Flynn tilted his head towards her and looked at her with such tenderness. He took both her hands and pulled her in, she rested her head against his bare, wet chest and could hear the thumping of his heart. Every inch of her tingled with desire. The intensity between them felt hotter than the afternoon sun, and she had to remind herself to breathe. For a moment they stayed in each other's arms, then gazed at each other in a contemplative silence. Flynn tucked her hair behind her ears before gently cupping her face in his hands. Julia was willing him to kiss her, and Flynn never took his eyes off her as he lowered his lips to hers. His kiss was soft, then long and deep. Julia savoured every second.

After a moment they pulled away and rested their heads against each other with huge beams on their faces. 'Come on, see that rock over there...' he pointed. 'That part is shallow, it's a great place to sit and watch the fish.'

Holding Julia's hand tightly he walked slowly, and Julia trailed behind him. It had been a long time since she'd held a man's hand, and she had forgotten how comforting it was. There were still a few rocks on the seabed, but it was mostly now sandy. 'Steady now, this part is a little deeper.' He held her hand a little tighter and gave it a squeeze, she found herself squeezing his back.

He glanced back at her from time to time to make sure she was okay. Julia was astonished that the deeper water had become extremely shallow, and she was suddenly hit by very warm water that lapped only around her ankles. 'Well just look at that,' Julia sat down and cupped her hands under the water. Tiny fish squirmed in her hands. 'There's hundreds of them.' Julia was amazed, she'd never seen so many fish in one place before.

'This is one of my favourite places,' Flynn admitted, sitting next to her in the water. 'It's just magical isn't it?'

'Beyond magical,' Julia was blown away by the whole afternoon, everything had been just perfect.

They were sat amongst the fish for nearly ten minutes before Flynn noticed the black clouds beginning to drift towards them. 'I think we are in for a summer shower. Come on, I'll race you back to the shore.' Flynn sprang to his feet, quickly followed by Julia. They splashed like a couple of kids until they collapsed in a heap on the picnic blanket.

'I was right, here we go.' Flynn held his hands up towards the sky. Large dollops of rain began to fall.

'Oh my God,' feeling the droplets against her bare skin Julia grabbed a towel and wrapped it around her shoulders. In the distance there was a low growl of thunder.

They began to pack everything up quickly and within seconds they were running across the small bay like they didn't have a care in the world. They reached the boat just before the lightning zig-zagged across the horizon. They fell onto the deck laughing like a couple of teenagers, wiping the rain from their faces. 'That came from nowhere,' remarked Julia, staring up at the sky.

Flynn ragged his hair with the towel before throwing it on the back of the chair.

'If you want to get out of those wet clothes be my guest.'

Julia cocked her head to one side. 'What, right here?' she joked playfully, but knowing exactly what he meant.

Flynn's eyes brimmed with laughter. 'That really did come out wrong. What I meant was, if you want to go and get a shower, be my guest.'

'That would be perfect,' she replied smiling, heading towards the bathroom. She stopped and turned back towards him. 'Flynn?'

'Yes,' he replied.

'I'm having the best day.'

Chapter Twenty-Three

TWO WEEKS LATER

'Are you nearly ready?' Callie shouted up the stairs. She'd been waiting for Julia to be ready for the last thirty minutes. 'It's not Royal Ascot you know.'

'I'm coming!' Julia bellowed, taking one last look in the mirror. She dabbed on her lip gloss, grabbed her bag, and declared herself ready.

'Finally,' joked Callie, hearing movement at the top of the stairs. Callie's phone pinged for the umpteenth time this afternoon and she looked at her messages. It was Dan... again. Callie sighed. 'He's just not getting the message,' muttered Callie.

'Is it really over? Are you 100-percent sure?' asked Julia, lifting up her dress and trying not to trip on it as she walked down the stairs.

'It is, even though he's not believing it himself at the moment. He thinks I'm just throwing a tantrum, but never mind that, look at you!' beamed Callie, admiring her cousin's choice of dress. 'Full of charm and elegance.'

With an open back and a peplum waist, Julia was wearing an absolute showstopper. Hand-designed floral print on a soft taupe base, with delicate ruffles of rose and blush finished with contrast lace trims. She dropped the dress as she reached the bottom stair and it hung perfectly above the ground.

'Look at your face, you are absolutely glowing. Give me a spin!' ordered Callie, turning her around. 'Amazing.'

'You don't look too bad yourself,' replied Julia, slipping her feet into a pair of ballet shoes. 'It has just been the best couple of weeks.'

The B&B had fully re-opened and the guests were bowled over by the opportunity to use the facilities at Starcross Manor. Word had spread on the Facebook business page, and Eleni had been busy all week taking new bookings. Julia and Flynn had spent every free moment together, and she knew she was high on life and in the first flush of love.

Today Starcross Manor was officially opening its doors for an exclusive garden party for the village, and Julia had been out of her mind and driving Flynn completely mad after trawling through the internet in search of the perfect dress for today's grand opening. To her surprise, Julia had received a delivery from Flynn with a handwritten note that read, 'Just for you! x.' After carefully opening the rectangular box, she'd peeled back the delicate tissue to reveal the stunning dress she was now wearing. Julia couldn't thank him enough.

'Where's Eleni? I thought she was meeting us here?' Julia stepped outside into the sunshine, where she spotted Eleni walking up the road, twizzling her parasol over her head. 'Here she is.'

'What a gorgeous day,' beamed Eleni, giving a low whistle when she spotted Julia. 'Look at you. I think you are going to find yourself all over the covers of the magazine dressed like that.'

'She will if I have anything to do with it!' They spun round to see Allie, waving her camera in the air. 'Guess who's covering this story today. I just can't keep away, and I wasn't going to miss this chance, and look at you all... stunning.' Allie flicked off the lens cap and began to take pictures.

The three of them posed, then giggled.

'People say life begins at forty, and since I've turned forty, I'm having the best time,' announced Julia, linking her arm through Callie's.

'Who'd have thought you'd be dating a handsome millionaire and have fallen completely head over heels? Even Martha would never have predicted that with her crystal ball,' grinned Allie.

They all wandered down the lane and took the short walk towards Starcross Manor. Allie gave them an update on Rory, who was due home for a visit soon, and chatted about the ongoing renovation project at Clover Cottage. Allie had been bowled over by the work done so far.

'And your building work starts on Monday,' added Callie. 'It's all going on.'

'I can't wait,' interrupted Eleni, with a smitten look on her face.

'We know why you can't wait! Would that have something to do with Jack being at the B&B every day until the building work is complete?'

'Might have!' replied Eleni smiling.

It didn't take them long to reach the long driveway of Starcross Manor. All the villagers were out in full force, dressed up to the nines. All the women kitted out in long flowing dresses, while the men looked striking in their linen summer shirts and kilts. Everyone was dressed to impress.

Once they'd stopped in the gardens, Julia looked around for Flynn, but she couldn't see him. Then Callie pointed. 'Over there.' He was surrounded by a handful of journalists and looked in good spirits, answering their questions and posing for photographs. Julia couldn't take her eyes off him; he was gorgeous, kind, genuine, the whole package. She knew it was very early days, but her heart told her this was the man for her, and she was excited to see what the future held.

All the guests followed the signposted arrows, and the outdoor lanterns that would look spectacular once the sun went down, to the grounds at the back of the hotel. There were waiters wandering between the guests offering canapés and cocktails. At the far end of the lawn was a giant brick stove, and Andrew Glossop looked like he was already cooking up a storm. On the tables next to him was a feast laid out, fit for a king.

'Wow! Look at that,' exclaimed Eleni, pointing at the oversized tumble tower blocks towering in front of them. There were skittles laid out on the lawn, and croquet hoops set out amongst comfy-looking deckchairs for the spectators. There were numerous gazebos, seating in shady areas perfect for people watching, and a bar area too.

'Are you sure we aren't at the royal palace?' exclaimed Callie, taking a cocktail from a nearby waiter.

Flynn had slipped behind Julia, causing her to jump. 'There she is! And you look absolutely amazing,' Flynn kissed her cheek and held both her hands. Taking a step back, he glanced over the dress. 'Beautiful,' he said, kissing her cheek once more.

'Thank you, you don't scrub up badly yourself,' she replied, squeezing his hand. 'This turnout is amazing.'

'I have you to thank for that, I think everyone in the village is here. Now, see that man over there,' Flynn nodded over to the far side of the lawn. 'Come and have you photo taken with me. That journalist works for *Scottish Life* and the tourist board. It will be good publicity for the B&B too, and then apparently I need to make a small speech before I can relax and enjoy the afternoon.' Hand-in-hand, Flynn and Julia strolled over the freshly mown lawns to where the journalist was standing. After answering numerous questions, and posing for more pictures, the journalist asked Julia for her name, to reference it in the article.

'Julia Coleman, my girlfriend,' answered Flynn proudly on her behalf.

The smile on Julia's face was instant. She couldn't believe that until a few weeks ago life had just gone on as normal – until Flynn had turned up in the village. After a shaky start between them, he had utterly melted her heart. Once more she thought back to a saying her grandad was fond of, 'You just never know what is around the corner,' and he had been right.

'I think it's time for you to say a few words,' suggested Jack, who'd wandered over with Eleni by his side.

'On my way.' Flynn saluted. They all walked over to the podium where the villagers began to gather round. It only took a few seconds for the villagers to settle before Flynn began to speak.

'Welcome to Starcross Manor, a place that has been a part of the village for a very long time, even though it was forgotten for a while. Some of you may not know, but as a boy I used to spend my summers around these parts, as my grandparents owned a small restaurant not far from here. So Heartcross has always held a special place in my heart. When I saw the news eighteen months ago, when this tiny village was cut off from civilisation after the bridge collapsed, I followed the story of how you all pulled together and raised the money to rebuild the bridge. All of you are an inspiration, the community of Heartcross is one I admire.' Flynn took a breath and glanced quickly at Julia before turning back towards the crowd standing in front of him.

'I know at first when I turned up you weren't too sure about me, but hopefully now that is all behind us.'

There were cheers from the crowd gathered in front of him.

'Can I just turn your attention to our resident chef, Andrew,' Flynn gestured over towards the brick stoves. 'Andrew will be in charge of all the food this afternoon, so do help yourselves.'

Flynn was interrupted by a round of applause for Andrew who waved his chef's hat in the air.

'We have drinks from the bar, or grab a glass from the waiters that will be circulating amongst you all,' continued Flynn, who then paused for a second. He scanned the crowd and gave a nod to Seb the waiter, who hurried towards the podium carrying a stunning bouquet of flowers, featuring pink oriental lilies and large roses hand-tied with eucalyptus.

'Today, I want to thank Julia, for making all this possible and ensuring I wasn't driven out of the village.'

The crowd laughed as Flynn turned towards Julia. 'These are for you.'

Coming over all emotional, Julia fanned her hand in front of her face before taking the flowers from Flynn. 'Oh my, they are beautiful, what have I done to deserve these?'

'For just being you,' he replied, leaning forward and kissing her lightly on the lips. Julia felt she was going to burst with happiness.

'Now, there's only one thing left for me to say,' he turned

back towards the gathered crowd. 'Eat, drink and be merry!'

Everyone applauded and Flynn stepped down from the podium, straight into Julia's arms. She couldn't thank him enough for the stunning flowers. 'They are gorgeous,' she gushed, taking in the aroma.

'Just like you. I've said it before and I'll say it again, I know we didn't get off to the best start, but I have a good feeling about you Julia Coleman, a good feeling about us.'

'Me too,' she replied, feeling a fizz of excitement.

The afternoon was magical, with everyone thoroughly enjoying the day. The children were mesmerised by the gigantic tumbling blocks, whilst the villagers sat in the deckchairs, drinking Pimms and watching the world go by – all of the community enjoying everything that Starcross Manor had to offer.

After just the best day, Julia and Flynn were the last ones standing. Under the night sky they walked hand-in-hand over to the lake and stared out over the beauty of it all. Flynn slipped his arms around Julia's waist, and she leant back onto his chest as he lightly kissed the top of her head.

'It's been a strange few weeks, hasn't it,' murmured Julia.

'It has that… Apparently, I've been a heartbreaker, a liar, and an all-round rat,' he replied light-heartedly.

'And I've been an idiot, but you have forgiven me, haven't you?'

'Without a doubt… quick, look up,' Flynn's voice rose, and he pointed up into the sky.

Immediately Julia swung her gaze upwards to see the most wonderful sight. 'Oh my, it's amazing.'

'A shooting star... quick, make a wish,' whispered Flynn, the white light shining all the brighter for the darkness around.

'It's the most perfect backdrop for Starcross Manor.' Julia squeezed her eyes shut and made a wish.

'Well, what did you wish for?' Flynn hugged her tightly.

Julia turned round and kissed him lightly on the lips. 'I can't tell you that, otherwise it won't come true, and this is one wish I hope will come true one day.'

Flynn's eyes were deep, hazel, and alive. 'Julia Coleman, I think we are in for an exciting future.'

'I think so too, Flynn Carter.'

They stared at the night sky a moment longer. Julia was the happiest she'd been in a very long time. All the uncertainty of the past few weeks was very much behind her. She couldn't wait for the rest of her life to begin. Julia knew difficult roads often lead to beautiful destinations, and even though she and Flynn began their journey on a bumpy road, Julia had every intention of making her wish come true.

A Letter from Christie

Dear Readers,

Firstly, if you're reading this letter, thank you for choosing to read *Starcross Manor*.

I sincerely hope you enjoyed reading this book, if you did I would be grateful if you'd leave a review. Your recommendations can always help other readers to discover my books.

I really can't believe my eleventh book is published; writing for a living is truly the best job in the world and I love spending my time in a fictional land.

I'm particularly proud of this novel and this storyline was inspired by a recent trip to a quaint B&B in the middle of the countryside which I absolutely adored. I was accompanied by a friend whose business was in trouble and she was in a quandary about what to do next so the idea was born.

The characters Flynn and Julia have become a huge part of my life for the last few months and you may stumble across them again very soon as there will be more books to come based around the little village of Heartcross in the Scottish Highlands.

Huge thanks and much love to everyone who has been involved in this project. I truly value each and every one of you and it's an absolute joy to hear from all my readers via Twitter, Facebook and Instagram.

Please do keep in touch!

Warm wishes,

Christie x

Acknowledgments

My eleventh book has been published; I really can't quite believe it! There is a long list of truly fabulous folk I need to thank who have been instrumental in crafting *Starcross Manor* into a book I'm truly proud of.

As always thanks and much love to my family, Emily, Jack, Ruby and Tilly for all your cheering, flag-waving and constant support.

Much love to Woody (my mad cocker spaniel) and Nell (my bonkers labradoodle) you are both my writing partners in crime and are always by my side.

Endless love for my best friend Anita Redfern, you laugh, I laugh. You cry, I cry. You jump off a high cliff, I yell do a flip! You are simply the best and everyone should have a friend like you.

Group hug to all the family at One More Chapter, especially Charlotte Ledger, who goes far beyond the call of duty to encourage, inspire and make the magic happen. I love being a part of this fantastic publishing team and am truly grateful for all your hard work turning my stories into books.

Thank you to my amazing editor Emily Ruston who must hold her head in her hands every time she receives my first draft but then in the most amazing way makes my books the best they can be.

To Bella Osborne for teaching me that post-it notes are a must and sometimes I can't just fly by the seat of my pants, planning is the way to go. You rock!

A special shout out to Glynis Peters, Deborah Carr and Terri Nixon – The survivors!

Team Barlow! Huge love to my merry band of supporters and friends, Kiren Parmar, Suzan Holder, Louise Speight, Suzanne Toner, Catherine Snook, Sue Miller, Janet Baldwin, Kathy Ford, Bhasker Patel, Angela Anderson, Pam Howes and John Jackson and all of the members of the Romantic Novelist Association. I am truly grateful for your support and friendship and your constant shout-outs and sharing of posts never go unnoticed – Thank you.

Finally high fives and a big thank you to everyone who enjoys, reads and reviews by books, especially Rachel Gilbey, Claire Knight, Lorraine Rugman, Sarah Hardy, Noelle Holten, Annette Hannah, Joanne Roberston, Amanda Oughton, Elaine Brent, Donna Maguire, Steph Lawrence, Kerry Ann Parsons, Jenn Webley, Kelly Disley and Sharon Hunt, who champion my writing on blog tours and always shout loudly about the Love Heart series.

I have without a doubt enjoyed writing every second of

this book and I really hope you enjoy hanging out at Starcross Manor with Flynn and Julia. Please do let me know!

Warm wishes,

Christie xx

ONE MORE CHAPTER

One More Chapter is an
award-winning global
division of HarperCollins.

Sign up to our newsletter to get our
latest eBook deals and stay up to date
with our weekly Book Club!
Subscribe here.

Meet the team at
www.onemorechapter.com

Follow us!

 @OneMoreChapter_

 @OneMoreChapter

 @onemorechapterhc

Do you write unputdownable fiction?
We love to hear from new voices.
Find out how to submit your novel at
www.onemorechapter.com/submissions